DREADNOUGHT

THE ROYAL MARINE SPACE COMMANDOS
BOOK 5

JAMES EVANS

JON EVANS

IMAGINARY BROTHER

PROLOGUE

Senior Lieutenant Lucas Silva cleared his throat, unable to shake the feeling something was out of place. Was his dress uniform correctly pressed? Perhaps he'd overlooked lint on his trousers, or maybe missed a whisker while shaving.

But it was far too late to check now, and that worsened his discomfort.

A giant viewscreen displayed his presentation. Facing it, he could almost forget the women and men seated behind him at the briefing table. Almost.

Everyone outranked him. Even the aides were older with higher security clearance.

Bluntly put, he'd been stitched up.

Silva hadn't expected to brief anyone this morning. Even the intelligence reports he received shortly after arriving for his duty shift hadn't prepared him for a meeting like this. He simply took the bad news to his boss, who escalated it with indecent haste. His boss's boss, Admiral Mkembe, should have been giving the briefing.

Except Admiral Mkembe had put him in the firing line and suggested he – Silva – present to the assembled dignitaries, and his immediate superior of course enthusiastically agreed. He didn't understand why they'd thrust the responsibility on him.

Or maybe he did. He knew how deep a hole he'd landed in. Silva was the messenger, and nobody wanted to take his role.

He should have been overseeing an analysis of data on enemy movements. But here he was, addressing two dozen admirals of various specialities of the Naval High Command, and behind them their senior staff and aides.

The only people even vaguely close to Silva's rank were a couple of tech specialists and the unfortunate intern serving coffee and breakfast pastries with shredded goat. They scurried away as soon as their jobs were done.

Silva cleared his throat, in a failed attempt to buy time. It only made him feel more self-conscious. He gulped and plunged on.

"Early this morning," he began, nerves making his voice higher than normal, "we received an intelligence update via wormhole transmission from one of the in-system monitors deployed to Commonwealth space. A new fleet, under the command of Admiral Morgan of the Commonwealth Royal Navy, has left the planet they call 'New Bristol' to travel to the system displayed on the viewscreen."

The screen switched to a video showing Morgan's fleet leaving New Bristol on one side, and a readout of the ship types, headcount, armament and other, more esoteric details on the other.

"Their immediate target seems to be the system where, just a few weeks ago, Admiral Morgan's fleet was destroyed by Admiral Tomsk. We believe that first fleet was to have assaulted Shipyard Delta. The interception prevented disruption of operations at Delta and gave us a significant victory."

Admiral Erikson spoke up when Silva paused. "This makes no sense. Why would they send a new fleet to the system where the last one was wiped out?"

"Er, yes, Admiral. Our conclusion, based on archive material and historical actions, is that the Royal Navy has a protocol requiring them to investigate a battle site and determine if there are survivors."

"You think they're going back to the site of a devastating ambush, hoping it won't happen again, merely to find a few escape pods?" Erikson pressed, not bothering to hide her scepticism.

"We do. They seem to have ethical qualms about simultaneous co-existence of clones of the same person, and we believe they prefer to confirm the crews are deceased before redeploying their backups to new clones," said Silva, feeling a little more confident now he was into the meat of the analysis.

But then Admiral Wagner leaned forward, bunched his huge fists and began to growl a question. Silva's confidence drained away. Wagner stood out amongst his colleagues. Indeed, due to his preference of clone type, he stood out amongst all Koschites. Admiral Wagner always used a Warmonger clone, a hulking brute of a thing designed to carry heavy weapons and lead major assaults. The Navy typically used standard officer clones, but Wagner preferred to rule by intimidation. He was nothing if not eccentric.

Silva wondered if Wagner's gruff voice was attributable to his clone's design, or if he'd sound gravelly and brusque even in his own body. In other circumstances, Silva might have found the admiral's clone amusing, but here the giant figure was simply terrifying.

"You said this Admiral Morgan is leading this fleet, but how can he be if they won't redeploy without confirmation of death? How do they know Morgan is dead?"

Silva shot a glance at Admiral Mkembe. "Our intelligence suggests the Commonwealth is aware that the Admiral's flagship, HMS *Duke of Norfolk*, has been lost with all hands."

"What sort of intelligence?" pressed Wagner. "How would you get that intelligence from the drones you have near New Bristol?"

Silva hesitated, "We...well, that is to say..." he began, frantically trying to work out how to answer.

"There are aspects of our intelligence gathering methods that we are not at liberty to share in a public forum," interjected Admiral Mkembe, much to Silva's relief, "or to discuss with those who lack the requisite security clearance."

At least she didn't totally abandon me, thought Silva. He knew information about the source was restricted – even he didn't know where it came from – but it hadn't occurred to him the admirals might not have the requisite clearance. His mouth dried as he realised he had no idea which officers possessed clearance for these advanced intelligence gathering technologies, and which did not. He had been a hair's breadth from inadvertently committing a court-martial offence.

Wagner shot to his feet and hammered his fist into the table, unaware of Silva's angst. Silva was almost certain the man was irritated, but reading people wasn't his speciality. He much preferred the company of data, which didn't lie even when they sometimes concealed multiple truths. Teasing information from a sea of data was Silva's one true joy.

"This is outrageous!" thundered Wagner as Silva rocked back, thoroughly intimidated. "How can any of us, the admirals of the Koschite Navy, lack clearance for the origin of the intelligence you present to us? We must know its provenance. It was your intelligence failings, Mkembe, that led to the situation on New Bristol in the first place. Had we been properly informed, we could have delivered overwhelming numbers of troops and crushed the colony utterly. The planet would now be securely in our hands."

Admiral Mkembe smiled, a thin, flat-looking expression Silva knew to take as a warning rather than an invitation of friendship. Of course, Silva hadn't deciphered her facial expressions himself; his colleagues had warned him to avoid the admiral when she looked like that. Empathy wasn't his strong point, but he had an excellent memory. It had occurred to him that his colleagues might have been teasing him. But his social therapist had taught him a range of things to look for, and he hadn't spotted any of them. His colleagues, it seemed, had been entirely honest and accurate.

Except for the bit where they likened Mkembe to a shark, which clearly wasn't true at all. He had checked, and all members of the Earth-clade selachimorpha had gills and fins, features Mkembe's clone obviously lacked. It was a puzzle.

"You may request higher security clearance," said Mkembe, "if you wish to be privy to the most sensitive intelligence work."

"Then I formally request my clearance be raised," said Admiral Wagner triumphantly.

Mkembe shook her head. "No, Admiral Wagner, you misunderstand. You must request higher clearance from the Admiral of the Fleet, and the request must then be approved by the Interior Minister responsible for interstellar security. I cannot authorise it, else all the power would lie with me."

"I will submit a formal request," said Wagner slowly as he lowered himself back into his seat.

Silva thought he detected a hint of menace in Wagner's tone and by the way he stared at Admiral Mkembe. But the tests he knew for anger and threat emotions worked poorly on the Warmonger clone. He wondered if he should talk to his social therapist about this, then decided he didn't really care.

"Are there any other questions?" he asked, hoping to bring the briefing to a close.

"What course of action do you recommend? How should we respond to this enemy movement?" said Erikson.

"We believe Admiral Morgan, once he has investigated the scene of the battle, will resume the earlier mission and proceed to Shipyard Delta. Even a moderately successful attack on the shipyard would represent a devastating setback that we can ill afford," said Silva, glancing at Admiral Mkembe for support.

"And so we recommend that the High Command consider an all-out attack – an ambush – on this new fleet," said Mkembe. "It must be prevented from reaching Delta at all costs."

There wasn't any immediate dissent and no-one seemed about to interrupt, so Silva continued with the most difficult portion of the presentation; convincing them to do something they probably wouldn't want to.

"Admiral Tomsk's briefing notes suggest Morgan may be an inferior commander, but subsequent events cast doubt on that assessment." There was a rumble of disquiet around the room. Tomsk's initial victory had been tainted by his later defeats, and all of his 'discoveries' were now viewed in a different, more hostile, light. "Naval

Intelligence proposes augmenting the standard naval forces with ships of the intelligence fleet. Rather than destroy the Commonwealth fleet outright, we plan to seize their ships, gather intelligence, and capture enemy personnel for interrogation."

And now the disagreement was immediate. Even Silva recognised the sharp intakes of breath, the creased eyebrows, and the muttered curses. The Admirals were not impressed.

Erikson spoke first, "That's a big request to make. You do realise that we'll lose a great deal by doing as you ask?"

"There is some risk," admitted Silva, "but we feel–"

"Feelings are irrelevant," interrupted Wagner. "We will lose ships if we fight to capture enemy vessels and crew. The risk to our long-term strategy is too high. We cannot expose an attack fleet to a high-risk battle scenario for the mere chance we might learn something beneficial. We should simply obliterate the enemy and move on."

"I agree," said Erikson, in a rare show of unity. "The intelligence you want to gather from this exercise has to be balanced against the cost in materiel. You know our overall war strategy. Does it strike you as wise to put a fleet at risk merely to find out more about the Royal Navy? How much do you think Admiral Morgan knows that could affect our long-term strategy? How will this help us win the war?"

Silva looked again at Mkembe, but this time she merely stared back, waiting for him to respond.

"Nothing is more valuable than knowing the enemy, ma'am. Admiral Morgan may be no Mark Antony, but he is an experienced, high-ranking Commonwealth officer. Our background information is out of date and our knowledge of their current status wholly inadequate, but we do know that Morgan was most recently in logistics and supply."

"Hah. He's not even a war leader? He's a quartermaster?" Wagner scoffed before breaking into full-throated laughter.

Admiral Mkembe leaned forward. "We don't need their battle plans, Wagner, we need to know what their fleets are doing, how many ships they have, where they are, how much is provisioned to support them, where their fuel comes from and so on. Morgan is far from a poor choice to interrogate," said Mkembe, ticking each point off on her fingers as she listed them.

"You are convinced this is worth the risk, Mkembe?" said Erikson, her scepticism obvious even to Silva.

"Yes," said Mkembe simply. "The potential intelligence coup is huge. I recommend you give the proposal serious consideration and proceed if you feel you can accomplish the mission. Once the ships are captured and cleared, my teams will move in to retrieve any physical or data intelligence, but the primary goal is to secure Morgan for interrogation. It is your prerogative as the war council responsible for this sector to pursue total victory if you prefer, Admiral Erikson, but you would be missing an invaluable opportunity."

"Then we shall vote," Erikson said, tapping his data slate. Silva couldn't see the screens but the consensus came through quickly.

"Very well, ladies and gentlemen," said Erikson. "We will work together, intercept their fleet, and take their pawn from the board."

Admiral Mkembe nodded and left the room. Behind her, Silva hurried to keep up, his mind racing. They were going to do it.

His little report might decide the fate of the entire campaign.

1

Admiral Morgan thumped his fist on the arm of his chair. "Not again!"

His voice was little more than a shattered croak after an hour of barking orders at his bridge crew. *What cruel twist of fate brought them to this bitter end?* he wondered.

The powers that be had insisted, against his protests of course, that this fleet would be sufficient for their purposes. He'd wanted to wait until the fleet was reinforced with a second round of ships, but the standing orders were clear: survivors of naval engagements, on either side, were to be rescued. Any commander found negligent in this duty, would be court-martialled.

As soon as his new fleet had arrived, Morgan had taken command of the flagship and renamed it HMS *Duke of Norfolk II* in a hasty ceremony. The crew had grumbled and muttered superstitiously about renaming a ship before it went to war, but he was damned if he was flying a flagship named HMS *Southampton*. The very idea of a flagship named after a merchant port made his eye twitch.

There was no need to worry, the analysts had said. This fleet, gathered to scour the site of the Battle of Akbar, was significantly larger than the last, and they were convinced that no Deathless naval force could possibly stand against such might. Morgan knew that he, too, was better prepared for a battle. Prepared to do everything in his power to ensure the confidence shown in him had not been misplaced.

When they set out from New Bristol, confidence filled Morgan. He'd been sure that those he reported to would welcome him as a conquering hero and any stain on his record to date would soon be expunged. Now he was in the terrifying reality of a battle in space for the second time in only a few weeks, and there was a real risk he might not survive, despite taking every precaution to the contrary.

And if he did not, the valuable insight he alone held into the conflict between the Deathless and the Commonwealth would be lost forever.

He had to survive. He simply had to. His was a once in a generation mind, he knew. Without him, the whole plan for the war would be thrown into disarray.

Yet despite his high value, he was still out here in the middle of nowhere, his flagship full of holes from railgun rounds and missiles. The Deathless had even tried to ablate the forward armour of *Duke of Norfolk II* with archaic laser batteries! This level of damage shouldn't have happened. The present situation was in direct opposition to the plan he formulated with his peers in the Commonwealth. His instructions had been so precise, so lovingly crafted. Try as he might, the crew couldn't get his elegant design right. They kept deviating from it.

His shipboard backup would undoubtedly be destroyed, along with his capital ship. There was no chance of broadcasting his latest backup to a relay station; *Duke of Norfolk II*'s wormhole transmission capability had been one of the first things destroyed.

Dimly, he became aware of a voice intruding on his reverie. "Hmm?"

"Admiral, what are your orders, sir?" asked Lieutenant Sturgis. Tactical, that was his role. Sturgis's job was to maintain an overview of the battle and find opportunities to recommend to the captain. A 'wargamer', to use the derisive nickname such officers attracted for their dispassionate view of crews and ships as mere pieces in a game.

"My orders?"

"Sir, should we engage this group of ships?" said Sturgis, highlighting a small cluster of vessels on the edge of the engagement zone. "They haven't joined the battle and appear to be ill-equipped for conflict. My estimation is that they are too valuable to risk and we should therefore seek to destroy them."

"No!" snapped Morgan. He couldn't have this upstart idiot dictating the course of the battle. "Ignore them. Navigation," he said, turning away from Sturgis, "plot me a course to that capital ship," he ordered, picking out the biggest of the Deathless vessels on the holographic display hovering in mid-air between the bridge consoles.

A course appeared on the display, weaving around an enemy cruiser and an area seeded with autonomous weapons platforms. "Did I tell you to plot an indirect course, Ms. Lam?" sneered Morgan.

The young officer whirled in her seat, her face a picture of surprise.

No imagination, that's the problem with these Academy recruits, thought Morgan.

"But a direct course would take us through an enemy cruiser. We would ram it!" she protested.

"You're an inch away from insubordination, Midshipman Lamb! Plot the direct course. What do you think a cruiser will do when they see *Duke of Norfolk II* intends to ram them, eh?" he barked.

"They'll...they'll...they'll take evasive action, sir! Laying course in now."

Idiots, he thought. *I'm surrounded by idiots.* How would he and his peers ever be able to bring the righteous side to victory if their ranks were swelled by people without vision? These people needed to be purged from the command structure for the good of humanity.

"Helm, full steam ahead!" Morgan bellowed unnecessarily, ordering a round of stims from his combat med-suite. His eyes snapped alert and his heart pounded in his chest.

"Weapons, get me a firing solution on that cruiser. If it moves, I want it filled full of holes. If it doesn't move, I want it obliterated before we hit it," he ordered.

"Ay ay, sir," echoed his two weapons officers, Barnes and Rees. No impudently insubordinate questions from them, at least. He laid out his orders, and they carried them out. They didn't see themselves as being above it all, they simply shot what he told them to shoot. He wished everyone under his command was like that, acting as an extension of his will, an automaton.

"Communications, broadcast the following order to the fleet. HMS *Duke of Norfolk II* is leading the assault, all ships are to support us in wedge formation as we drive into the heart of the enemy fleet and crush them. The Commonwealth expects every man to do their duty, Admiral Morgan out," Morgan said firmly.

They were pressed firmly into their chairs as the acceleration increased. It would only be a few minutes until they collided with the cruiser. Unless it moved, of course, in which case they would rake it with railgun fire as they passed by.

"Launching counter-measures," said Ellis as a flurry of high-G missiles shot from the prow. Able to accelerate far more rapidly than the humans in the ship could tolerate, the missiles would disperse active chaff once they were sufficiently far ahead of *Norfolk*.

The tiny drones were equipped with a variety of signal-confusing equipment, each specialising in one form of jamming or another. Useless against railgun rounds, they were hugely effective against guided weaponry such as missiles. If they were close enough to an enemy ship, they could even prevent their targeting computers calculating a solution for railgun fire.

"Enemy cruiser is making a move, sir!" blurted Lamb excitedly.

Morgan leaned forward in his seat, eager to see the fate of the cruiser as it passed on their flank, "Rees, Barnes, make ready to give it hell."

They waited. The distance between *Norfolk* and the enemy capital ship closed. From all around, Deathless ships pummelled them with fire, and Commonwealth ships returned it in good measure. The wedge Morgan ordered was taking shape, although technically, it was more of a cone.

"Enemy fleet is adjusting to our attack, sir, they're changing formation in response to the wedge," Sturgis advised.

"Irrelevant, we have them now, and we'll start with that capital ship," said Morgan. They had lost eight ships already to this Deathless assault, which he knew to be the act of a cunning and dishonourable mind. It was considered poor form to attack ships sent to retrieve escape pods.

Which was ridiculous, of course; attack was exactly what a brilliant strategist should do. Morgan was sure he was the only admiral in the entire Commonwealth with the depth of insight needed to give such an idea its due respect.

The wedge formation would accomplish his goals. He could already see how it would happen. Future generations would probably call this *Morgan's Gambit* and study his tactics in the Academy. His peers would be the only people in the galaxy who could truly appreciate his strategic brilliance as he prosecuted this war.

Norfolk's starboard railgun batteries began to spew forth fire. Less than a minute later at least one round found its way home to a critical system, and the Deathless cruiser was suddenly ruptured by a series of internal explosions. The bridge crew cheered, congratulating Barnes and Rees on their shooting.

Morgan smiled. His path to the enemy capital ship was now clear. He watched as it slowly manoeuvred to bring its forward batteries into play.

Admiral Morgan's thin smile broadened into a triumphant grin. He had them now.

It was time to spring the trap.

"The fools, utter fools! Why didn't they follow my orders?" hissed Morgan at the bridge in general. No-one answered. No-one even looked at him.

"Sir, we have incoming," said Sturgis, his tone close to panic.

"Incoming what, Sturgis?" bared Morgan.

Sturgis turned to him with a wild-eyed expression, "Everything, sir. Everything." The lieutenant flicked a control and raised a sweaty hand to a secondary viewscreen. A host of icons was headed directly for *Duke of Norfolk II*. "Railgun rounds, then missiles, at least two squadrons of fast-flit attack craft, and a heavy cruiser," said Sturgis as his laser pointer highlighted each cluster of icons.

"Weapons, full defensive fire. Helm, evasive manoeuvres. Counter-measures, target those missiles," Morgan barked, his heart pounding in his chest. *Why is the engagement failing to go as planned?* he fumed to himself.

His aide, Barber, approached the command chair and leaned in to whisper in his ear. "Sir, the battle is lost. We should get you to the escape pod."

Morgan turned to reject the very notion, his face flushing with anger. He barely kept his response from escalating to a shout. "No! Not yet," he whispered. "We have to be certain of the outcome."

"Very good, sir. I will prep the escape sequence," said Barber obsequiously.

"Yes, of course! Do I have to tell you to do everything?" Morgan snapped at her. Honestly, she had been an aide for years, he shouldn't have to tell her such obvious things.

"First impact in fifteen seconds," said Sturgis.

"Impact? Of what? I ordered evasive action," replied Morgan.

"Yes, sir. *Norfolk* is not fast enough to evade all incoming fire. Our aft section is about to be hit. Damage estimate is non-critical."

"That's something, I suppose," Barber muttered.

"Something? Something!" Morgan yelled. "What's good about this exactly, Barber? The aft is where the bloody engines are. If we lose them, we won't be able to engage the enemy!"

"Yes, sir. Sorry, sir."

Morgan threw up his hands. "Weapons. Status?"

"Thirty per cent of incoming missiles destroyed, sir," Barnes answered.

"So low?" said Morgan, frowning.

"Brace for impact!" yelled Sturgis.

Railgun rounds ripped into the hull. Every impact sent shock-waves through the ship which Morgan felt through the seat of his trousers. It was as if a drummer beat a staccato riff on the hull with sticks of weeping gelignite. He gripped the arms of his chair until his knuckles went white, waiting for the juddering to subside. All the while, he stared at the screen Sturgis had put up, counting down the seconds until the missiles arrived.

"Damage reports," he said belatedly.

"Engine capacity at sixty-one per cent," said Church from the helm position.

"Multiple hull breaches, across all decks," said Sturgis. "Compromised compartments are being sealed, thirty-nine crew deceased."

"Weapons functional," said Rees.

"Then get the rest of those missiles down!" snarled Morgan.

"Firing counter-measures," said Ellis softly. Morgan rolled his eyes but ignored the man.

Missiles struck the length of the ship. Every alarm that wasn't already going off, started to bleep, and everyone on the bridge began to scream over the warnings. Damage reports ticked through the status screens faster than they could be read.

Morgan stared at the consoles, waiting for one to burst into flame like they did on the holo-vids.

Commander Barber, somehow still managing to stand beside Morgan's command chair, tapped him on the forearm. He glanced up at her and nodded.

"Sturgis. Order the crew to the escape pods. Get everyone off the bridge."

"Yes, sir. Immediately," said Sturgis, moving towards the door. The young officer paused and turned back to him. "And you, sir?"

"I shall be along presently. I'm going to see if the old girl can't do some final damage to that bloody capital ship before I leave."

Sturgis threw him a salute and he snapped one back. "Best of luck, sir."

Morgan nodded and turned to his comms panel. He tapped a few icons.

"Admiral Morgan to fleet. *Duke of Norfolk II* is critically damaged. We are abandoning ship. Do not go down without a fight, we must give the Deathless a bloody nose if it's the last thing we do. Morgan out."

He punched in a few commands to the nav console, setting the ship to begin maximum acceleration and removing the human safety limits with one final command from his HUD.

He looked around the bridge. The Deathless had been lucky today. Lucky the Admiralty had sent him such ineffective captains to form his fleet. Lucky his orders had been ignored or disobeyed. Lucky not everyone in the fleet was as dedicated to their mission as he was.

Yes, the Deathless would have been in trouble, were it not for their luck.

He snapped a final salute to the ship, in honour of her service, then followed Barber and fled for the nearest escape pod.

2

"Gentlemen," said Vice Admiral Staines in a strained tone. "Take a seat."

Lieutenant Commander Cohen and Lieutenant White of the Royal Navy took seats opposite the admiral's desk. Captain Warden of the Royal Marines Space Commandos, by far the most junior office in the room, pulled a chair from beside the wall to sit behind his colleagues. They were in Staines's command suite behind the bridge of his flagship, HMS *Iron Duke*, in orbit around the Commonwealth planet New Bristol.

"Admiral Morgan's fleet has been ambushed," said Staines, diving straight into the topic of the briefing, "and distress messages suggest it has been largely, if not entirely, destroyed."

The room was silent as the message of Staines's words sank slowly in.

Cohen cleared his throat. "I'm sorry, sir," he asked cautiously, "Admiral Morgan's fleet has been destroyed? Again?"

"Don't give me that look of polite incomprehension," snapped Staines, clearly feeling the pressure of the situation. "Yes, Admiral Morgan has lost a second fleet, or so it seems."

"To lose one fleet may be regarded as a misfortune," muttered

Warden. The admiral glared, and he coughed, embarrassed. "Sorry, sir."

"Carelessness doesn't enter into it," said Staines firmly, his face darkening. "This smacks of deceit and betrayal. Somehow, somewhere, we have a leak. A spy – possibly more than one – feeding information to the Deathless so they can draw us out and slap us around, one piece at a time."

"Someone's spying for the Deathless?" asked Cohen, frowning at the concept.

"Yes, dammit," snarled Staines, "someone's spying for the Deathless and now they've taken two of our fleets. At this rate, we'll bloody well run out, so stop asking stupid questions and let's see if we can make it through this briefing before we lose a third."

"Sorry, sir," said Cohen.

Staines blew out a long breath and got his temper under control.

"We couldn't afford to lose the first fleet and we certainly can't afford to lose the second. We have ships rushing in from all over, but if the Deathless were to attack now we would surely be forced to cede New Bristol and that, gentlemen, is simply not acceptable." He paused to poke at a data slate on his desk. An image flashed onto the main display. "This is the trajectory Admiral Morgan took, following the path of the first fleet. Your mission is to take *Dreadnought* and investigate, but for pity's sake be careful. We cannot afford to lose any more ships."

"Understood, sir," said Cohen carefully; he no more wished to lose another ship than Staines. "But *Dreadnought* is in a bad way. We really need more time to finish equipping and outfitting."

"The new fab units went in yesterday," said White, "and they're fitting the first of the weapons arrays at the moment, sir. But there are another two dozen to install to restore *Dreadnought*'s close-range capabilities. Her other weapon systems will take even longer."

"I don't care what the problems are," said Staines firmly. "Load your vital supplies and get moving. I want you underway within twelve hours. I've assigned *Palmerston* to you under Lieutenant

Ruskin. Make good use of Ruskin, and the shortcomings of *Dreadnought* should be easier to cope with."

The admiral paused and Cohen nodded his assent.

"Find the second fleet, Lieutenant Commander, collect any survivors, and then come straight back here. Is that clear?"

"Yes, Admiral," said Cohen as White nodded his support.

"Good. Captain Warden," said Staines, turning to the Marine, "your company has completed their redeployment, I see. You're to join *Dreadnought* for the duration of this war. You'll receive formal orders shortly from General Bonneville. Assist where possible, otherwise stay out of trouble."

"Yes, sir," said Warden. "I understand."

"Good. Don't let me keep you from your work, gentlemen."

~

Cohen walked into the mess on *Dreadnought* and was somewhat surprised to find the tables full. There was a scraping of chairs when the crew stood, but he quickly waved them back to their seats.

"At ease," he muttered, striding to the dais at the other end of the hall. He looked out across the room at the sizeable number of people now under his command.

"It's good to see so many of you back in RN standard clones," he said. Like Cohen himself, most of the crew opted to return to normal RN bodies as soon as the need to impersonate the Deathless was over. There were still a few lizardmen dotted around the room, but even most of the Marines had redeployed.

"There are few ships with longer pedigrees or more honourable histories than *Dreadnought*," said Cohen as he addressed the crew. "You know her achievements as well as I, but now it is time to begin a new page, to take *Dreadnought* into the future and to gather new honours in our conflict with the Deathless." He paused to look around, checking that everyone was listening.

"We had all hoped for a break from action, for time to re-fit the ship and bring her up to modern standards." There was a murmur of

disquiet from the crew and no small degree of uncomfortable shuffling. That the re-fit was needed was obvious, and the mere fact that
Cohen had mentioned it meant, obviously, that they would be doing
without.

"Unfortunately, circumstances have contrived to deny us the
required refit time. Instead," he paused again to glance at White.
"Instead, we will be taking on supplies now – all that we can carry
and that New Bristol can provide – with the intention of departing
within twelve hours."

Now the murmurs turned to outright surprise and alarm. There
was no way *Dreadnought* could be made ready within twelve hours,
and the crew knew it. To set out from New Bristol without completing
the refit was, at best, risky.

"I know this isn't the news you had hoped for," said Cohen with
hands raised, "but Admiral Staines has ordered us to pursue the fleet
and learn their fate. We will not be engaging the enemy, we go merely
to inspect and observe."

Down towards the back of the room, someone laughed, a short,
high-pitched snigger.

"*Palmerston* will accompany us. Captain Ruskin and I have agreed
that she will shadow *Dreadnought* to give us broader firing solutions,
just in case we need them. But this is a rescue mission. We don't
expect to even see the enemy, let alone engage them."

There was another round of mumbling, but whether scepticism
at the mission profile or doubt about encountering the enemy was
unclear.

"That's it, people. Get to work." And with that, he strode from the
mess with White in tow.

"We're going to be a little short-handed," observed White
when they reached the bridge. Unlike modern vessels,
Dreadnought was designed for a large bridge crew, each highly
specialised and working within clearly defined areas.

"They'll have to adjust," replied Cohen, walking across the bridge and into the command suite. He nodded as he looked around. The room was large, and Mantle's team had already been through and fitted it with new displays and equipment, unlike the rest of the ship. There was even a modern coffee machine, well-stocked with beans and gleaming in one corner.

"It doesn't work," said Lieutenant Eve Mantle, striding into the command suite as White poked at the machine. "We haven't had time to plumb it in yet, but there's a kettle and a jar of coffee granules in the cupboard." She nodded at the cupboard beneath the coffee machine and White gave her a pained expression. "It's perfectly drinkable," snapped Mantle defensively, "and there's always tea if you prefer."

"Just a glass of water, I think," said Cohen, pulling out a data slate. "What news on the ship?"

Mantle sat down and frowned at the captain over her slate. "We need another six months, sir, and even then we'll only have done the basics. In twelve hours, all I can do is load supplies."

"And the guns?" asked White as he passed around three mugs of water.

"Two railgun batteries installed in the bows, eight more being loaded. The rest – as well as the missile launchers and the counter-measure systems – will need to be fabricated as we go." She paused to fix Cohen with a grim stare. "This really isn't the way to do it, sir. Just want to state that for the record, in case it isn't clear. We should not be leaving New Bristol in our current state."

"Noted, Sub Lieutenant, but there's nothing we can do about it. Admiral Morgan's fleet is absent, feared lost, and we are – awful though it might seem – the best placed ship to run search and rescue. And don't forget we'll have *Palmerston* along for backup."

"What else can you tell us, Mantle?" asked White to divert the engineer from the full-blown rant she was clearly working towards.

Mantle sniffed, then flicked at her data slate. "Life support is working everywhere except the lower six decks. The main bays and hangers are in decent shape, although the doors work only in the starboard bay. The others haven't been used in decades and are frozen shut. The engines and hyperspace drive work, but don't go getting excited about our speed or manoeuvrability, both of which are significantly lower than *Ascendant's*."

Cohen frowned. "Really? I thought the engines took up a third of our volume?"

"They do, sir, with their accompanying fusion generators," said Mantle in the slow tones one might use with a child, "but they're old, inefficient and poorly maintained. At full power, we'll muster only half the force of *Ascendant* but with about fifteen times the mass."

"I hadn't realised it was that bad," muttered Cohen, poking at his slate to review Mantle's report. "I mean, I knew the engines were a bit tired, but I hadn't realised they were quite so feeble."

"Nothing happens quickly on a ship this big," Mantle went on, "so get used to giving orders far earlier. Manoeuvring thrusters are less effective as well, which is just as well because the acceleration couches are worn and uncomfortable. In fact, apart from this room, all the furniture is antique, as are most of the displays and processors, the internal comms system, the wormhole communicator, the mess and galley, the ammunition manufactories and the management systems. The only things that are vaguely modern, we've fitted ourselves."

Until an hour before, Cohen had thought that they had months for this refit and he'd paid less attention than he maybe should have. Now, with only hours to go, it was far too late to catch up, but he was damned well going to try.

"Right," he said decisively, checking the countdown on his slate. "We have only eleven hours. Do what you can with the weapons – the more we have, the better. We'll take everything that we can get from the supply ships, and anything from *Iron Duke* that isn't nailed down. We'll call it the admiral's contribution to the cause."

"I can handle that," said White. Then he gave an evil little grin. "I'll get Warden to give me some bodies. The Marines will enjoy the challenge of liberating supplies from our hosts."

"What about the Valkyr?" asked Mantle.

Cohen groaned at the mention of the three Valkyr citizens assigned to the crew. Trygstad was no trouble at all, and Agent O – the research AI – was hardly a burden. But Frida Skar, the research scientist who accompanied Agent O, was a difficult and prickly character.

"Just keep them occupied and a long way from me," said Cohen.

"I would, but *our friend* has been making suggestions. It's getting annoying, especially as she's invariably right." Agent O – or *our friend* when the crew wanted to talk about her rather than to her – had inserted her routines into *Dreadnought's* systems as soon as she had been brought aboard. Now, she listened for her name and would join conversations as soon as she was mentioned. "She's proposed new designs for the fabricators based on the systems the Valkyr use. They're streets ahead of our current machines, but we don't have time to build or install them."

"She's an AI," countered Cohen. "Give her a problem, set the parameters, and let her come up with the solution." Mantle opened her mouth to object but Cohen merely held up a hand. "We have too much to do. Let *our friend* help, just keep an eye on her to make sure she isn't going rogue."

The journey through hyperspace from New Bristol had gone smoother than Cohen had anticipated. The engine, despite being old, inefficient and obsolete, worked as well as anyone could have wanted, pulling *Dreadnought* through hyperspace without a hitch. It was, as White observed, exactly as boring as everyone always wanted interstellar travel to be.

Boring, but not quiet. The entire crew worked double shifts or more to construct, install or upgrade the ship's systems and equipment. The job was far from complete – in most areas they hadn't done more than scratch the surface of what needed to be done – but their efforts had given them a modern flight control system and upgraded navigation systems. They'd made changes to some of the internal doors as well, which had an annoying tendency to lock when closed.

"We're coming out of hyperspace in a few minutes, sir," reported White, hovering at the edge of the command suite. The internal communications system was still on the blink, so the crew were resorting to walking around the ship to pass messages.

Cohen grunted and stood up to follow White back to the bridge. At least this was a short walk; to send a message to someone in the aft cabins or service areas might mean a long walk with a good chance the recipient would have left by the time the messenger arrived.

The bridge was huge, far bigger than *Ascendant*'s had been, and it seemed most of the ship's officers were present. Chief Science Office Mueller was off to one side, intent on a slate. Sub Lieutenant Mantle had also found an excuse to be there, straying from the engineering department that was her natural habitat. Captain Warden was also on the bridge with, Cohen noticed with no small amount of annoyance, the Penal Marine, X. Cohen still hadn't figured out why Marine X was on active duty rather than imprisoned somewhere, but Warden had assured him that the situation was above board.

"Sixty seconds to normal space, sir," said Midshipman Susie Martin at the helm.

"Very good, Ms Martin. Let's put the sensor feeds on the screen and see what's going on around us."

"Aye, sir," said Wood at communications, punching at his controls.

"Coming out of hyperspace now," said Martin a few seconds later. There was a familiar lurch, then the displays changed to show the area of real space around the ship.

"No hostiles, sir," reported Midshipman Tiobaid MacCaibe at the fire control console.

"No incoming communications, sir," said Wood.

Dreadnought left hyperspace some distance from the point Admiral Morgan's fleet emerged. Nobody wanted to give the Deathless a chance to launch yet another ambush.

But from out here they could see little. Even the expanding clouds of debris produced by exploding star ships had dispersed to the point where they were no longer obvious.

"Take us in towards the rendezvous, Ms Martin," ordered Cohen. "Let's see what's going on."

"Aye, sir," said Martin. "One hundred and twenty second main engine burn at full power in three, two, one." She triggered the controls as her count reached zero, but instead of the punch in the back Cohen expected, *Dreadnought* simply accelerated gently away.

"Is that it, Ms Martin?" asked White, frowning.

"Aye, sir. The generators are working and the engine is reporting full power burn. No problems so far."

"Except we're barely moving," observed Cohen. "Any thoughts, Mantle?"

The chief engineer shrugged. "The engine is underpowered for the size of the ship. It was never very good, and it hasn't improved with age."

"Is this the best we can expect?"

"For now, yes."

"I may be able to help," said Agent O, her voice floating out of the ship's speakers. "There are parts of the engine that are inefficient and that could easily be replaced, yielding a fifty per cent increase in power."

Cohen looked at Mantle, who shrugged.

"Maybe later, Agent O, when we have completed this part of the mission."

"I understand, Captain. I will prepare implementation plans and a schedule for Sub Lieutenant Mantle to review."

"Scanners show a school of life pods ahead, sir," said MacCaibe. "Dozens of 'em, but no sign of any star ships."

"Plot a course, Mr Parks. Let's take a closer look at these life pods."

"Aye, sir, plotting now."

"Keep scanning, Mr MacCaibe. I don't want to get caught by surprise."

"Scanning continuously, sir, although it mebbe won't do much good. These scanners are ancient, fit for scrap but nothing more."

Cohen sighed and nodded. The scanners – both active and passive – were of such low resolution compared to their modern equivalents that anything smaller than a battleship wasn't likely to show up until they were practically ready to dock.

"The life pods are pinging their position and contents, sir. Looks like we have crew members from most of the larger vessels."

"Bloody hell," said Cohen as the details flashed onto the screen. The life pods – about the size of a shuttle and far from luxurious – were designed to support life for weeks at a time, albeit without any degree of real comfort. The list of pods, parent ships and crew members scrolled onto the screen as the tiny ships broadcast both their locations and the current status of their inhabitants.

"No sign of the Deathless, sir," said MacCaibe. "But they could be anywhere, just waiting to pounce, and we'd never know with these sensors."

"Thank you, Mr MacCaibe. Mr Wood, let's see if we can reach one of the pods."

"Aye, sir, working on it now." There was a pause, then a holding symbol appeared on the main display before the channel opened to show an unshaven face.

"This is Rear Admiral David Harper of HMS *Marlborough*. We require assistance."

"This is Lieutenant Commander Cohen of HMS *Dreadnought*. We will be alongside shortly to render assistance. Do you have reason to believe the enemy may be in the vicinity?"

"No, but we are short of food and we have people in need of medical attention."

"Understood, sir," said Cohen. "We will be with you in," he paused to glance at Martin, who held up her hands. "about six hours."

"Acknowledged," said Harper. "Good to see you, *Dreadnought*. Out." The channel closed and Cohen sat back, thinking hard.

"Get me a count of the life pods, Mr Wood, and a list of their occupants. I want to know who we'll be bringing aboard and which ships they represent."

"Aye, sir, working on it now."

"Did Admiral Morgan go down with the fleet?" mused White as Wood pulled together his list.

Cohen glanced at him, frowning, and White shrugged.

"Just wondered why Admiral Harper took the call instead of Morgan."

"Something strange here, sir," said Wood as he peered at his screen. Cohen pushed himself from his seat and stood behind the midshipman. "The life pods log their occupants," said Wood, pointing at his screen, "and they aggregate the information and include it when they send their distress calls. Admiral Morgan is listed as escaping from HMS *Duke of Norfolk II*, but his life pod is not here, sir."

"Not here? Then where it is?"

"I don't know, sir, but it can't have gone far – these things have a top speed in the hundreds of kilometres per hour."

"Nothing on the sensors, sir," said MacCaibe when Cohen shot him a questioning glance.

"The Mystery of the Disappearing Admiral," muttered Cohen as he sank back into his command chair. "Let's see what the survivors have to say."

The survivors had a lot to say, as it turned out. Apart from the criticism – both veiled and open – levelled against the Admiral's choice of tactics, the survivors mostly told a tale of Morgan's subsequent capture.

"Say that again," said Admiral Staines when Cohen contacted him to report their findings.

"Taken, sir, by the Deathless. It seems an enemy capital ship drew alongside the life pods, extracted Admiral Morgan's vessel from the collection, then departed into hyperspace almost immediately. The other survivors are somewhat indignant."

"I'm not at all surprised," muttered Staines, his face darkening.

"It's bad enough to lose the fleet without having our crews abandoned to their fates by the enemy. I'll talk to the Admiralty about this. In the meantime, we need to find and recover the Admiral."

Cohen frowned at the screen. "Find him, sir?"

"He's been kidnapped or taken prisoner. If the Deathless abandon people to the void, they surely won't hesitate to interrogate an admiral. We have to recover him." Staines leaned forward and jabbed a finger. "*You* have to recover him, Captain, or prove that he is dead and recover his backup from the life pod."

"Understood, sir," said Cohen stiffly, although he couldn't see a way to complete his orders.

"Keep me informed, Captain. Staines out."

Cohen sat back as the vidscreen switched to show the Royal Navy's screen saver.

"Bugger," he muttered. Then he stood up and straightened his jacket. No point moping around. It was time to get cracking.

3

"What do we know, people?" said Cohen as he strode back onto *Dreadnought*'s oversized bridge. "Give me something to work with."

"There are debris shells ahead, sir," reported MacCaibe. "Can't say which ships yet."

"Enough for the whole fleet?" asked Cohen as he slid his to his chair.

"Don't know yet, sir. We've found a hulk as well, dead and floating. Looks like HMS *Chelsea*, but the range is extreme."

Cohen nodded. It was a grim picture of defeat. "Pull it all together, Mr MacCaibe. We'll send it all home once we've collected the survivors."

"Aye, sir."

"How long till we're alongside the pods, Ms Martin?"

"Just over five hours, sir. I've set a rendezvous point three kilometres from the pods to avoid over wash from *Dreadnought*'s engine burn. It will take a few hours to dock all the pods but there is plenty of room in the forward starboard bay."

"Good. Let's keep things tight, people. I don't want to be here any longer than necessary."

A chorus of confirmations sounded off from the bridge crew as they turned to their tasks. Cohen turned to Mueller, who was hunched over a console.

"A Deathless capital ship kidnapped Admiral Morgan," said Cohen, summarising the situation. CSO Mueller nodded absent-mindedly, as if to suggest admirals ought to know better. "Admiral Staines wants us to recover him. Quickly."

Mueller looked up, frowning.

"That's not going to be possible without knowing where he's been taken," the scientist pointed out.

"Quite," said Cohen. "Which is where you come in."

"But we can't simply follow a trail through hyperspace," protested Mueller. "It doesn't work like that."

"We have a starting point, an initial direction, and knowledge of the surrounding Deathless systems," said Cohen, ticking the points off on his fingers. "We don't need certainty, just a well-educated guess. I'm sure Agent O would be happy to help."

Mueller made a sour face at the mention of the Valkyr AI, but even he could see the value in recovering the admiral.

"I want a list before we finish loading the life pods, Mr Mueller."

"Let me see what I can do."

Loading the life pods took longer than anyone expected, but producing a list of likely destination systems turned out to be somewhat easier than Mueller had suggested. By the time the first of the life pods had been safely stowed in the starboard bay, Mueller was able to present the list to Captain Cohen.

"There's only one system on this list," said Cohen. "How sure are you about this?"

"Certainty is impossible, Captain," said Agent O, "but our confidence is in excess of eighty per cent. The Koschites have a small facility in this system and it is the first that might be reached along the direction of travel taken by Admiral Morgan's captors."

"And if they skipped this system and went straight to the next?"

"The next system in that direction is another seventy-four weeks' travel," said Mueller, "and it isn't claimed by the Deathless according to the information Agent O holds."

"That is correct, Mr Mueller. There is no logical reason for the Koschites to travel to such a system."

"Unless they feared pursuit," muttered Cohen, "and they wanted to throw us off the scent."

"There will be no way to follow them if that is indeed what they have done, Captain."

"What sort of facility do they have in this system?"

"That is unclear," said Agent O. "According to my records, the facility is not listed as a civilian outpost, which suggests military purpose. Beyond that, I cannot say."

"Very well. Ms Martin, lay in a course for this system and prepare for hyperspace travel as soon as the pods are loaded."

"Aye, sir. Calculating now."

"Sir, Admiral Harper is asking to see you," said Midshipman Wood. "He's in the command suite."

Cohen frowned. The life pods were docking in the unpressurised forward starboard bay, so Harper must have donned an environmental suit to cross the open area to the internal airlock.

"Over to you, Mr White," said Cohen as he stood up and headed for the command suite. "Admiral," he said, closing the door behind him, "welcome to HMS *Dreadnought*."

"Thank you, Captain Cohen," said Harper, rising to shake Cohen's hand. The helmet of an environmental suit sat on the table next to a data slate. "What do you plan to do next, Captain?"

Cohen described Admiral Staines's orders and outlined his plan. Harper nodded along, seemingly in agreement.

"And we plan to use the rescued engineering personnel to help accelerate our refit efforts, sir. *Dreadnought* is still not fit for active service."

"Very well. Keep me informed, but for the moment I don't expect to take command," said Harper.

Cohen ground his teeth but nodded politely. "Of course, sir. I will keep you fully apprised of the situation."

"Good. Now, what about accommodation, food and fresh clothes?"

"Ah, yes. Refurbished and habitable quarters are limited, I'm afraid, but we have plenty of food and water for washing. Let me have someone show you to the assigned areas."

Cohen waited until the admiral had been escorted away from the command suite before he headed back to the bridge to oversee the rest of the life pod rescue mission. Three hours later, all pods had been secured and the crew were being given medical care, food and fresh clothes.

Nine and a half hours after entering the system, *Dreadnought* re-engaged her hyperspace engines and set off in pursuit of Admiral Morgan's captors.

And on the gently tumbling hull of HMS *Chelsea*, unseen eyes watched *Dreadnought* arrive, collect the life pods, and depart. As the great ship vanished, the Deathless observation drone fired up its wormhole communicator and reported all it had seen.

"Six, sir," said Mantle. "That's the best we can do." Despite being loaded as finished units to be fitted into the existing weapons ports, installing the new railgun batteries had fallen behind estimations.

"But we're also having to replace the cabling, ammunition delivery systems, fire control processors, targeting computers and rework the mounting points. It's a big job."

"Six, though?" asked Cohen.

"At best. Six installed, three ready for use, the rest are in progress."

He sighed. "Fine, we'll manage with six. What's next?"

They worked their way through the daily list, updating the status on the repairs. This was a daily chore - review, reprioritise, amend, plan - but progress had improved with the help of the rescued engineers. *Dreadnought* was starting to come together, even if she was still far from ready for action.

And there was still the mission to rescue Admiral Morgan to discuss.

"This is the ship that captured his life pod," said Mueller, pushing a still image from his slate to the main display. "Video from the life pods allows us to estimate her size and function."

"She's smaller than *Ascendant*, lightly armed and probably slow. A cargo hauler, not a clipper," said White, summarising their findings.

"A standard design," interjected Agent O, "built quickly to a common pattern. The Koschites have hundreds of such vessels."

Admiral Harper did little to conceal his outrage over Agent O's presence, especially after discovering her involvement in *Dreadnought*'s refit programme. His discomfort was matched by a disquieted shuffle around the conference table. Most of the crew had quickly become accustomed to Agent O's presence and assistance, but the command team and the rescued officers from Morgan's fleet still harboured suspicions. He was set to reignite his earlier rant, but becoming incandescent with rage would do little good against their current mission.

"But she will be faster than *Dreadnought*," Agent O went on, "if she is even still in the system."

"This is ridiculous," snapped Admiral Harper. "Whatever they're doing with Admiral Morgan, they're hardly likely to hang around waiting for us, are they?"

Cohen ground his teeth and forced a polite expression onto his face. "Maybe not, sir, but we owe it to Admiral Morgan to investigate, even if it is a hopeless action."

"And what do you hope to achieve when you find he isn't there? Tell me that, Cohen. What will you do?"

"If the Koschites took the admiral to this system," said Agent O, "it is because that is where they wanted him to be. They allowed the life pods to observe the jump to hyperspace, which suggests either supreme arrogance or deliberate intent."

"It's a trap," said Cohen.

"Or a gambit," said Agent O.

Cohen shook his head, although the suggestion that the Koschites might act elsewhere while *Dreadnought* was distracted was unsettling. "Doesn't matter. We have to pursue. Trap, gambit or wild goose chase, we have to know."

"Madness, Captain. We should return at once to New Bristol," said Admiral Harper.

"My orders are clear, sir. And *Dreadnought* is not without resource." He paused to glance at Warden. "If an opportunity is presented, we will attack and seize what we can." Warden gave a curt nod. It was all the confirmation Cohen needed that the Marines were standing by, should he order a boarding action.

"I hope you know what you're doing, Captain," hissed Harper. "For your sake and ours."

～

"Coming out of hyperspace in three, two, one."

Dreadnought flashed back into real space at action stations and with weapons ready. A thousand kilometres away, *Palmerston* emerged from hyperspace a few seconds later.

"No sign of the enemy vessel, sir," reported MacCaibe. "And no pings from *Norfolk*'s life pod."

"Understood. Mr Wood, let's ask *Palmerston* what they see. Their sensors are better than ours."

"Relaying the request, sir," said Wood. There was a pause while they waited for a response. "Negative, *Palmerston* reports no sign of any vessel within at least thirty light seconds."

"Dammit," muttered Cohen. This had always been a slim chance, but it was a blow nonetheless.

"Let's drop a couple of survey drones and see what they learn. Ms Martin, find us a flight solution to the inner system. I want to see it for myself before we head back to New Bristol."

"Drone deployment in progress, sir," said Wood. "Sixty seconds to launch."

"Flight solution laid in, sir." A flight plan appeared on the main display, *Dreadnought's* path shown in red.

"If I might suggest an alternative," said Agent O. A second flight plan appeared. "This solution would put us close to the Koschite facility and might allow us to establish why Admiral Morgan was brought to this system."

"You still think he was?" asked Cohen.

"Yes, Captain. Absence of the vessel we seek does not change the probability that this was their destination, and there is no other reason to come here if not to visit that station."

Cohen drummed his fingers on the arm of his chair for a few long seconds as he thought it through. "Agreed. Ms Martin, we'll use Agent O's solution and swing past this facility. Make things ready."

"Aye, sir."

"We'll depart in one thousand seconds and take a closer look at this station. Very close. Captain Warden, ready a team for an intelligence gathering assault. We'll make the final decision when we get there."

"Acknowledged," said Warden, pushing out of his seat and heading for the door as a timer began to count down on the main display.

"Mr Mueller, your insights on the station, its moon and the planet it orbits, please."

"The moon is large, almost a planet in its own right. It's covered in a dense but low-lying layer of vegetation and orbits a large rocky planet that seems to be geologically active. There are signs of volcanic activity and," – he paused to study something at his console – "quakes. Probably why they built on the moon rather than the planet itself," mused Mueller. Then he cleared his throat. "We'll learn more when we're closer."

"Stand by, everyone. We jump to hyperspace when the counter hits zero."

"It looks like a prison," said Cohen, frowning at the image of the Deathless facility. It sat on the planet like a monstrous concrete carbuncle, festooned with communication antennae and surrounded by a wall.

"Good place to hold a captured admiral, then," said White, although he too was suspicious.

Prisons, insofar as they were still needed, tended to be virtual. There was no point building an expensive physical building when a simple download allowed someone to be kept in a virtual prison for as long as necessary.

"Bring us into launch position, Ms Martin."

"Aye, sir, plotting now."

"Captain Warden," said Cohen, opening a channel to the Marine captain, "we'll have you in position in a few minutes. Not much moving on the surface and nothing in the air. We'll keep the rain off your heads, but you're on your own as soon as you hit the atmosphere. Get in, find the admiral, and get out. Clear?"

"As crystal, sir," replied Warden.

"Good luck."

"A Troop, load up," said Warden. "Launch in three hundred seconds, full armour, hostiles are probably aware of us. *Dreadnought* will provide support from orbit, but everything we need to worry about is down there."

"All this for a single admiral?" Marine X sounded sceptical as he checked the fittings around Goodwin's helmet.

"And the rest of the crew in the life pod," said Goodwin. "Can't leave anyone behind."

"Fair point. You're good to go, Gooders," said Ten, slapping Goodwin's armoured shoulder.

"Dropship, people," said Colour Sergeant Milton, clapping her hands. "Get moving."

The Marines made their way up the ramp and found seats on the dropship, which was perched at the edge of *Dreadnought*'s bay, ready to launch. Marine X took one next the door, settled his weapon into its spot beside his seat, put his head back and went to sleep.

"Amazing," muttered Milton as the rest of the Marines filed past and strapped themselves in.

"Shall I wake him?" asked Goodwin, hand poised.

"It'll just make him grumpy," said Milton, shaking her head. Then she turned her attention to the rest of the troop, checking that everyone was present, secure and ready to go.

"That's it, Captain, we're ready to rock and roll," she said, standing at the top of the dropship's ramp. Warden looked up from his slate, the face plate of his helmet up as he checked the latest information from the survey sensors. He glanced suspiciously at Marine X and took his seat beside Milton as the ramp closed behind him.

Unlike the Deathless dropships, this was a standard Royal Navy vessel built purely to deliver and recover troops from a planet's surface. It was fast, sleek and small, carrying nothing more than the equipment it needed to deliver its cargo and keep them alive on the surface for a few days.

<We're ready> Warden sent to the dropship's flight crew.

<Acknowledged, prepping for launch>

There was a rush of wind as the atmosphere in *Dreadnought*'s bay was sucked away. A screen at the end of the troop bay showed a launch countdown, and when the timer hit zero, the dropship – DS *Wickham* – fired its thrusters and nudged gently out of *Dreadnought*'s main bay.

<*Wickham* clear, firing main engines>

<Acknowledged, *Wickham*. Good luck. *Dreadnought* out>

There was a kick as the engines fired, and *Wickham* began its descent towards the target base.

"This is your pilot, Lieutenant Jordan. Thank you for choosing Wickham Air on this short trip to a hostile planet."

"Oh, shit," muttered Milton, "a comedian." Warden shook his head and closed his eyes.

"Flight time will be approximately forty-five minutes with increasing heavy turbulence and risk of serious injury or death towards the end. A safe landing is sincerely hoped for, and if we're really lucky we might be able to get you home again afterwards. Have fun."

Jordan was thankfully quiet for the next forty minutes and the Marines sat mostly in silence as *Wickham* shot towards its landing point.

"Final approach, ladies and jellyspoons. Buckle up," said Jordan over the intercom. Milton rolled her eyes.

Wickham began to bump and shake through the moon's thin atmosphere, braking as it fell towards the surface. The craft's stubby wings slowed its descent, dragging at the meagre air to scrub speed.

"No sign of hostiles yet," said Jordan in a jolly voice, "but we're approaching the daylight terminator. The wings are glowing nicely at the edge of their operating envelope, but we're almost down to atmosphere-appropriate flight speed, so it looks like entry burn isn't going to kill us today, folks."

"Might be less painful if it did," murmured Milton, and Warden could only agree.

The bouncing subsided as *Wickham*'s speed fell.

Marine X awoke with a snort. "Did I miss anything?"

Milton gave him a sour look.

"Five hundred metres and falling," said Jordan. "You'll be on the ground in two shakes of a lamb's tail."

"What the fuck...?" said Marine X, looking at Milton. She shrugged.

"He's a character, but we're not dead yet."

Which was good, but a fairly low bar for success at this stage of the mission.

A message arrived in Warden's HUD and he sat up.

<Be advised, *Dreadnought* under attack from orbital stations>

He acknowledged the message then opened a channel to A Troop. "*Dreadnought* is engaged, so we're on our own. Let's keep this tight."

There was a round of quiet muttering from the Marines. They checked their armour and weapons again, adjusting straps and shuffling webbing for the best possible fit.

"Goodwin, grab anything that might be of interest – files, documents, slates," said Warden.

"Of course, sir," said Goodwin. "Got my hacking kit all ready to go."

"Thirty seconds," said Jordan over the intercom, "good luck, and drop me a postcard if you get a chance."

The ramp lowered in preparation for landing, giving the Marines a view of the scrawny vegetation covering the moon's surface. *Wickham* was only fifty metres above the ground and slowing rapidly. Jordan heaved her around in preparation for landing and the greenery trembled in *Wickham*'s wake.

"Ten seconds," warned Jordan. "Looks like you'll need to breach the wall."

"Acknowledged," said Warden. "Heavy weapons to the fore, give us a breach, we're going in hot and fast."

There was a final burst of brutal deceleration and *Wickham* thumped down on its landing gear.

"Go, go, go!" yelled Warden over the radio, face hidden behind the helmet's armoured plate.

Marine X charged off the end of the ramp and into the brush, swinging around in search for hostiles. Warden followed with Milton close behind, and in seconds A Troop were dispersing across the surface, ready to bring their own special brand of entertainment to the locals.

"Give me a shout when you're done," said Jordan in one last message, then *Wickham* leapt back into the air and shot away, heading for the relative safety of the nearby hills.

Even before the sound of her engines had died away, the heavy weapons team had setup their tripod-mounted rocket launcher.

"Firing now," said Marine Victor Maxwell, using his HUD to

target a point on the wall of the Deathless facility The rocket launched, streaking away above the shrub. "Reload, same target."

A dull roar confirmed a direct hit, and then the second rocket was away, following the path of the first.

"Target hit," announced Marine Terry Lee, who was spotting for the heavy weapons team. "I reckon one more hit'll give us a workable breach."

The Marines fanned out, quickly approaching the wall through the shrubbery, well away from the diversionary breach the heavy weapons team were creating.

"Hit it again," said Milton, "then follow Section One over the wall."

"Will do, Colours," said Maxwell, triggering the loading of a third rocket. "A little to the left," he muttered, trimming the aim. "One more into the breach," he said with a grin as the third rocket raced towards the wall and blasted fragments of foamcrete across the open ground.

"Let's go!" shouted Milton, waving the heavy weapons team to follow close behind, racing across the open ground to catch the rest of the troop.

Dark smoke from the shattered wall drifted across the open ground. Marine X was first to the wall, closely followed by Goodwin and the rest of Section One. Section Two rocked up on the other side of the breach, while Section Three went to ground amidst the limited cover outside the wall.

"Up we go," said Marine X, firing his grappling line. The motor whirred, pulling the line taught, then he sprang onto the wall and heaved himself up and over. He dropped to the ground on the other side, the legs of his power armour taking the shock of landing. Marine X unslung his rifle and prowled forward, searching for enemies as the rest of the section followed his lead.

"Across there," signalled Corporal Drummond, waving at the entrance to the main building. Inside, the compound was clear. On the far side of twenty metres of open ground, the bulk of the prison reared up in a sheer concrete cliff three stories high.

Section One crossed the ground quickly, half the team bounding forwards, the rest holding back to give covering fire. Section Two came in from the side, hugging the building to reach the entrance.

"So far, so good," said Marine X as he squatted down next to a large cargo door, his back to the cool foamcrete. Section Two were already at the heavily fortified personnel entrance, checking for opposition while Marine Parker mined the door.

"Ten, shift," snapped Drummond. Ten looked around and realised the cargo door had been mined as well. He shuffled away from the shaped charges, grinning weakly inside his helmet.

"Syncing detonators," said Drummond on the common channel. "Three, Two, One." The charges fired in a series of loud bangs and Drummond nudged the door open. The Marines streamed forwards. Micro-drones flitted overhead, mapping the interior and searching for Deathless troopers.

Marine X led the way into the cargo area, a large open room with double doors on each wall. Drummond gestured, splitting his team to cover each entrance.

<Contact> sent Corporal Campbell of Section Two. The message was followed by several short bursts of fire. <Clear>

Marine X took the exit on the far side of the room with Goodwin and Harrington right behind him. The steel doors slid into the wall to reveal another huge room, this time with a platform lift in the middle. They circled, but the room was clear.

"Going down?" suggested Goodwin, but Ten snorted and shook his head. The doors on the east wall opened and the Marines whirled, weapons raised, only to be confronted by the rest of Section One, who had circled through another entrance from the cargo bay.

"That way," said Drummond, pointing at the last set of doors. The drones had already mapped the space on the other side and when Goodwin slid the doors back, a friendly face greeted them.

"Section Three are in the compound," said Warden. "It's quiet out there."

"Quiet isn't good," muttered Ten. He liked to know where the enemy were.

The two sections gathered in an open space with passenger elevators and staircases.

"Section One, downstairs with me," said Warden. "Section Two, upstairs with Milton."

Marine X took the lead, following his rifle down the stairs with the rest of Section One close behind. Halfway down the stairs the painted walls gave way to plain foamcrete, as if it wasn't worth decorating down here.

Marine X paused at a corner and a drone whipped past. A burst of fire drilled into the walls throwing, blasting chunks of foamcrete onto the floor. There was a curt shout of command and the firing stopped.

The drone rocketed past the Deathless position and headed deeper into the basement.

<Grenades> he sent, bouncing a couple of small devices down the stairs and into the corrodor below. There was a frenzied shout and the clatter of running feet before two sharp bangs tore through the air. Marine X eased around the corner and barrelled through the smoke, HUD switching to infra-red to peer through the murk.

Two guards lay in the corridor. Stunned, according to the HUD's AI. He kicked away their weapons and moved on.

<Contact> he sent redundantly. A brief burst of gunfire floated down the stairwell as Section Two worked their way onto the first floor, then things were quiet again.

A pair of heavy double doors slid open. There was a yell and someone opened fire. Marine X hurled himself to one side, rifle spitting as he went, and a half-seen figure fell back. For a moment, a gun sprayed bullets wildly into the corridor then it stopped, replaced by a chorus of panicked shouting from inside the room.

Marine X pushed himself to his feet and edged forwards, peering around the doorframe. It was a large room furnished with desks, chairs and sofas, with armoured windows looking out into an exercise compound of some sort. A lizardman was sprawled across the floor, blood leaking from a hole in his chest. A dozen Deathless prison guards in standard lizardman clones were standing around, hands up, all terrified.

Marine X edged into the room. None of the lizardmen was armed, and they stood very still as Ten eyeballed them down the sights of his rifle.

"On your knees," said Ten. "Hands behind head." His HUD translated the words into Koschite and played them through the helmet's external speakers. As Drummond came in, the lizardmen tumbled to the floor, hands behind their heads.

"Keep an eye on them," said Ten, moving to check the other rooms. An accommodation area, a kitchen and a shower block yielded a few more bodies in various states of dress and readiness, and the Marines herded them into the guard room.

Downstairs, the rest of Section One cleared the lower basement and captured their own bevy of unenthusiastic guards. The floor plan was pretty much identical – cells, a central exercise area and facilities for the guards.

"I don't think they're equipped for a surprise attack," said Milton as the guards sat quietly on the floor with their hands on their heads. "They're more used to handling unarmed prisoners than facing off against assault troops."

"Harly any weapons, no armour. Guards, not soldiers," said Marine X, nodding his agreement.

<First floor clear> reported Corporal Campbell. <No casualties, thirty-four prisoners in the mess>

<Acknowledged. Keep them there, we'll bring our prisoners to you> replied Warden.

"Where is Admiral Morgan?" said Warden, relying on the translation system to make his words intelligible. Nobody answered, but whether from ignorance or a lingering determination not to help, Warden couldn't tell. He repeated the question, but the silence of the Deathless guards merely deepened.

"Bugger it," he muttered to himself. He looked around, counting their prisoners. "A nice round twenty. Get them upstairs with the others," he said to Drummond. "Hand them over to Campbell then sweep the building again. Find the control centre and make sure we aren't surprised."

"Sir," said Drummond, issuing orders to his team. The Marines ushered the guards away, clattering up the stairs in a long line. The basement fell quiet.

"I hadn't expected a prison," said Warden as he walked down the line of heavy steel doors. "I thought it would be more like a barracks."

"Got something," called Goodwin from the guard room. Warden hurried back along the corridor and joined Milton and Marine X in a cluster around the terminal Goodwin was working at.

"Prisoner list," she said, scrolling down a page of text and reading the translations in her HUD. "Try cell four."

"Right," said Marine X, jogging back down the corridor with Milton. He stopped outside the door, rifle raised. "Ready," he called to Goodwin.

There was a clunk as the locks disengaged and the door slid open. Inside, a bright but plain cell held four bunks, four chairs, and four thin, tired-looking Royal Navy personnel. They stared at Marine X, clearly expecting him to be hostile. He lowered his weapon and flicked up the faceplate on his helmet.

"Morning, chaps," he said brightly. "Royal Marines, at your service. If you'd like to come this way, we have a taxi waiting to take you home."

There was a moment's pause, then three of the men hurried from the cell and down the corridor. The fourth stopped outside the door and extended his hand.

"Lieutenant Haddon," he said, "HMS *Molesworth*. You're a welcome sight. We thought we'd been forgotten."

"Call me Ten, sir," said Marine X, shaking the lieutenant's hand. "You sure you're not from *Duke of Norfolk II*?"

"I'm unshaven, Marine, not addled," said the lieutenant. "The crew from *Norfolk* are in another cell. Most of us are from *Molesworth* or *Apollo*."

"How many in total, sir?"

"Ninety. Seven newly arrived from *Norfolk*, the rest of us have been here rather longer."

"Shit," muttered Ten. He signalled Goodwin to keep opening

doors. She nodded and flicked down the list. All along the corridor, steel doors slid open and dazed crew stumbled out.

"Listen up," shouted Marine X, parade ground voice booming above the hubbub. "Head out, up the stairs, wait in the loading area."

Captain Warden strode down the corridor with Milton, helmets open as people streamed past and up the stairs. "What the hell is going on?" he asked, frowning.

"Ninety prisoners, sir," said Marine X, explaining the situation. "This is Lieutenant Haddon. No sign of the admiral."

"Admiral Morgan?" asked Haddon. "He never arrived. They took him away while *Norfolk*'s survivors were in transit, then dropped the others into this godforsaken hole with the rest of us."

"Bugger," muttered Warden, "that makes things difficult."

"Fuck Morgan," snapped the Lieutenant. "He's the reason we're in this mess. What about New Bristol? Is it still ours? Did we win?" There was a pregnant pause as the Marines looked at each other. "The attack?" Haddon went on. "The Deathless attack on New Bristol?"

"I think we'd better get back to *Dreadnought*," said Warden quietly.

"*Dreadnought*? HMS *Dreadnought*?" said Haddon, his eyes boggling.

"Let's get our people above ground," said Warden, "and I'll explain everything."

4

L ifting ninety rescued personnel from the surface of the prison moon required *Dreadnought* to send a second dropship, and Lieutenant Haddon fretted and fidgeted through the entire journey, desperate to make his report.

"It was an open secret," he said when he reached the safety of *Dreadnought* and was delivered to Cohen's command suite. He insisted on going straight to the Captain, refusing both food and medical aid in his haste to share his knowledge.

"They all knew about it, they baited us with it. The guards, the crew, the soldiers. They were going back to New Bristol to raid the system and teach us a lesson."

"You're sure?" asked Cohen.

"Of course I'm sure," snapped Haddon, his patience clearly frayed after weeks of captivity. "Sir," he added. "They were looking forward to it, planning what they were going to do and what sort of keepsakes they were going to collect."

Cohen glanced at his slate. Ninety minutes before the second dropship returned with the rest of the prisoners and the Marines. He nodded to White, his XO.

"Get ready to put us underway. I want us in hyperspace as soon as the bay doors close behind the dropship."

"Sir," said White, returning to the bridge.

"But we have to get word to Admiral Staines," protested Haddon, appalled at Cohen's lack of urgency. "You have a wormhole communicator, sir?"

"Had," said Cohen through gritted teeth. "We had a wormhole communicator, Lieutenant. The prison moon's orbital defences were largely ineffective, but it turns out that *Dreadnought*'s WC is considerably more susceptible to attack than we'd expected."

Haddon stared in horror, his mouth hanging open.

"It's just one of the weaknesses of flying a ship that was decommissioned before we were born, Lieutenant. It's completely obsolete, and rather fragile. You'll get used to it."

$\sim$

D*readnought*'s hyperspace engine fired as soon as the second dropship was safely secured in the main bay. The giant ship disappeared from real space to begin its journey back to New Bristol. The rest of the rescued prisoners were contemptuous of Admiral Morgan and his attempts to manage his fleets. Fed, medicated and properly clothed, they told their stories at considerable length, fleshing out the details of the ambushes into which Morgan had led his fleets.

"One moment we were at action stations, everything under control," reported a rating from *Duke of Norfolk II*. "The next, *Norfolk* was falling apart and we were abandoning ship. Morgan squirmed his way into our life pod, the cockroach, and we watched the vidscreens as the ship blew itself apart behind us. They came for our life pod only an hour after that, and that was the last we saw of the admiral."

"They grabbed him? Just like that?" White made a note on his slate, although everything was being recorded and transcribed. This rating was the fourth *Norfolk* crew member he'd spoken to, all with the same tale.

"As soon as we stepped out of the life pod on their transport, sir. They seemed to know who he was, just marched up and pulled him away. We were left there for hours while they worked out what to do with us, then they bundled us into a suite, locked the door and dumped us on that bloody rock to rot."

Later, there was a briefing conference for the officers of *Dreadnought*, *Palmerston* and *Molesworth* to bring everyone up to speed. Cohen stood at the front of the room with his XO, Lieutenant White. Captain Warden was amongst the last to file in, accompanied by Colour Sergeant Milton and, for reasons Cohen decided to leave till later, the Penal Marine, X.

"I'll keep this brief," he said by way of introduction as the stragglers found seats. "We believe New Bristol is about to be, or may already have been, attacked by a Deathless fleet. This intelligence comes from interviewing the personnel rescued from the prison moon. We're unable to notify Admiral Staines directly due to damage to the wormhole communicator sustained during our recent engagement, so we're en route to deliver the message in person.

"We hope to arrive before the attack, and thus play some part in the defence of the system." He paused to look around the room. "But we must face the possibility that we will arrive too late. After our raid on the prison, the Deathless know the secret is out and they must attack as soon as they are able. The longer they leave it, the greater their risk."

"And they don't know about our WC failure," said White, "so they'll be motivated to move sooner than they might have liked."

"It will take us almost a hundred and eighty hours to reach New Bristol," said Cohen, "and I want to make sure we're absolutely at peak readiness when we hit the system. Sub Lieutenant Mantle is our lead engineer and, with the assistance of Agent O, will be handing out maintenance and repair assignments. This work is vital, so push your teams as hard as you can.

"Any questions?"

"Where's Morgan?" said someone near the back of the room. Cohen searched for the questioner but couldn't be sure who had spoken.

"Unknown," said Cohen. "Although I hate to admit it, there's nothing more we can do for the admiral at the moment."

~

*D*readnought dropped out of hyperspace and engaged her main engines, accelerating sedately towards New Bristol. *Palmerston* – smaller, more modern – ripped past, diving in towards the skeleton of the London-class star base whose construction was being overseen by Admiral Staines.

"Battle debris, sir," said MacCaibe. "Still hot."

"Open a channel to HMS *Iron Duke*, Mr Wood," said Cohen, "and let's find out what's going on." *Iron Duke* was Admiral Staines's ship, and should be nearby.

If it's still in one piece, thought Cohen, burying the fear they might have arrived too late.

"*Dreadnought*?" said Staines when the comms channel opened. "Is that you, Cohen?"

"Aye, sir. Sorry we're late."

"Don't worry about it. They caught us unawares a couple of hours ago, gave us a right pasting. Now they're out near the asteroid belt doing who knows what."

"They're still here?" asked Cohen in surprise. A fast attack followed by a rapid retreat would be normal. Get in, do some damage, and get away before the enemy could respond. Hanging around suggested something else altogether.

"They're arrogant bastards," said Staines, "but we have nothing left to respond with. Until you turned up, we were just waiting for them to stick the boot in again."

"Understood, sir. We're still not fully operational, but I think we can give them a fright."

"Good. Give them a taste of cold steel, then get back here. Staines out."

Staines's head disappeared from the display screen. A tactical overview of the system flashed up in its place.

"Enemy fleet is out amongst the asteroids, sir, just like the admiral said," said MacCaibe. "Looks like a squadron of those fast attack craft."

"Nasty little bleeders," muttered White.

"Very well. Throw us into hyperspace, Mr Jackson. Five light seconds past New Bristol, then turn us around to face the enemy."

"Aye, sir, laying in the course now," said Midshipman Jackson at the navigation console, "Ready to go, sir."

"Let's go, Ms Martin."

"Aye, sir. Course is confirmed, engaging now," said Midshipman Martin at the helm.

Dreadnought flicked into hyperspace and reappeared almost immediately.

"Hyperspace transit complete," reported Martin, "turning to face the enemy. Manoeuvring thrusters firing." There was a pause as the thrusters strained to turn *Dreadnought*'s bulk. "Complete."

"Full ahead, three hundred second burn on the main engines," ordered Cohen.

"Aye, sir, full ahead it is."

There was a punch as *Dreadnought*'s main engines fired and the ship began to accelerate.

"Not quite as nimble as *Ascendant*, is she?" muttered White. "Time for a coffee, while she gets up to speed."

Cohen grunted as the engines pushed *Dreadnought* along, accelerating gradually but continuously.

"At three hundred seconds, Mr Jackson, I want to engage the hyperspace engines and emerge within five thousand metres of the enemy. Clear?"

"Five thousand metres, sir?" asked Jackson doubtfully. "I'll do my best."

"And we'll be firing as we go, Mr MacCaibe, everything you have, continuous fire, at as many targets as you can hit."

"Aye, sir. Locking it in now," said MacCaibe, selecting targets at his console. On the main display, the small cluster of enemy ships were prioritised and tagged. "Firing patterns laid in. Should work," he said, "if we don't fly right past them and emerge on the far side, o' course."

"Twenty seconds left on the main engine burn," said Martin.

"Hyperspace flight plan locked and ready to go," said Jackson. "The computer will be controlling it all, but there's still a decent chance we'll overshoot."

"Noted, Midshipman," said Cohen, settling back in his chair. The counter on the main engine burn hit zero and the acceleration ended. "Go, Ms Martin."

"Aye, sir, triggering sequence now."

The hyperspace engines engaged and *Dreadnought* wrenched. Almost immediately they disengaged and *Dreadnought* dropped back into real space. The targeting computer relocated its designated targets and began firing, exactly as ordered. Hurtling along at a little under three kilometres a second, they were past the enemy ships before their crews even had time to register their presence, and disappeared into the darkness.

"Report, please, Mr MacCaibe," said Cohen as the enemy fell far behind.

"Four enemy ships targeted, sir. We came out of hyperspace a gnat's breadth beyond the fourth ship," said MacCaibe, glancing up from his vidscreen to glance at Jackson, who shrugged, "so the guns could only fire on the first three. Looks like we hit all of them. One destroyed, one incapacitated, one maybe damaged. Difficult to tell."

"Excellent," said Cohen. "And what are the survivors doing?"

"Looks like they're bugging out, sir. Engines firing, they seem to be heading towards home."

"Good," said Cohen nodding. "Let's get after them. Turn us around, Mr Jackson."

"Aye, sir. Calculating burn pattern for manoeuvring thrusters and main engine."

"And then we'll see how these buggers do when they're being chased, shall we?"

But *Dreadnought* did nothing quickly. Pointing the great ship in a new direction was easy, but executing an about turn meant first slowing her vast mass and accelerating back the other way. Five hundred seconds passed before *Dreadnought* was moving in the right direction.

And that gave Sub Lieutenant Mantle an opportunity to contact Cohen. "Sir, what the hell are you doing to my hyperdrive engines?"

"Your engines, Mantle? Is there a problem?"

"They're not designed to be used like this, sir," said Mantle firmly. "If we keep doing this, they'll break."

"How soon?"

"What? I don't know!"

"Very good," said Cohen. "Let me know if it becomes imminent." He cut the channel. It was childish, but sometimes he just didn't want to hear Mantle's paranoid warnings.

"Plotting an intercept course," said Midshipman Jackson. "They're faster than us, sir, so we'll need to blip through hyperspace, and they'll know what we're doing as soon as we engage the hyperspace drive."

"If we're not careful, we'll run right into an ambush," said White. "Maybe we've done enough for now?"

Cohen glanced at his XO, then shook his head. "Engage the enemy, that was the order, and chase them from the system. We can hardly do that if we drop back now, eh? Anyway, blipping through hyperspace like this is a new tactic, so they're hardly likely to expect it."

White sat back in his chair, unconvinced. "New for us, maybe," he said quietly, "but wasn't this exactly the tactic they used to shred Admiral Morgan's fleet and cripple *Ascendant*?"

Cohen gave him a worried frown, but the heat of the chase was upon him and he shook off his doubts. It was time to carry the battle to the enemy.

5

"We destroyed one enemy craft and incapacitated a second, sir," said Cohen. Admiral Staines listened intently to the report from the vidscreen. "We are in pursuit of the last four. They're all small gunships, like the ones we faced at Akbar."

"Good work, Cohen. Chase them off, then come back here. Don't stray too far, though. We don't know where the rest of their fleet is."

"Understood, sir. Cohen out."

"What's the fifth ship doing, Mr MacCaibe," said White, dividing his attention between the four fleeing craft on the main screen and the incapacitated vessel shown on a side panel.

"Not much, sir. Looks like it's well and truly dead."

"Let's keep an eye on it, just in case it's just pretending."

"Aye, sir."

"What's your game?" murmured Cohen, leaning forward in his chair and resting his chin in his upturned palm. "Why run under conventional engines? Why not simply drop into hyperspace?"

"We're ready to blip through hyperspace again, sir," said Midshipman Martin.

"What's our firing status, Mr MacCaibe?"

"Ammunition stocks at seventy-four per cent, sir. Replenishment from stores is underway, fabrication of further ammunition is scheduled to begin once we leave action stations."

"Very good. Target the four ships, just as before, and let's see if we can give them another smack."

"Aye, sir, setting up the firing solutions now."

"How long will the hyperspace engines be engaged, Ms Martin?"

"One point four seconds, sir."

Cohen sniffed. Mantle wasn't going to like this, and it was bound to stress the engines, but they were short of options.

"Right, let's make this work, people. Fire the engines, Ms Martin."

"Aye, sir. Firing in three, two, one."

Dreadnought entered hyperspace, immediately dropping back out again. Cohen's data slate lit up with an angry message from Sub Lieutenant Mantle warning that the engines had been critically stressed. He swiped it away and turned back to the main display.

"That's weird," muttered MacCaibe as he searched through the reports from the scanners. Cohen turned to the weapons office. He gave a gentle cough and MacCaibe shook himself. "Sorry, sir. The enemy vessels have gone. There's nothing to target."

"Nothing to...So where the hell are they?" said Cohen, walking to the weapons console to peer over MacCaibe's shoulder. "Show me where they were."

MacCaibe's hands flicked over the console. "There, sir," he said, the tactical overview on the display updating to show the entire extent of the battle. The position of the enemy ships was marked with a blue ring, with *Dreadnought*'s trajectory in yellow.

Cohen stared at it for a few moments. "They disappeared while we were in hyperspace," he muttered to himself, "so it was coordinated, planned." Something about it felt off.

What was Warden's mantra? he thought. *If it feels wrong, it probably is.*

Cohen was suddenly chilled.

"Put us into hyperspace, Ms Martin. Ten seconds to anywhere!" he said urgently.

"We, er, negative, sir. Hyperspace engines are offline."

Cohen shot her a glare and punched open a channel to the Engineering Department. "Mantle," he barked, "what's going on with the hyperspace engines?"

"They're broken, just as I warned."

"They won't be the only thing that's broken if we can't get out of here!" Cohen snapped.

"Six hours, minimum."

Cohen closed the channel and swore under his breath. "Turn us around, Ms Martin. Get us out of here before…"

A proximity warning sounded and the tactical display updated to show enemy craft entering from hyperspace.

"Fire main engines now, Ms Martin!" snapped Cohen.

"Ay, sir. Firing now." *Dreadnought*'s engines pushed her forwards.

"Incoming," said MacCaibe. "Railgun fire, brace for impact."

"Target them, Mr MacCaibe," said White, fingers flying over his data slate, seeking damage reports from the automated monitors.

"Negative, sir. They've gone."

"Are you sure?"

"Yes, sir. Clear hyperspace engine signatures. They're away home for sure."

"Kill the engines, turn us back to New Bristol and get us there as quickly as possible," said Cohen.

"Aye, sir. Plotting flight plan now."

"Damage, White?"

"Remarkably little, sir. Firing the main engines was a genius move – it put us just beyond where they expected us to be and half their rounds missed entirely. They were firing as they left hyperspace, no time to correct."

"Genius my arse," said Cohen, shaking his head angrily. "It was blind luck."

"Mostly cosmetic damage, minor disruption to sensors and there are holes in the door of the port cargo bay. There's a team heading over to investigate."

Cohen sat back in his chair. "Looks like we got away with it," he muttered. Then he looked at Navigation. "Do we have a flight plan yet, Mr Jackson?"

"Aye, sir, laying it in now."

"Take us home, Ms Martin. White, command suite. Get Mantle." And he strode off the bridge.

~

"Some damned good flying," observed White, studying the replayed videos of the attack on the main display of the command suite. "Highly coordinated, very fast, very precise weapons fire. We'd have taken a lot more hits if we hadn't changed course."

Cohen snorted. "We fell for it. We fell into exactly the trap that caught Admiral Morgan."

"Twice," said White.

"Yes. Twice. These tactics have been theoretical for decades. Looks like the Deathless have solved the problems."

"They worked for us as well, though. Fast-flit hyperspace looks like the way to go."

"Except it damages the hyperspace engines," said Mantle, striding into the command suite. She sat down next to White, pulling out a data slate and flicked at it until a monitoring dashboard appeared on the main screen. "The power couplings are burned out; the central drive is stressed and the containment fields will need to be reworked before we fire the engine again. We're damned lucky not to have shattered the fuel containment system."

"But the dilithium crystals are okay, yes?" joked White. He grinned, then stowed his humour as Mantle and Cohen both glared at him. "Too soon, sorry."

"How long to get it running again?"

"About eighteen hours, sir," said Mantle. "But it wouldn't be a bad idea to take the whole system offline for a month and give her a complete overhaul."

"We don't have that sort of time. Do what you can. Use the

rescued crew, if they have the skills. When we reach New Bristol, we'll review."

"If I may make a suggestion, Captain Cohen," said Agent O, her voice floating out of the air.

"What did we say about eavesdropping, Agent O?" said Cohen.

"My apologies, Captain, but I wasn't eavesdropping. I'm running an observational experiment into post-combat stress amongst the command team, which involves analysing facial expressions, physical performance, vocal patterns and cognitive abilities. Listening to your conversation was an unavoidable side effect."

White shrugged indifferently, and Mantle frowned, clearly disturbed.

"That's not really within the spirit of our agreement, Agent O," pointed out Cohen.

"I'm sorry, Captain. I don't understand the relevance of ghosts. Can you explain?"

"Never mind," said Cohen, giving up in the face of what he recognised to be deliberately obtuse thinking. It seemed even AIs weren't above playing dumb with officers. "What was your suggestion?"

"The hyperspace engines on *Dreadnought* are old and inefficient," observed Agent O. "Restoring them, as Sub Lieutenant Mantle suggests, will take no more than twelve hours and twenty minutes given current resource availability. Naturally, that merely returns Dreadnought to operational readiness."

"That's the whole point, O," snapped Mantle, not even slightly pleased to have her nicely padded repair estimates slashed by the AI.

"Yes, but the next phase of the project should be to replace the engines entirely, not to overhaul them. I have prepared a work schedule and a design that would fit within *Dreadnought* and allow us to work on the system without requiring extended downtime."

"That's preposterous," snorted Mantle. "Replacing the engine will require us to open the hull and exchange major components. We're talking at least a year's time in dock plus three months post re-fit testing and trials."

"The design is far smaller and more efficient than the current engines, Sub Lieutenant, and I calculate construction could be handled in situ by a dedicated team of assembly fabricators we would build on board. We would need to scavenge elements from the current engine, or take delivery of additional materials, but given power and adequate resources, fabrication and installation should take no longer than fifty-four hours. I'm afraid it would take at least thirty hours to fabricate and program the required assembly units, though."

There was a stunned silence in the command suite as Agent O went on.

"This is my proposed schedule," said the AI as a Gantt chart flashed onto the room's main display. "As you can see, the longest task is the dismantling and removal of the current engines, which is a difficult task that would likely benefit from human assistance. At the end of the programme, *Dreadnought* would have far smaller, but vastly superior hyperspace engines. She would, I venture, be the envy of the fleet."

"I see you've allowed six hours as float," said Cohen weakly.

"Indeed, Captain. It makes sense in a complicated project to allow time for unforeseen circumstances."

"Can you give us a little time to think it over, Agent O? In private?"

"Of course. I expect Frida Skar to require assistance soon on the next stage of our research project, so I will then be fully occupied for the next few hours. Agent O out."

There was a click as Agent O disconnected from the command suite's audio-visual system.

"Has she gone?" muttered White, poking at the AV controls.

"Well?" said Cohen, failing to gain Mantle's attention.

Mantle flicked through the designs with her mouth open. Occasionally she snorted to herself or gave a little smile.

"Mantle," said Cohen after another minute. She looked up sharply, seeming to remember where she was. "Well?"

"It *might* work," she conceded. "It's years ahead of anything the Commonwealth has, or anyone in Sol, for that matter. Parts of this design are ground-breaking. The power delivery system is revolutionary."

"Would it allow *Dreadnought* to employ fast-flit tactics?"

"Maybe," said Mantle grudgingly. "Maybe. But we'll need to check it out. I'm not at all keen to simply launch into this without prototyping or trialling it in a test vessel."

"Agreed. Let's get the repairs done on the engine and think about this more once we're safely back at New Bristol. I'm all for improving the ship, but this feels like a big change."

"Huge," agreed Mantle, "and unproven."

"But if it worked..." said White.

"Quite," said Cohen, "we'd have an edge."

"We just have to hope our friendly AI doesn't start editing the ship while we sleep."

There was a pause while they all pondered this.

"I'll talk to Skar," said Cohen, "and make sure that both she and Agent O understand the limits."

"Do they have any interest in cloning or biology?"

"Not that I know of," said Cohen, frowning. "Why?"

White shrugged. "They're improvers. I'd hate to wake up with an extra arm."

6

Dreadnought reached the safety of her New Bristol orbit, and HMS *Iron Duke* was a welcome sight. Admiral Staines's flagship floated serenely through space with her support ship, *Albion*, just as she had done when *Dreadnought* left.

But they were no longer alone. The space around New Bristol teemed with ships.

Dwarfing them all, the new London-class orbital station that would become the fleet's regional base was slowly taking shape. The station's skeleton hung above New Bristol like the part-assembled wheel of a bicycle. Small two-man or AI-controlled assembly craft were everywhere. They shifted and installed components, steadily adding flesh to the bones.

A vast bulk freighter, bigger than *Dreadnought* but made up almost entirely of hold space, hung a thousand metres from the station. Its main bay doors were open and a stream of material flowed out, ferried by tugs to the staging area which circled the construction site. Three more were queued behind the freighter, awaiting their turn to unload.

On the far side of New Bristol, a growing number of locally-built low-gravity fabrication units – dozens of them – fed on the resources beginning to arrive from the newly established mining operations in the asteroid belt.

Some of their output went to the planet's surface to speed construction of Ashton's nascent space port, or to build the new hyperloop system that would soon link the colony's settlements. Some would be used to refit the mothballed ships trickling into the system, or to create new resource processing plants to further increase the system's output. And the rest would go back to the asteroid belt as new automated extraction plants to accelerate the mining efforts and increase the rate at which the elements and minerals required by the fabricators were generated.

But most of the system's output was being sent as finished components to the space station, ferried away by a small fleet of haulage tugs to be slotted into the rapidly growing structure.

Cohen, White, Warden and Mantle observed it all from the shuttle carrying them to *Iron Duke* from *Dreadnought*. They were ushered quickly to a conference room whose windows gave them a view of the construction zone.

"I think this must be the beginning of the end," said White, taking in the vast quantity of materials being brought to bear in the Deathless conflict.

"Impressive, isn't it?" said Governor Denmead as she came into the room with Colonel Atticus and Admiral Staines. "But I'm afraid this isn't even the end of the beginning, let alone the beginning of the end."

"Although it might be the beginning of the beginning, if you get my drift," said Staines. He shook hands with the visitors, gesturing for them to sit.

"We'll keep this brief," said Staines. "New Bristol is secure, for the moment. Or at least as secure as we can make it."

"It's also now the fastest-growing colony in the Commonwealth," said Denmead. "We're building new cloning facilities on the surface and soon the rate of new arrivals will exceed a thousand a day. From there, it will only accelerate."

"Wow," muttered White.

"You don't need to know the details," said Atticus, "but this sleepy backwater is now on the front line, and investment in both civilian and military infrastructure has been hugely increased."

"The Government's full attention has now fallen upon this matter," Admiral Staines went on, gesturing at the windows. "The might of the Commonwealth is being brought to bear, and from here on, the pace will increase. The fleets gather. This is not the only station under construction, and we will soon see the greatest military deployment in centuries."

"Where does *Dreadnought* fit into all of this, sir?" asked Cohen. "If everything's under control, does *Dreadnought* even have a role?"

"Appearances can be deceptive," growled Staines. "If the Deathless arrive in force before we're ready, everything could change. If they guess at our plans, or learn of them from a privileged source, our efforts will have been in vain."

"Which is why the whereabouts of Admiral Morgan is a high priority," said Atticus. "If he lives – worse, if he's been captured – then he presents a security risk."

"And that's where *Dreadnought* comes in. We might all wish it wasn't the case, but *Dreadnought* is still our best option despite our recent losses. We have more information now, thanks to your efforts, so you're going back out there, today, and you're going to complete the mission. Find Admiral Morgan, bring him home, and bring me whatever information you can about the Deathless and their plans."

"Sir, *Dreadnought* needs a full refit," began Mantle. Staines cut her off.

"Noted, Sub Lieutenant, but you're going anyway. Make the best of it, do what you need to do to keep the ship running and cut whatever corners must be cut. Is that clear?"

"Yes, sir, but–"

"Then that concludes today's briefing. Good luck to you all," said Staines, striding from the room with Governor Denmead following.

"Things are a bit busy around here, Tom," said Atticus by way of explanation, "but it was good to see you." He grinned. "Opportunities for glory and promotion abound, ladies and gentlemen, but time is short and there is much to do. If you'll excuse me." And Atticus was gone.

"Promotions, eh?" said White. "I could fancy a little promotion."

"Coming from the Old Boy, who famously resisted promotion beyond Captain longer than any Marine on record, I can't say the prospect of promotion fills me with enthusiasm," said Warden.

"There'll be no promotions if we don't find the admiral," pointed out Cohen. "So let's stop gawping at the view and get back to work."

7

Morgan inspected his pristine fingernails for any of the filth commonly found on a poorly-maintained ship. He'd already counted the panels in the ceiling and walls. He'd tried counting the rivets before realising that he was drifting down the path to madness. He'd tried sleeping, but the table – like the chair, the floor, the ceiling and the walls – was made of metal and about as comfortable as a rock. No matter how he sat, slumped or lay down, he couldn't relax.

He needed to distract himself from the awesome boredom of his confinement. He closed his eyes and imagined he was on his favourite golf course about to tee off. Morgan sank into his daydream and focussed on the smell of the grass, the swing of the club and the feel of wind on his cheek.

When the door eventually opened, Morgan was momentarily startled. He'd adjusted to the solitude and the noise was a terrible intrusion.

He pulled himself together as two figures entered. He sat up straight, gripped the waist of his uniform jacket, and tugged it a little straighter. There wasn't much he could do about the unsightly stubble, the yellow staining of his collar or the ungentlemanly stink that rose from his armpits, but these barbarians hadn't seen fit to provide him with even a sink and a razor.

Morgan gave his interrogators his best stony glare as they sat down opposite him. The junior one, judging by his uniform, set down coffee cups and pushed one across the table. Morgan turned his scowl to the cups, made from some kind of recycled synthetic and so thin they were almost transparent. They didn't use proper china, even for an admiral, and that was as calculated an insult as he had ever received.

"Good morning, Admiral Morgan," said the lead interrogator in lightly accented English against all evidence to the contrary.

Morgan fumed for a few seconds before grudgingly responding. "Good morning."

"You can drink the coffee, it is not drugged."

"How very gracious of you," sneered Morgan, leaving the cup untouched.

"I am Senior Lieutenant Lucas Silva, and this is my colleague, Agent Alexandra Romanov. We are Naval Intelligence officers of the Koschite Republic."

When Morgan didn't respond, Silva smiled, "Tell me, Admiral, what went wrong at the Battle of...what do you call it?" The man swiped through pages on his data slate until he found the information he sought. "Ah yes, The Battle of Akbar. That is a strange name to give a battle, is it not?"

Morgan took a sip of the coffee to buy thinking time, and grimaced. It wasn't actually bad, but he didn't feel like praising his captors.

"We weren't naming the battle, we were naming the system. HMS *Akbar* has been the name of several ships, this time we used it for a system. It's just a codename, picked at random from a list. There's nothing special about it."

"I see. And what went wrong in the Akbar system? What mistakes did you make, Admiral, hmm?" Silva asked.

Morgan felt his neck flush, "Nothing went wrong, my plan was carried out to the letter. To the letter, I say!"

Romanov rolled her eyes and sighed.

"Really, Admiral? Your plan did everything you set out to accomplish?" pressed Silva.

"This is outrageous!" protested Morgan. "You keep me locked up like some common criminal, you question my plans, and then you have some wet behind the ears junior officer interrogate me. This is beyond the pale. Beyond the pale, I tell you!"

Agent Romanov leaned back, locked her fingers together and cracked her knuckles with a series of revolting pops.

"What did you expect, Admiral? To be welcomed with open arms? Your people and mine are at war, in case it had escaped your notice," said Silva calmly.

"I'm an Admiral, damnit! I demand the respect due to my rank. If you must pester me with questions, I insist you find a senior officer to speak to me, not some underling."

There was a faint snickering sound and Morgan's eyes flicked toward Romanov. She was fiddling with her forearm. No, she was drawing a long thin blade from a sheath strapped to her arm inside her sleeve.

Silva tutted softly. "Now, Admiral, I hardly think you want that. Aboard this ship, the ranking officer is the captain. She is, you understand a very busy woman and like many Koschite officers, she takes a direct approach to her work. I really do not think you would enjoy it if she conducted this interview."

Romanov balanced the blade on the tip of her finger, slowly moving her hand to keep it upright. She shook her head slowly to confirm that no, Admiral Morgan really wouldn't want to speak to the captain.

Morgan swallowed drily and took another swig of the coffee to cover his sudden fear.

"Admiral," said Silva, his tone friendly but firm, "I need you to tell me what happened in the battle. Come now, it is in the past, it can do no harm for you to speak openly, can it?"

Romanov flipped the knife end over end between her fingers. It was wickedly sharp, but Morgan could sense she wasn't going to cut herself. He'd known people who had the irritating habit of fiddling like this with a pen or a data slate stylus, but never a stiletto. The woman was clearly cracked in the head.

Morgan drew his attention back to Silva, licking his lips and trying to ignore the blade-wielding nutjob to Silva's left.

"I acted as I thought best for the future of the Commonwealth," said Morgan stiffly.

"I am sure you did, Admiral, I am sure you did. And that was very brave of you."

"So brave, so bold, so heroic," crooned Romanov, cocking her head and smiling at him. Morgan shuffled uneasily in his seat. He felt like he was being sized up by a cobra.

"What happened wasn't my fault," said Morgan.

"I see. It was not your fault," Silva said, making a note on his data slate. He sighed softly. "Admiral, I would like very much to be able to make a good report to my superiors, do you understand?"

"Yes, of course."

"Good. Then you will understand when I say that, at Naval Intelligence, we are expected to present facts. Detailed facts. Interpretation and opinion have their place, to be sure, but we always start with facts. I am sure the same is true in the Royal Navy of the Commonwealth, is it not? Your intelligence branch does not simply guess at their conclusions, they gather data, they check it, they analyse, they find facts, and then they interpret. Yes?"

"Yes, I suppose so," conceded Morgan.

"I hope you appreciate, then, that the only thing standing between you and a prisoner of war camp on some long-forgotten asteroid, is the quality of my report?"

Morgan recoiled in horror. "Now just you wait a minute," he snarled. "You can't threaten me! How dare you, you little pipsqueak! This is not how you treat a high-ranking officer, regardless of which side they're on."

"I dare because we are at war, Admiral," said Silva, leaning back in his seat as if he hadn't a care in the world. "Are you going to be more forthcoming? My commanding officer wants useful information, and she wants it last week."

"I don't give a tuppenny-fuck what she wants, Senior Lieutenant Silva," sneered Morgan. "You will respect my rank or you and your freakish colleague can fuck off and die for all I care."

Quick as a snake, Romanov was around the table. She twisted Morgan's arm up and around, locking out his wrist and subsequently pinning it to the table. The knife appeared, twirling, and slammed into the table so fast it sliced into the metal top between Morgan's middle and ring fingers. Morgan stared, eyes wide, barely able to breathe.

Silva winced, and his face screwed up in the exact expression of someone who couldn't bear to watch a horror holovid.

"Fucking talk, you pompous windbag!" Romanov hissed.

A bead of sweat trickled down Morgan's temple. There was something behind those eyes, something animal, something barely held in check.

"Alright, alright!" Morgan howled. "What do you want to know?"

Silva barely opened his mouth to speak before Romanov snarled, "Tell us about the battle! Talk!"

"We...we arrived at Akbar, as planned. The fleet was to deploy a network of surveillance drones and a wormhole transmitter in each system as we checked for a Deathless presence."

"Deathless? Who is Deathless?" Romanov barked, looking meaningfully at the razor-bladed knife she still twisted between Morgan's fingers.

"You are!" Morgan blurted. He could feel bile rising in his throat as he anticipated the knife doing its bloody work on his hand. "It's what we call your people."

"Why for you call us this?" demanded Romanov.

"Agent Romanov, please," said Silva with forced politeness. "I don't think we care what nickname they use for us, and you are obviously aware that it is because the Ark of our ancestors was called Koschei the Deathless. Kindly let the Admiral speak."

"Yes, right," Morgan cleared his throat. "As I was trying to say," he said, licking his lips nervously. "I say, would you mind taking that away?" He looked at the blade resting a mere hairs breadth from the skin between his fingers.

Romanov looked down at it, then back up at him. "Yes."

"Yes, what?"

"Yes. I mind. Continue."

Morgan stared for a few seconds before he went on. "The fleet emerged from hyperspace in Akbar, and we were to execute the same procedures we'd already carried out several times in different systems."

"And?" Silva prompted.

"The Deathless fleet arrived, just a couple of small ships at first," explained Morgan, looking from Silva to Romanov. "I repeated the order for the fleet to stay in formation and not to provoke the enemy or attack, until ordered to do so."

Romanov snorted. "You think they obey such an order?"

"Of course," Morgan said indignantly. "They have to obey orders. I'm their admiral."

"Agent Romanov, would you mind dropping the comedy English, I know you speak the language fluently," Silva said. The woman rolled her eyes and groaned.

"Why did they lumber me with you, Silva? I had him just where I needed him," she said in Koschite.

"He's talking, Alexandra," said Silva, "that's where we need him. Please, sit down so we can get this over with." Romanov grunted and unthreaded the knife from between Morgan's fingers, backing away to return to her seat.

"Now, Admiral Morgan," said Silva, switching back to English, "you were saying. You ordered your fleet to hold position."

"Yes, of course. I didn't want them starting an all-out attack."

"But why not?" said Silva. "Would that not have been the best thing for them to do, given the sudden appearance of our fleet?"

"As long as they followed your orders. Why did you think they would do that, when it was clearly suicidal?"

Morgan straightened his jacket again and pushed his chin up.

"Because, sir, the Royal Navy follows orders. It's what we do. Wouldn't your fleet follow the orders of their admirals?"

Romanov snorted again. "No, our fleet would never follow an admiral who gave such incompetent orders. The captains would order the attack if the admiral put them at risk like that."

"Then your fleet are ill-disciplined scum, madam," Morgan sneered.

"Scum who win," she pointed out.

"Our ancestors were not quite as bloody as yours, Admiral," Silva said.

"Speak for yourself, Silva," said Romanov. "Mine were every bit as bloody a bunch of bastards as Morgan's."

"Aye, my ancestors were a pretty rum lot, but by the *Beagle* they were brave," Morgan said.

"My point," said Silva, "is that your Navy measures its traditions by the century, whereas the Koschite Navy measures its traditions by the decade, and there are precious few of them. Our ancestors came to live in peace, but now we are at war, and we have no choice but to win, no matter the cost. Your crews held their discipline, even after the first shots were fired. You had complete control, and yet your plan didn't work, did it?"

"I knew what I was doing. I laid the plan perfectly. There was no way it could go wrong."

"But there's the crux of the problem, Admiral. It did go wrong, didn't it?"

Morgan scowled and looked away. "The plan was sound," he insisted. "The plan didn't go wrong."

"Then how did *Ascendant* escape, Admiral?"

The admiral seemed upset by the accusation, but Silva couldn't be certain. He wondered if these Commonwealth clones had different emotional tells, different signs he should be searching for.

"How did *Ascendant* escape, Admiral?" he repeated.

"That jumped up little prick Cohen, that's how."

Silva looked at his data slate. "Lieutenant Commander Cohen. A relatively junior officer. What about him?"

"He turned and fled, along with HMS *Palmerston*."

"Ahh yes, *Palmerston*. Which later destroyed a ship escorting the flagship of Admiral Tomsk, of the Koschite Republic Navy. A tiny ship armed with a simple kinetic weapon built purely for orbital bombardment."

Morgan nodded.

"And these two ships escaped the ambush, despite your best efforts."

"That's not my fault. I gave you the fleet on a platter, and your people ballsed it up. You and your ill-disciplined navy of scum," sneered Morgan.

"We can argue about fault later," said Silva, "but we followed your plan, exactly as agreed. It was supposed to result in the annihilation of the entire fleet. Not most of it, the entire fleet."

"I gave you more than enough information to do that. I brought them to your door like lambs to the slaughter, as requested. Any failure is entirely on your part, Lieutenant."

"Senior Lieutenant," corrected Silva. "Admiral Tomsk's assessment is different. He feels you undersold the capabilities of *Ascendant* and her captain."

Morgan laughed out loud. "How did I do that, precisely? I gave you his complete personnel file, along with that of every other bridge officer in the fleet. What else did you need?"

"For Cohen to defeat Tomsk with only the training indicated in your files and with the ships he had available is inconceivable," said Romanov.

"You use that word, but your dictionary must be leading you astray. It doesn't mean what you think it means."

"He must have had more specialist training," persisted Silva, "and those ships must have been more than was claimed. What aren't you telling us?"

Morgan laughed at him again. "You can't be serious? *Ascendant*

was your ship, you must know its capabilities. If they made any modifications to it, it wasn't to add a super weapon, not even close."

"And what about Captain Cohen?"

"What about him? He's a cunning sod, but he has no special training. If he'd had advanced training of any kind, it would be listed in
his file. I have access to all personnel files of junior officers. If there
were anything above my clearance, there would still be evidence of it
in the files. No, I'm afraid the devious little shit simply outwitted
Tomsk. I should probably have thrown him into the frontline. There,
I admit it, Tomsk's defeat is all my fault because I failed to put the
captain of a captured enemy vessel at the front of the battle order.
Mea culpa. Happy now?" asked Morgan.

Silva shrugged. "It is not me you want to please," he said quietly.
"It is Admiral Tomsk."

"No, I honestly don't. I've done what I said I would do, and Tomsk
fucked up his end of the operation. So what are you going to do about
Cohen and his band of misfits?"

Romanov paced back and forth, waiting for Silva to return and
wrap things up with this traitor. Tempting though it was, she
wasn't planning to interrupt second time, unless Morgan got
belligerent again, which didn't seem likely. In her estimation, he was
a venal coward.

The sooner Silva passed on the orders from Admiral Tomsk, the
sooner they could leave this system and get on with something more
useful to the wider war effort.

Turning an enemy officer into an intelligence asset was her stock
in trade, and usually she found it professionally fulfilling. Morgan
hadn't been one of her agents and, having met him, she was glad she
hadn't dealt with him before.

The man was a disgrace to his people. Not just a traitor, but an
arrogant, slimy buffoon. Even dealing with this debrief was distaste-
ful. He hadn't turned because of any deeply held belief or because of

his ethical stance. His motivation for betraying his people had to come from amongst the more disreputable reasons. For Morgan, she deduced, it was about ego, power and self-interest, not a high-minded philosophy of self-sacrifice in the fight for the future of humanity.

She glanced at her HUD for the time. Damnit, Silva had asked her to keep an eye on the admiral, leaving the room for something he said would take ten minutes. They were now approaching sixteen. Why was it some people couldn't estimate task durations accurately, she wondered? Over the years, she had learned no-one else meant it when they said they would be there in five minutes; friends and colleagues would give vague times with no real concept of how far they had to come or how long it would take.

Romanov looked at the back of Morgan's head. He was studiously ignoring her, taking occasional sips from the bottle of water they'd given him. It was tempting to spend a few minutes using her considerable skills to beat more information from him, but she knew Silva would report it and she'd be sent on some kind of self-control course, or have to have a long and boring conversation with her superiors that would keep her out of the field even longer.

She spent a happy few minutes visualising the smug egotist's head being slammed into the desk to punctuate the questions she would put to him. Then she considered breaking his fingers, one by one. With most subjects, she wouldn't even dream of using physical torture because she believed it unreliable and of course, morally reprehensible. But if ever there was someone for whom the rules were meant to be broken, it was Morgan. The man was a perfect candidate, an obvious coward and bully, someone she felt sure deserved everything that happened to him, on some level.

Romanov had barely begun picturing his response to water-boarding when Silva returned to the room.

"Where the hell have you been?" she demanded in Koschite, in a sweet tone to mask her displeasure from Morgan. She was buggered if she was going to show weakness in front of him.

"I've been trying to keep the brass happy. They want to know what we're going to do with Morgan, but they've left the decision to us."

"Really?" said Romanov, not able to hide her surprise. "So we can be their scapegoats?"

"Yes, that was my interpretation anyway."

"Could we just kill him?" she asked, hoping against hope.

"Mmm. I understand the temptation," said Silva, although he wasn't at all sure if Romanov was serious, "but I think they were looking for something more substantive than that. They want to know if he can be of use to us."

"For intelligence, or as an admiral?"

"The latter, it seems."

"You're joking," said Romanov.

Silva frowned; he was sure he hadn't made a joke.

"Did you explain what he's like? How 'competent' he really is? The man's an idiot." She glanced at Morgan, oblivious to the content of their conversation.

"Yes, of course, but they seemed to think I was exaggerating," replied Silva, his eyes showing resignation to the inevitable weight of bureaucracy.

"What do they want us to do, then?"

"He's to be tested."

Romanov perked up a little at this, "Tested. Is this about to get interesting?" The blade reappeared in her hand, and she glanced again at Morgan.

Silva frowned at her reaction. "No, they want his recommendation for dealing with Cohen. They want him to demonstrate his willingness to advise, and determine if he has any lingering loyalty to the Commonwealth."

Romanov cursed. "Because you and I aren't enough to determine that he's a cowardly weasel with no shred of loyalty for his own people."

Silva shrugged. He'd argued as hard as protocol would allow, but ultimately the decision belonged to those who outranked him. "We are to let him suggest something on his own."

"Of course," Romanov agreed. How else would they hear the truth? A man like Morgan would say whatever his superiors wanted to hear, or what he thought they wanted to hear, at least. Such men had always been a significant weakness for intelligence gathering; a capable intelligence officer looked for truth and detail from their assets, not embellishment and bias. A professional had to know when the assets they nurtured were telling them what they wanted to hear, rather than what they needed to know.

"What do you think he'll do?"

Romanov considered the question. "He's a weak man, he'll want to protect himself from Cohen. He'll suggest we hunt down his ship no matter the cost in order to protect himself from discovery. He wants a way back if he doesn't like how things play out with us. If he's not uncovered, he'll be able to slip back into their command structure with ease, and he wants to preserve that."

Silva nodded his agreement and sat down. Romanov sat beside him, arms folded, giving every indication she was not about to spring into violence. She wanted Morgan as relaxed as possible for a man of his nervous disposition.

"I'm afraid I have to report that Captain Cohen and his new ship, *Dreadnought*, are still active. They appear to be searching for you. Of course, we don't know for certain, since you are no longer providing us with live intelligence," said Silva.

"That can't happen," said Morgan. "He can't be allowed to capture me. You must send a fleet to intercept him. Destroy him and *Dreadnought* before he causes any more damage or works out what's going on."

Silva forced himself not to look at Romanov, then waved a hand to dismiss Morgan's suggestion. "We can't send a fleet after every Commonwealth ship, especially one as venerable as *Dreadnought*. We must manage our resources and strike to maximum advantage."

Morgan slapped the table with his palm. "Damnit. This is advantageous. Cohen is a thorn in my side and a threat to everything we've been working for. He must be brought to heel."

"If we destroy *Dreadnought*," said Silva, "won't they just give him a new ship?"

Morgan shook his head, "No. He's lost one already. If he loses another, and a capital ship at that, he'll be demoted. He'll be blamed for the loss, and he'll end up with a desk job or a bridge position under another officer. It'll be years – decades maybe – before they'll risk giving him another command, by which time this will all be over."

"That sounds like revenge," said Romanov.

"It's not," Morgan blustered, "it's sound strategic thinking. Sooner or later, Cohen will work something out, find some incongruous piece of information and get suspicious. The longer you let him pursue this mission, the sooner he'll work out there's a mole in their midst."

Romanov chose not to correct him on his use of the singular. "You think he could expose you? How will targeting him help?"

"Because, madam, if he is given a new position he'll either be desk-bound and unable to investigate, or he'll be too busy with the day to day business of a warship and integrating with the crew. He won't have time to think about my activities, much less the resources to investigate anything. Once he stops pursuing me, there won't be anyone looking. So have at it, I say. Find out where he is, if you don't already know, and hit him hard." He paused and sat back, looking from one to the other. "Will you take that to your superiors?"

Romanov glanced at Silva, who gave a slight nod.

"As you wish, Admiral," she said, her stony face betraying none of the satisfaction she felt at being proved correct. "We'll present your suggestions and see where they lead."

8

"Sixty seconds to System Four, sir," reported Midshipman Martin. The journey from New Bristol had been a non-stop sequence of upgrades, improvements to the ship, training and more upgrades., all aimed at getting the crew ready for this moment.

"You know the drill," said Cohen from the command chair. "Let's get this done, people. Nice and tidy."

"Schedule is on screen," reported Wood, throwing the script onto the main display.

"Where's Mueller?" snapped Cohen, glaring at the only empty seat on the bridge.

"Fifteen seconds," said Martin.

A flustered Mueller hurried in.

"Glad you could join us, Mr Mueller," said Cohen as the Chief Science Officer finally took his seat.

"Three, two, one." Martin counted down to *Dreadnought*'s emergence from hyperspace. System Four's star filled half the main display, as *Dreadnought* shot past, well within the orbit of the system's innermost planet.

"Scanning, all bands," said MacCaibe.

"Drone launch underway, six seconds remaining."

"Course laid in, hyperspace engine engaging in ten seconds," said Martin.

"Drone launch complete, comms links check out, good to go."

"Scan complete," said MacCaibe.

"Engines firing in three, two, one," said Martin.

Dreadnought dropped safely back into hyperspace and tore away from System Four, heading for the anonymous safety of interstellar space.

"In system time was nine point eight seconds," reported Martin.

"Excellent work, people," said Cohen. "Begin stage two manoeuvres."

An hour later, *Dreadnought* dropped out of hyperspace beyond the range of any scanners the Deathless might have deployed to monitor System Four. The surveillance drones they left behind during their short visit began transmitting data to *Dreadnought*, feeding it a continuous stream of intelligence.

"The base is on the planet in the northern hemisphere, exactly as Agent O described," said White when the command team convened to review the analyses. "But there's an orbital platform as well, and that's protected by a small fleet of corvette-class ships – six, as far as we can tell, although two are a long way out – and there may be other automated systems we haven't found yet."

"The survey drones are working well and gathering information about movements in System Four," said Mueller, for once engaged and enthusiastic. "The gravimeters and hyperspace anomaly detectors are spreading out and mapping the system in ever greater detail, and we'll soon know the location and velocity of every object over a kilometre in diameter."

"A kilometre? That's great, but what about smaller things, like ships?" asked Cohen.

"Oh, them too, yes, but scientifically they're far less interesting. If they're moving or transmitting, they should be fairly easy to spot." Mueller beamed, but it wasn't entirely clear what he was pleased about. "Our information will further improve as the drones move apart and their baseline of operation widens."

"We've tweaked the stage two flight plan to take account of the positioning of the corvettes," said White, throwing the revised plan onto the main display. "They're all small – far smaller than *Dreadnought* – but we don't know how they're armed, so we're not taking any chances. Two hours to first position. If they stay where they are," – it was a big 'if', and they all knew it – "we'll have a chance of smacking them all."

"Weapons?" asked Cohen.

"We've done all we can," said Mantle flatly.

Cohen waited, but she didn't seem keen to elaborate.

"Marines?"

"Prepping now," said Warden. "Dropships are ready to fly, pods are locked and loaded. Add Marines, and we're good to go."

"*Palmerston*?"

"In position, ready to rock and roll," said the hologram of Captain Ruskin, who was safely ensconced on her own cramped bridge aboard the gunboat, HMS *Palmerston*.

"Then let's get moving, people. We'll only get one chance to rescue Morgan."

∿

"Are you ready, Mr MacCaibe?"

"Aye, sir, poised and ready to leap."

"Then let's see if Agent O's hyperspace engine design is as good as everyone believes."

"Five seconds to normal space," said Martin.

The counter on the main display reached zero and *Dreadnought* emerged, gun ports open and ready to fire. On the main display, the view switched to show the way ahead.

"*Target One*, dead ahead, right where we left her," reported MacCaibe pointlessly. *Dreadnought* had emerged from hyperspace almost on top of the unfortunate *Target One*. The Deathless vessel, long, sleek and gleaming, was laid out ahead of them, completely unprepared for the imminent attack.

"Two thousand metres, closing at one hundred and twenty metres per second," said Martin.

"Give it everything, Mr MacCaibe."

"Firing now. Forward railgun batteries, sustained burst, everything else firing as opportunity allows. Whew, look at those numbers."

The fire rate, as Mantle had promised, was impressive. The number of rounds in the magazine fell with astonishing swiftness, so fast it couldn't be tracked by eye. The railgun rounds raced across the tiny distance between *Dreadnought* and *Target One*, puncturing a neat spread of holes across the vessel's midships.

"That's it," said MacCaibe a few seconds later. "Fifty per cent depletion, one hundred per cent hit rate. Missiles away, no sign of countermeasures."

Dreadnought's missiles slammed into *Target One*, ripping great holes in her weakened flank and tearing into her sensitive innards. Every missile struck home, pounding the ship in a stunning ferocious display.

"*Target One* at eight hundred metres. Hyperspace in three, two, one."

Dreadnought lurched back into hyperspace for less than a heartbeat's length.

"And back to real space," announced Martin after *Dreadnought's* fast flit through hyperspace.

"Deploying surveillance drones," announced Mueller, apparently disinterested in the one-sided battle through which *Dreadnought* now flew.

"*Target Two* at fourteen hundred metres, firing all weapons."

"No incoming communications," said Wood.

"No sign of enemy fire," reported MacCaibe as *Dreadnought* sped on, spewing death and destruction as she went.

The collision warning sounded as *Dreadnought* approached within five hundred metres of *Target Two*, a hulking dark grey ship festooned with gun ports and missile silos. She stared back across the void, obliquely aligned to *Dreadnought*'s attack vector, exposing her entire starboard flank to MacCaibe's withering railgun fire.

"Railgun magazine depleted, all missiles away, collision imminent," reported MacCaibe, unconsciously leaning back in his seat as if that might have any effect at all.

"Hyperspace engine firing now," said Martin as *Target Two*'s hull sprouted gouts of fire and filled the forward display. "Clear of enemy vessels, course laid in."

"Railgun reload in progress. Missile silos being restocked."

"Damage reports?"

"Nothing so far, sir," reported White happily. "Looks like we came through without a scratch."

"Sixteen minutes to real space, thirty seconds of manoeuvring, then thirty minutes of hyperspace jumps to reposition for attack run two, sir," reported Martin.

"Good work, people," muttered Cohen. "Let's hope our luck holds a little longer."

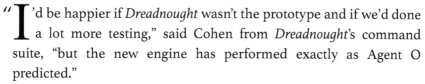

"I'd be happier if *Dreadnought* wasn't the prototype and if we'd done a lot more testing," said Cohen from *Dreadnought*'s command suite, "but the new engine has performed exactly as Agent O predicted."

Admiral Staines was on his ship, HMS *Iron Duke*, but the newly installed holographic display system made it seem as if he were sitting opposite Cohen on *Dreadnought*.

"This is not the time for timidity, Captain. We are beset on all fronts by an overwhelmingly powerful enemy and must take opportunities as they present themselves."

"I agree with Admiral Staines," said Governor Denmead. Her

holographic avatar was seated opposite the admiral's. "And we all appreciate the risks you're taking on our behalf."

"Thank you, Governor."

"You have your orders," said Staines, leaning in. "Hurt them, Captain, and bring back Admiral Morgan."

"Aye, sir. We'll do our best."

The holograms disappeared and the lights came up to reveal the rest of the room. White, Mantle, Mueller and Warden were all waiting for him.

"Right," said Cohen. "Status?"

"The work done by Agent O is exceptional," said Mueller. "To design, install and test a new hyperspace engine technology in under a week is nothing short of astonishing, and then to have all the tests check out as predicted is simply unheard of."

"Frida Skar isn't happy about it," said White. "Says she's not getting enough of Agent O's time for her research."

"Never mind that," said Cohen. "We leave in six hours. What's left?"

"Ha," snorted Mantle. "Almost everything. The hyperspace engine checks out, but the main engine is still a piece of antiquated junk. We don't have a full suite of railgun emplacements, our fire control solutions are patchy, internal comms and management systems are a joke, and half the internal systems are still awaiting review, let alone replacement."

"Don't hold back," said White, "give us the bad news."

Mantle glared at him. "The wormhole communicator has been repaired and we've added more shielding, but it needs a wholesale upgrade. The Shard Storm launchers are still in the main bay because we don't have fitting points or launch systems, the kitchens are disgusting, some of the bathrooms are indescribable and there are whole sections of the ship we can't get to reliably because the doors don't work properly. Frankly, this ship needs to be gutted and docked for a three-year refit. Until that's done, systems might fail at any time."

"Milton found one of your dodgy doors this morning," said

Warden, ignoring White's warning frown. "Went into a storeroom, door closed behind her and wouldn't open. She was in there for ninety minutes before anyone noticed." He shrugged when Mantle gave him the evil eye. "We raised a ticket."

"Doors aren't important. What about the railguns?"

"Upgrades on the forward battery are in progress and will be finished by the time you need it," said Mantle.

"And the effect will be...?"

"Higher fire rate, less chance of overheating, improved barrel lifetime."

"Nice to have some good news," muttered White.

"Indeed. Six hours," repeated Cohen. "Do what you can."

Mantle and Mueller left, leaving only Cohen, Warden and White.

"The analysis of the intelligence from the prison," said Cohen, holding up his slate. "I don't like it. Are we sure it's genuine?"

"The Admiralty went through it with a fine-toothed comb," said White, "but the Deathless wouldn't be the first people to plant material to deceive an enemy."

"Goodwin ripped it from their computers," said Warden. "It seemed real at the time."

"We plan as if it were accurate, but watch for anything suspicious," said Cohen. "It's just too convenient that we find information leading to a captured high-value prisoner in the first place we looked."

"Agent O, any thoughts on this information?" asked White.

"The system is controlled by the Koschite Republic," said Agent O. "It has one sparsely populated habitable planet, called Micarro for reasons I can't explain, mostly devoted to pastoral pursuits. There is an orbital facility that matches the name mentioned in the captured files, but I have no more information about it."

"Is that normal?" asked White. "I mean, is it secret or just outside your cached knowledge?"

"Possibly both," admitted Agent O. "I have background information on Koschite systems, but my focus is their research. This is not a relevant research facility, so if I ever knew more, the information has been deleted."

"Could be a trap," mused Cohen.

"So avoid the obvious," said Warden. "Come in from an unexpected angle, use *Dreadnought*'s new fast-flit capabilities. We have the technology, let's make it work for us."

9

"Tomsk," said the Koschite admiral, focused on something on his desk, taking the call without deigning to look at the screen.

"Admiral Tomsk, we need to talk," said Morgan, biting back his annoyance at the Koschite's attitude.

Tomsk looked up and openly scowled at him. "Morgan. What do you want? I'm busy." He spoke Koschite – another calculated insult – and Morgan had to look away to read the translation before he could respond.

"Cohen has attacked, and your cruisers are not faring well. I need you to get me out of here before he overruns your facilities and captures me," said Morgan.

Tomsk snorted. "Absolutely not. You have the resources you need. He has only one old ship that's barely able to move and should have been broken up decades ago."

"He's wreaking havoc here, there's something wrong about our intelligence."

"The information we have on – what is it, HMS *Dreadnought*? – came from you, Morgan. You assured us your information was valuable and accurate," said Tomsk, frowning. "Are you sure you told us everything about this ship?"

"Yes, of course, and the information I have is of high value, I assure you."

"Good. Then it shouldn't be a problem for you to exploit the weaknesses of this decrepit antique of a vessel and destroy it."

"I'm telling you, something has changed," insisted Morgan. "They're moving like nothing I've ever seen before. It's as if they disappear and reappear elsewhere."

"Sounds like a local sensor anomaly to me. Destroy him and have done with it."

"I need a ship to get out of here, in case he survives. I can't be captured."

"Denied."

"You made assurances to me!" raged Morgan, banging his fist on his desk. "You owe me, Tomsk, we had a deal. I sacrificed the fleet to you, and you were to give me the life you promised. At this rate, I'll end up back at New Bristol. Get me out of here. Now!"

Tomsk leaned back in his chair, his face falling into shadow. He steepled his fingers and tipped his head forward until they pressed against his lips. He was silent for a moment, then his eyes flicked up again.

"I see two possible paths. If you cannot defeat *Dreadnought*, you will be found and captured by Cohen's Marine complement. In that event, you would indeed be returned to New Bristol and tried for treason if they somehow discover your role. If, on the other hand, you defeat Cohen with the ships available to you, you will be safe from Commonwealth justice and we can talk about resettling you. I suggest the latter is the better option for you."

"Damnit, there's a third path!" snapped Morgan. "I could leave now. Your ships have commanders, they don't need me to deal with this. Get me out of here, and I can provide you with everything I know about the Commonwealth, the Navy, the Marines, their fleets. Everything."

Tomsk shrugged. "That would be a possible path if I were willing to grant you another ship, but I'm not. Win the battle, Morgan, or you will return to New Bristol and keep supplying us with intelligence until you prove your value and another opportunity for extraction arises. You likely won't be in command of a fleet if you go back, so you'll have to work to get yourself an assignment that allows you to forward sufficiently valuable intelligence."

Morgan felt his skin pale. "No, you can't be serious. I can't go back. If they work out what I've done, I'll be done for!"

"If they decide you're dead, they'll redeploy you anyway. You were always likely to be going back, one way or another."

"But that would be some other person," protested Morgan. "That wouldn't be me! I need to stay here, where I'm most valuable."

"Then do as I've ordered. Stop complaining to me, Admiral, and win your battle. Then we can reward you."

Tomsk cut the connection and Morgan slumped in his chair. He stared at the screens above him, wracking his brain for a way to defeat Cohen's assault.

"That little shit is the source of my troubles," he whispered. "He's caused all of this." He pushed on the arms of his chair and left the ready room to return to the command centre.

"Admiral on deck," an unenthusiastic junior lieutenant said as his fingers danced across his console's controls.

"At ease," Morgan growled out of habit. "We have work to do."

But how to do it, that was the question. And Morgan didn't have the answers.

10

"What's that?" asked Cohen, pointing at a new tally at the bottom of *Dreadnought*'s main display.

White looked up from his seat on the bridge and grinned.

"Kills, sir. Deathless ships we've destroyed since *Dreadnought* came out of storage."

Cohen frowned but said nothing more. Logging kills was a little macabre, but this was a warship and those tallies represented, by one measure, a record of their success.

"Final adjustments to attack run locked in," said Martin. On *Dreadnought*'s last blip through real space, the surveillance drones showed that *Target Three* beginning to move, although it wasn't clear where she was heading. "Thirty seconds to the start of the next attack run."

"Weapons primed, sir," reported MacCaibe, rubbing his hands and grinning at his screens.

"Ten seconds to normal space."

"Fire as soon as you have the enemy in sight, Mr MacCaibe," said Cohen.

"Aye, sir."

The countdown hit zero and *Dreadnought* fell back into normal space. Ahead, only three thousand metres, lay *Target Three*, a slim cigar-shaped vessel with bulbous engines at one end and blue-tinged weapons ports clustered around its prow.

"Firing railguns, missiles away," announced MacCaibe happily.

"Deploying weapons platforms," said White as four autonomous vessels were launched from *Dreadnought*'s flanks.

The rest of the bridge crew were silent. *Dreadnought* tore towards *Target Three* and the ammunition counters dropped rapidly towards fifty per cent. Ahead, *Target Three*'s engines fired and she accelerated, pushing hard but far too late.

"No getting away from this," said MacCaibe. "Take that, you little beauty!"

The magnified view from *Dreadnought*'s forward sensors showed *Target Three* taking railgun and missile strikes along her length. An explosion punched fire and debris from the top of the stricken ship and her engines failed. There was a small cheer from the bridge crew.

"Three seconds to hyperspace," said Martin as *Dreadnought* bore down on *Target Three*.

"Ammunition at fifty per cent," said MacCaibe.

"Entering hyperspace," reported Martin. "And back into real space."

"*Target Four* has moved," said MacCaibe. "Firing now, but the angle isn't all it should be." He frowned and leaned forward, peering at his screens. "Something floating around near *Target Four*, sir. Could be nasty."

"Anything we can do about it, Mr MacCaibe?"

"Not a damned thing, sir. All our guns are firing on *Target Four*, everything's committed and automated."

"Fingers crossed, then," murmured Cohen, nervously licking his lips.

"Four more weapons platforms launched," reported White. "They're running silent now, configured for delayed stealth assaults as opportunities arise."

"Incoming fire," interrupted MacCaibe. "Railgun and missile fire. Countermeasures away."

"Three seconds to end of run," said Martin.

The tactical overview on *Dreadnought*'s main display showed the flight paths of every ship in System Four, and it looked like all the surviving corvettes were on the move.

"Ammunition depleted," said MacCaibe. "Reload commencing."

There was a shudder as something struck *Dreadnought*'s hull.

"What was that?" asked Cohen, flicking at his slate to bring up the monitor reports.

"Entering hyperspace."

"Some sort of mine or autonomous weapon system," said White. "Hull breach near the forward railgun battery."

"Sneaky bastards," muttered Cohen.

"Looks like they mined the volume around *Target Four.* Two attack runs might have been pushing our luck a little."

"Get down there," said Cohen to his XO. "Find out what's going on and get things under control."

"Aye, sir," said White.

Klaxons wailed as Mantle and her team ran the length of the ship to reach the breach in the forward compartments.

"Shut the bloody siren off!" yelled Mantle as she picked her way over a stack of folding tables that had been thrown from a storeroom at some point on the voyage.

This part of the ship was largely unused. The junk accumulated over the ship's years of service as a museum filled the rooms and, on occasion, overflowed into the corridors. The naval architects built big when laying down *Dreadnought*, and everything in this area was setup for large numbers of people or the easy movement of stores and supplies on semi-autonomous loading vehicles. That meant corridors four metres wide and four tall, with large sliding doors and even bigger rooms set with heavyweight floor-to-ceiling racking.

"And get this bloody corridor cleared."

Mantle's team, following behind in environment suits, began removing the rubbish and stuffing it back into the rooms that lined it.

"This is it," said Mantle, stopping outside a door showing a red 'vacuum beyond' warning. She fitted her helmet and checked her seals while her team secured the corridor. "Ready?" She waited till each of the three engineers tapped the thumbs up status icon in their HUDs to indicate they were ready for vacuum.

She triggered the evacuation of air from the short section of corridor between the target area and the pressure door behind them. Nothing happened. She tapped it again then opened a channel back to engineering.

"It's reporting as evacuated," said Hodges, her second, when Mantle described the problem.

"Well, it's not," snapped Mantle. "Log a ticket, see if you can override the check."

"Okay, if I reset the sensor and force the issue...Right. Here goes." There was a hiss of air leaving the room that quickly fell away. Mantle checked her HUD, which now reported vacuum outside her suit.

"That's done it. Opening the door." She tapped the control but nothing happened. "HUD, log another ticket for a broken door."

"Acknowledged," replied her HUD.

Mantle flipped open the panel beside the door and heaved on the manual release lever. She had to brace her foot against the wall, heaving hard until the grime of decades came free and the lever moved. The door slid halfway open, then stopped.

Muttering under her breath, Mantle pushed at the door till it was three-quarters open and she could squeeze through.

"What a mess," she whispered to herself. The room was huge, some sort of low-value storeroom originally, but lately used for – at a guess – visitors' lost property. "Get a couple of loaders up here and clear this rubbish away," she snapped, tossing aside what looked like a long-lost child's rucksack. "Get everything down to the recyclers, and let's get things tidied up."

The breach couldn't have been more obvious. A gaping hole, two metres in diameter, had been blown in *Dreadnought*'s heavily armoured outer hull. The explosion had punched back the layered plates and shattered the ceramics, but at least the door had held and the atmosphere loss had been minor. And nobody had been in there when it happened, so what they really had now was a weakness in the hull that they couldn't easily fix.

"Shit," said Mantle as she surveyed the damage. "Lucky that's all it did, I suppose." Then paranoia crept in. She flipped open the channel to engineering. "Hodges, get a crew of crawler drones out to check that there aren't any more of these things waiting for an inopportune moment to punch a hole in our hull."

"Roger. Might take a while to survey the whole hull."

"Start at the front and work back then, but get it done."

"Aye, ma'am, we're on it."

"What's the news, Mantle?" asked White.

The engineer turned to see a suited Lieutenant White surveying the mess from the doorway.

"There's a breach, we're working on it," she said.

"Is that it?"

"What did you expect? We're working on it. I'll inform you if something changes." Mantle kicked aside discarded coats and boxes of ancient tablets to get closer to the breach.

"Right," muttered White. "Yeah. A breach. Carry on."

Mantle waited till he left, then she turned her attention back to the breach, peering out into the bleak emptiness of hyperspace. For a moment she imagined what it might be like to float out through the hole and disappear into it, never to return. Then she shuddered and started issuing orders.

"How long to close the breach?" asked Cohen. The timer on the start of the next attack run ticked steadily towards zero.

"Too long," replied Mantle. She muttered something then shouted an order. "Let me work."

She closed the channel. Cohen and the bridge crew were left with nothing to do but run their checks and keep an eye on the timer, hoping that Mantle could close the breach in time.

"This could get a bit sticky," said White.

"More than a bit," replied Cohen, "but we're committed."

What choice did they have? They needed to find Morgan, but they couldn't head to the planet's surface while there were enemy vessels prowling the systems. They had to be drawn out and smacked down.

"And to draw them out, we have to really hurt them," he murmured.

"Sir?"

"Nothing," said Cohen. "Just thinking out loud."

"Three hundred seconds," said Martin.

"Take us to action stations," ordered White, "and let's run a last check to make sure everything's ready." He opened a channel to Mantle. "You have only a few minutes. Clear the area."

"I can read a timer as well as you," snapped Mantle. "We'll leave when the job's done. Out."

"All stations report standing ready, sir," said Martin.

"How are we for ammunition, Mr MacCaibe?" said Cohen.

"Stuffed to the gunwales, sir."

"Then let rip with the railguns, but let's hold back on the missiles for now."

"Sir?" asked MacCaibe, confused. "The missiles are programmed and ready to go, it's no bother."

"Then change the programme. We don't need to destroy the station, merely render it unsafe so the Deathless are encouraged to do what they can to save their fellows and the station itself."

"Oh, aye," said MacCaibe, smiling as the light dawned. "Making the change now, sir."

∾

Dreadnought dropped back into real space and the proximity alarms sounded. The station lay right in front of them, only two thousand metres away and getting rapidly closer.

"Bigger than I'd expected," muttered White.

"Focus on the job," said Cohen, although his eyes were drawn to the huge circular orbital that hung in space before them, a giant toroid against the stars. At a kilometre in diameter, it was a large station for such a remote outpost

"Firing now, sir," said MacCaibe. "But there's some sort of autonomous weapons platform paying us some attention. Brace for impact."

There was a shudder as something exploded against the ship's hull.

"More mines," said White as he scanned the reports from the forward sensors. "They've laced this orbit with mines."

"Keep firing," said Cohen as another shudder ran through Dreadnought's decking.

"Targeting the mines and those wee weapons platforms," said MacCaibe.

"Three seconds to hyperspace," said Martin.

"Forward railgun ammunition exhausted. Port side weapons cluster is offline."

"Feels like we've swept the minefield clear," muttered White.

Another explosion banged through the hull and the lights on the bridge flickered. Midshipman Wood grumbled when his displays went dead.

"Hyperspace," said Martin, "and back to real space."

Dreadnought flashed through hyperspace so fast the crew barely registered the change, but it was enough to put them a hundred thousand kilometres clear of the station.

"Report!" snapped Cohen.

"Ninety per cent strike rate against the station, sir," said MacCaibe. "Reloading beginning now. No response from the port weapons cluster."

"At least three more mine strikes and a score of railgun impacts. Two more hull breaches, all crew and Marines accounted for, no sign of casualties."

"The station is sending off all kinds of comms chatter," said Wood, working from a slate while his displays rebooted. "Probably summoning help, but it's all encrypted."

"I want to know what they're saying," said Cohen. "Agent O, can you help?"

"No, Captain Cohen. The cipher used by the Koschite military is sophisticated and I don't have the keys. A brute force attack is theoretically possible, but under my current operating parameters, such an attack would take two to three decades."

"Never mind," said Cohen, dismissing the idea. "We can assume they're reporting up the chain and summoning help. How long, do you think?"

"For help to arrive? The two corvettes at the edge of the system lack advanced hyperspace drives and are powering in under normal engines. They will arrive in no more than sixteen hours. Craft from outside the system might arrive in two to seven days."

Cohen nodded, his decision made.

"White, coordinate with Mantle and get the repairs done as quickly as possible."

"Aye, sir, on my way."

"Miss Martin, put us in orbit to drop on the enemy base."

"Plotting course now, sir."

"Mr MacCaibe, sweep the area for mines and anything else that might do us harm."

"Working on it now, sir. We'll soon clear away the nasty wee beasties."

"Captain Ruskin," he said, opening a channel to *Palmerston*, "begin your attack run. I want the base defences nicely softened."

"Understood, sir. We'll be with you in fifteen minutes."

Cohen opened a channel to Warden, who was in the mess with the rest of the Marines.

"Be ready to launch in twenty minutes, Captain. It's time to recover the admiral."

"Roger. We're suited and ready to go."

"Then good luck, and good hunting. Cohen out."

11

"Sir, all orbital defence platforms have been destroyed or disabled. Both enemy ships are positioning for an attack run on this base."

Morgan fumed. And his teeth ached he clenched them so hard. He'd known this would happen, known it from the moment *Dreadnought* attacked the first Koschite vessel. Tomsk's forces were ill-disciplined and overconfident, and Cohen had defeated them with ease.

Now he was coming in for the kill, and Morgan couldn't see a way out. He cursed Tomsk under his breath. This was exactly the situation he'd foreseen, but Tomsk had refused to listen. Until the Koschite navy learned to outthink the Royal Navy commanders, or ensured they always had an overwhelming advantage in numbers and firepower, they would continue to have this problem.

"Time to firing range?" he asked.

"Less than twenty minutes, sir. The smaller ship is mounting a weapon designed for ground bombardment."

"I know that, Junior Lieutenant!" snapped Morgan.

"What is the yield, sir?"

Morgan shook his head, as if trying to free himself from an annoying thought. "More than sufficient to destroy any ground defences we have available," he said. "It's a mass driver," he went on, striding around as he babbled. "It uses inert material for orbital bombardment, but the yield from impact is more like a small nuclear weapon than a conventional projectile."

"I will get a firing solution and we will destroy the incoming fire before it strikes the surface!" said the junior lieutenant.

Morgan barked a manic laugh. "You think that'll work? They can just pull asteroids into their processing bay and create more missiles. We have to get lucky every time, they only need one hit per installation!" They were staring at him, all the little Koschite officers with their stupid uniforms and their ridiculous rules. Did they not realise what was going on?

He took a deep breath and forced his hands down by his side. "We can't win this fight on our own now," he said in a more normal tone. "So we play for time. Destroy as many of their shots as you can, it will delay their ground assault and hold back the Marines."

"Marines?" whispered one of the operations crew members, face white. They'd heard the stories. Rumours had filtered through the grapevine, and none of them were good. Most of them were nonsense, but the crew were scared. There was an edge of panic to the room.

Morgan scowled. He hated them for their weakness, their fear, their lack of training.

"Just get to work!" he snapped. "You have your orders. We will fight until we can do so no longer. Understood?" A muted chorus of acknowledgement was the only response. Their morale was so bad, he almost missed being aboard a Royal Navy vessel.

He shook loose from his melancholy and strode from the command centre. This installation was doomed. Cohen would be here in under an hour, and the little shit would send Marines to 'rescue' him.

"Find a pilot, find a pilot," he muttered under his breath.

"Sir?" Barber, his faithful aide, blocked his escape.

"Have to find a pilot," he murmured, "find a ship. Get away from here."

Commander Barber frowned. "Sir? Are you alright, sir?"

"Get in there," he said, pointing back at the command centre, "get in there and make sure they're doing their damned job."

"Sir," said Barber, but she didn't move, and Morgan left her there.

He had a short window of opportunity to find a ship he could pilot away from here. Out here, on the fringes of the Koschite Republic, defences were spotty but he knew they had huge fleets. If he could make it to one of the better-defended systems, Tomsk wouldn't be able to send him back.

"I'll be safe," he muttered.

The signs on the corners of the junction were useless. He had no idea what they meant and blast it, they didn't use icons in their signage. No handy spaceship graphic or a picture of a rocket to indicate which way the launch bay might be. But he knew they had one. It contained a number of hyperspace capable craft; he'd seen them when he arrived.

Not that he'd seen much else. The bastards had put a bag over his head when they unloaded him, so he had no idea where the landing bay was in relation to the rest of the base. They'd bagged him – an Admiral! – taken him straight to that damned cell and dumped him there until those two arseholes came in to interrogate him. Like he was some junior rating being summoned to the carpet for incompetence.

He turned left and took a few tentative steps down a corridor, paused and changed his mind.

The base wasn't enormous – the system was more of an outpost than a proper military site – and in any case, the orbital station was the bulk of the facilities in this system. Down here, on the planet's surface, it couldn't be too hard to find one of the largest rooms in the base.

He wished he had a map.

"No time, no time..." He realised he was talking to himself and wondered briefly if he was going mad. "Ridiculous, 'course you're not going mad. One of the greatest naval minds ever."

Sooner or later someone would look for him. He needed to get off the station before anyone could question it. He moved up to double time, then gave in and began to jog.

Morgan took a right into a long wide corridor with a different type of tile.

"Yes, this is it," he said, feeling some of his old confidence return in the familiarity of the corridor. It was wider to allow sleds to move gear around the base after unloading in the launch bay. This was definitely the right corridor.

But which way was it? There was nothing to indicate a direction except two arrows and a string of words that may as well have been hieroglyphs for all the good they did him. Left again.

He was running out of wind. He slowed to a walk and clutched at his sides. Even the bloody clone was letting him down. It was a conspiracy. Maybe Tomsk had done something to this clone. Yes, it was infected with a virus, that was it. Bloody Koschites! They'd sabotaged his clone to keep him under control, but it wasn't going to work. He'd show them what a Royal Navy officer could do, even in a crippled clone.

Another junction loomed, and he slowed to a stop to make sense of the signs. Was that a rocket on the sign pointing ahead, or just another letter from their pictographic alphabet?

Which genius came up with that one, he wondered. He could picture the meeting, "We should have our own alphabet, an original one designed to be better!" The tweed-wearing academics would have suggested this was an inspired spark of genius that would revolutionise society. They must have believed they could construct a language superior to the ones developed over millennia.

"Idiots." Instead of a neatly labelled direction in a sensible Latin alphabet he might reasonably be able to interpret, or a photograph of a rocket, he had this bullshit. The other directions had symbols as well, and they were even less helpful. Rocket it was, then.

But after ten metres he found his way blocked by two big Deathless troopers armed with bulky pistols and extendable batons.

They didn't salute, an oversight he ignored even though it infuriated him. These Deathless were so sloppy, so ill-disciplined. He would have to do something about that.

But not now. Now, he needed to concentrate on escape.

"Good afternoon gentlewomen," he said with a false smile, "just getting some exercise, got to keep the old waistline under control." He emphasised the jolly-officer routine with a couple of pats to his stomach, then made to move past them and down the corridor.

The troopers adjusted their stance in a subtle way that told him he wasn't getting through. He bristled at the insult.

"Now look here, I'm an Admiral. I demand you move immediately and let me through or I'll have you up on a charge!"

"We have orders," one said in heavily accented English.

"Orders? Orders from whom? And about what?" Morgan demanded.

"You must come with us, Admiral," said the second trooper.

"I will not!" replied Morgan indignantly. "Indeed, I will not. Be on your way," he gestured along the corridor as if waving the two troopers away.

"Admiral Tomsk's orders," said the first trooper. "We bring you to communications room." The trooper gestured back along the corridor, away from the landing bay.

"Later," said Morgan airily. "I'll speak to Admiral Tomsk after I finish my exercise, if I feel like it." He tried to push past the troopers, but they spun him around and lifted him up by his armpits as if he were a disobedient toddler.

"Put me down!" he demanded, his legs kicking as they frogmarched him all the way to the interrogation room and thrust him roughly into a chair. "What is the meaning of this? I demand to know what is going on!"

A viewscreen clicked on and Admiral Tomsk's face appeared.

Morgan glared at the screen. Tomsk was busy with a slate, paying no attention to his own screen.

"What's the meaning of this, Tomsk? I want these women on a charge! They laid hands on me, interrupted my daily exercise routine, and forced me into this cell!"

"Yes. I ordered them to. There won't be any charges."

Morgan's mouth dropped open.

"I wanted you to do your job," Tomsk went on, "but apparently you've failed, and the base will soon be under attack."

"It's not my fault your personnel are incompetent, Tomsk. You need to get me out of here before that bastard Cohen arrives and causes trouble," said Morgan.

"You wish to flee?"

Morgan snorted. The idea was ridiculous, but his resolve began to slip. "Not flee, Admiral," said Morgan, his tone withering. "A strategic withdrawal. I have valuable intelligence you need, remember. I'm not some junior rating you can afford to have recaptured."

Tomsk shrugged and shook his head.

"I can't protect you any longer," he said, leaning forward, cheeks flushing with anger. "I can't even issue a general evacuation order to salvage materiel because you've left the system too vulnerable for us to recover anything. Your failure is complete, Morgan, and you'll be returned to your original position as an agent."

"You want me to go back?" said Morgan, astonished that Tomsk might even consider the suggestion. "I won't do it."

"You will," said Tomsk, eyes flashing. "You will go back and gather more intelligence, something we can use." Tomsk paused and sat back, calmer, more controlled. "And then maybe, later in the war, we'll arrange an extraction. If you fulfil your obligations to the Koschite Republic."

"You can't be serious?"

"I am perfectly serious," said Tomsk. "You are clearly worthless as a military strategist or commander. Your only value is as a double agent."

"I won't do it!" Morgan shouted.

"You will, or you will die."

"Fine, they'll put me in a new clone straight away! Then I'll tell them all about you."

"Will you though? Would you even remember this conversation? Are you sure you won't wake up just as you were before the ambush?"

Morgan frowned, but something about Tomsk's tone gave him pause. "I'm backed up, they'll take the backups from the station before they leave, especially if they find me dead."

"Ah. You misunderstand. There is a backup of you, of course. But the one the Commonwealth forces will find isn't the you of right now. It's an amended copy. If they find you dead, they'll be convinced you held out till the end and revealed nothing of value. And if they redeploy you from that copy, so will you."

Morgan felt a chill go down his spine. Tampering with a person's backup was unconscionable, but Tomsk's threat seemed real. He could well imagine the slimy weasel playing such tricks.

"You wouldn't dare," he hissed.

"To win this war, I would do anything, Admiral. We must win. You will cooperate, willingly or not. We have a workable backup plan, but it would be better for us all to persuade the Commonwealth that you've been our unwilling prisoner and have resisted our interrogation attempts. It'll make you much more sympathetic, and they'll be less likely to suspect you are a duplicitous traitor. Don't you agree?"

Tomsk's tone was reasonable, almost friendly, as if he were discussing a minor question of philosophy with an equal. Morgan glared at him, then glanced at one of the troopers as she caressed the grip of the pistol holstered on her belt. She glared back with a look of disgust, as if he were something unpleasant she'd found on the sole of her boot.

Morgan saw no chance of dissuading Tomsk. The bastard had all the cards, and he wouldn't hesitate to have him killed to further his cause. The thought of being redeployed with false memories made him feel sick; he wouldn't even know Tomsk betrayed him, and there would never be an opportunity for revenge.

Pragmatism, that was the key to survival. And a cold, cold approach to revenge. When he finally defected, he would be a hero, and would destroy Tomsk.

There was nothing more satisfying than the demotion or sidelining of an opponent. Career officers like Tomsk never got over such a political retaliation; it destroyed them mentally. It was a tactic

Morgan had used repeatedly on his way up through the ranks of the Royal Navy.

The Deathless armed forces would be no different, and Tomsk was an obvious fanatic. Demotion or, even better, dishonourable discharge, would ruin his life. That would be the most delicious revenge.

His decision made, and with care to maintain his grudging attitude, Morgan made a tactical withdrawal. "Very well, I'll go back. But you'd better keep your side of the bargain. I want my reward for serving the Republic before this war is over."

"You'll get what's been agreed, Morgan," said Tomsk. "Sergeant, you have your orders. Make it look convincing, hmm?"

"Yes, sir," said one of the eerily similar women. She motioned to the other who moved behind Morgan and pulled his chair, with him in it, back from the table he'd been sitting at.

Before he knew what was happening, the sergeant delivered a right cross to his cheek. Morgan heard himself cry out a second before a meaty left swung his head back the other way. The corporal behind him slammed her hands down on his shoulders, holding him in place, and the sergeant methodically worked him over.

At some point, he lost track of the blows. His head swam, and his face was in agony. The metallic taste of blood filled his mouth.

The sergeant slammed a straight punch directly into his face and he heard a grinding noise as his nose broke. He had to spit blood before he could take another breath.

"Don't forget his ribs," said Tomsk conversationally. "They'll give him a medical, and we want this to look convincing." Through bleary eyes beginning to swell, Morgan saw Tomsk calmly working at something on his data slate.

"Fuck you, Tomsk!" snarled Morgan through his broken lips.

The sergeant's fists played a staccato rhythm on his ribcage. A low blow caught him in the kidney and he lost the ability to speak, and the will to live. He couldn't even scream.

It seemed to drag on for an eternity.

The unfamiliar violence stunned Morgan. He'd joined the Navy to serve the Commonwealth in a civilised part of the military. He wasn't a Marine, or sanity preserve him, a common army oik. What did the ratings call them? Pongos.

"Sergeant, I think he's pissed himself," the corporal behind him said.

Morgan coughed, head wobbling. That explained the wet heat. He thought he'd dribbled so much blood on his crotch his trousers were wet through, but apparently not. No, he'd messed himself like a child. Fuck them. Fuck Tomsk. Fuck the admiralty. Fuck the Deathless. He'd make them pay.

A few vicious kicks to his shins with the sergeant's sturdy boots brought fresh agony and he screamed hoarsely. He could have sworn he heard bones break when she stamped on his foot.

"How's he looking, sergeant?" said Tomsk offhandedly.

"Like he's got in the ring with a Warmonger, sir."

"Excellent. He looks a bit too clean and tidy, though. Rub some dirt in his face and hair, make it look like we've kept him in a filthy cell."

"Yes, sir," said the sergeant, nodding at the corporal, who let him go and left the room.

"He's right-handed, yes?"

"Yes, sir."

"Break a few fingers on his left hand then, make it look like we made him talk," said Tomsk with no trace of venom or emotion, as if he were ordering cocktails in a fancy wine bar.

Morgan tried to scream even before the sergeant touched his fingers, but his voice was lost. He whimpered and passed out when the first of his fingers snapped.

He barely felt the corporal rubbing a filthy hand against his face and through his hair. At least it smelled like soil from a plant pot or something, not shit from a latrine.

"I'm going to kill you, Tomsk," he tried to say, but the words came out wrong, mere gurgling nonsense, then he passed out again.

"I didn't catch that, was it important?"

The sergeant looked up at the corporal, whose expression

suggested she was absolutely not going to repeat Morgan's words to the admiral.

"No, sir. Just begging for mercy," said the sergeant. "He's passed out. Should we wake him and find out?"

"Oh no, I doubt it was anything I need to hear. Mess up the jacket and shirt. And make sure he has no metal or personal effects on him. Do anything else you think will sell the effect, just don't let him die," said Tomsk.

"Yes, sir."

"Excellent work, Sergeant. I'll add a commendation to your files."

"Thank you, sir."

"Make sure you are not taken alive. The enemy must not know that Morgan is a disgusting traitor. Tomsk out."

12

"Lock in the attack run," said Cohen. "Let's get things moving."

"Aye, sir," said Martin. "We're ready to go."

"Then let's make a start, Ms Martin."

"Manoeuvring thrusters for thirty seconds in three, two, one."

The automated flight plan began to unfold on the main display. The thrusters fired and *Dreadnought* swung neatly around to point towards the Deathless station orbiting Micarro. Woods focussed the forward camera array and pulled up a video of the station in one corner of the display.

The station was lit intermittently in some areas, and gas vented in sections, streaming continuously into space as the station spun on around the planet.

"Status report on the station, Mr MacCaibe," said Cohen.

"Evidence of life, sir, but they've no more control than a Mendollese sand-wright in a Karovian desert storm."

"A what in a what?" muttered White, frowning at MacCaibe. The man was like a miner's canary. When his metaphors and mannerisms dropped into broad Scots dialect, it was a clear sign the tension on the bridge was increasing.

"Are they a threat, Midshipman?"

"Nae chance, sir. The station's orbit is unstable. They will enter the planet's atmosphere in forty hours or less if they can't restart the manoeuvring engines. I don't think they'll be worrying about anything else for a while." A counter appeared alongside the icon representing the Deathless space station on the main tactical display, counting down from forty hours.

"Good. Mr Mueller, keep an eye on that station. I want to know as soon as there's any sign they've regained control," said Cohen.

"I'll do my best, Captain," said Mueller with a frown, "but I'm not sure what I'm looking for."

"Your best will be sufficient, Mr Mueller," said Cohen. "Mr MacCaibe, let's focus on the other satellites and the remaining corvettes. I don't want anything getting close enough to fire on the drop pods."

"Aye, sir. There are a number of orbital weapons platforms, but they're small and slow," said MacCaibe. "At least, the ones we've seen are small. Targeting now, shouldn't be a problem."

"Fire as soon as you're ready, Mr MacCaibe. Sweep them all away."

"Aye, sir. We'll be in range of the first platforms after the first hyperspace jump."

"And the corvettes?" asked White.

"*Target One* was destroyed," said MacCaibe, running through the report from the sensors. "There's a cloud of debris around her last position, and gravity distortions indicate a mass roughly equivalent to the estimate of *Target One*'s. Nothing bigger than a cargo container, and lots of hot atoms flying around. *Target Four* is mobile but heading out of system towards the asteroid belt. She appears to be in trouble. *Target Three* is right where we left her, just sitting there. *Target Two* is missing."

"Keep them under surveillance, Mr MacCaibe."

"Aye, sir."

"And find *Target Two*. I don't want her surprising us."

"Aye, sir. Running full sensor sweeps. If she emits so much as a squiggle of electro-magnetic radiation, we'll find her."

That sounded implausibly optimistic to Cohen given *Dreadnought*'s largely antique infrastructure, but there wasn't anything more they could do right now.

"Ready for next hyperspace jump, sir," said Martin.

"Punch it, Ms Martin," ordered Cohen.

Dreadnought flickered through hyperspace, reappearing in orbit around Micarro, oriented so the pod launchers pointed into the gravity well. The Deathless station was a bright spec in the distance.

"Twelve minutes to launch position," said Martin.

"Targeting weapons platforms," said MacCaibe. "The port side weapons cluster is still offline, launching self-guided missiles."

Dreadnought's tactical display updated with every new platform and mine found by the sensors. MacCaibe fired freely, whistling tunelessly under his breath.

"Have we found them all, Mr MacCaibe?" asked Cohen.

"Too soon to say, sir."

"Meaning?" Cohen pressed.

"If they're being sneaky, they might be sitting in the dark just waiting for us to get too close, like a hunter watching a young deer step closer to their hide."

Cohen raised an eyebrow, then shook his head.

"Then keep an eye out for hides, Mr MacCaibe."

"Aye, sir, will do."

"Here comes *Palmerston*, sir," said Wood as the gunboat dropped out of hyperspace to begin her attack run.

Palmerston wasn't going to orbit the planet. Instead she was coming in high and fast to maximise the impact of her projectiles.

Where *Dreadnought* was a massive and brutal generalist able to take on a wide range of tasks and combat scenarios, *Palmerston* was a tiny, high-precision specialist with a single role; to bombard enemy ground targets. Her principal weapon was a huge rail cannon capable of launching a spherical, three-metre projectile into a gravity well for high-precision destruction.

By the time the projectile reached the ground, it would be glowing red hot and travelling so fast the impact could flatten whole city blocks. By varying the angle of delivery and launch speed, *Palmerston* could adjust the destructive force to deliver exactly the right amount of shock.

<Targets are confirmed and locked> sent Lieutenant Ruskin, commander of *Palmerston,* the message scrolling onto *Dreadnought's* screens. <Three shots, ten-second separation. Firing position in thirty seconds>

"Last chance to abort, Mr Mueller. You're sure there are no civilian facilities down there?" asked Cohen, Admiral Staines' brief with permission for *Palmerston* to fire on the Deathless base fresh in his mind.

The rules of engagement were made clear.

"Make damned sure it *is* a military base," Staines had said. "We don't need civilian casualties coming back to cause us problems when we inevitably get around to talking."

"As sure as I can be, Captain," said Mueller. "The base has walls like those we've seen on other Deathless military facilities. There are no civilian structures – schools, parks, museums and the like – and the infrastructure is distinctly military." He flicked an image onto the main display and highlighted several parts. "A high-speed monorail, walls and towers, landing strip. So yes, I'm sure there are no civilian facilities in the target area."

"Good enough for me, Mr Mueller, good enough."

<Permission to fire> Cohen sent to Ruskin.

<Acknowledged. Firing in ten seconds>

Cohen switched his attention to the tactical display. *Palmerston* shot through the system, right on the agreed trajectory.

"First projectile away," reported MacCaibe. The display updated to show *Palmerston's* shot as it began its short journey to the surface. "Second projectile away," he said a few seconds later.

The seconds dragged on, but there was no sign of the third shot.

"Something's wrong," muttered White.

<What's going on, *Palmerston*?> sent Cohen.

There was no reply.

"Find *Palmerston*, Mr Woods. Bring her up on the screen."

"Aye, sir, working on it," said Woods, struggling to lock onto *Palmerston's* identification transponder. "Found her. She's on course but running dark."

The display updated and there was *Palmerston*, dark against the bright stars.

"No obvious damage," said White.

"Open a channel to Ruskin," said Cohen.

"Aye, sir, doing it now. Channel open, but audio only," said Woods.

"Ruskin, this is Cohen. What's your status?"

"Sorry sir," said Ruskin, "we took a hit from something – not sure yet whether it was an enemy attack or just bad luck – but it's gone right through our primary targeting systems. We'll be up and running with the backups in a few minutes, but we're past our firing window and we'll need to circle back. It'll take us an hour or more to reset, and that's assuming we can repair the rest of the damage or work around it."

"That's too long," said Cohen. "Get your ship together and meet us at the rendezvous point."

"Acknowledged. Good hunting, *Dreadnought*." The channel closed and Cohen sat back in his seat. *Palmerston's* first two projectiles were aimed at a heavily defended gatehouse in the wall and the monorail station. The third would have hit a building just inside the perimeter that appeared to be a power station.

"Although it could be a chemical processing plant, or maybe an automated manufactory of some sort," Chief Science Officer Mueller had said when they planned the attack. "It's really very difficult to be sure with just the low-res images from the visible light spectrum."

They'd decided to hit it anyway on the sound military principle that if it was important enough to warrant building it onsite, it was worth destroying. If only to annoy the Deathless. But with the third projectile still aboard *Palmerston*, that wasn't going to happen.

"Maybe Warden can have a pop at it," said Cohen.

"Sixty seconds to drop pod launch window," said Martin.

"We have a ship emerging from hyperspace," said MacCaibe, his hands flicking over his console. An image appeared on the main display. "Looks like *Target Two*. She's two hundred and sixty thousand kilometres and moving at–" MacCaibe tapped at his lagging console – as if that would make any difference. "Moving at about two thousand kilometres an hour, sir."

"Course?"

"She's manoeuvring, sir. Looks like she's setting up an attack run."

"From a quarter of a million kilometres away?" said Cohen. "Well, good luck to them. Keep an eye on her, but let's focus on the mission."

"Aye, sir. New targets coming into range, more of the weapons platforms and what looks like a brace of comms satellites. Firing now."

"Any change on that station, Mr Mueller?"

"No, Captain. They're still losing atmosphere and altitude."

"Ten seconds to pod launch."

Cohen opened a channel to the lead drop pod. "Get ready, Captain, and good luck."

"Thank you, sir. See you on the other side."

There was a brief silence as the timer counted down to zero. The display updated, showing the pods streaming away from *Dreadnought* on their one-way journey to the surface.

"Drop pods launched," said White.

Dreadnought shot through the upper atmosphere of Micarro. A camera tracked the pods on their descent towards the planet's surface.

"Perfect," said MacCaibe, nodding with satisfaction as the pods' trajectories were added to the tactical overview. A thick cord of red lines led from *Dreadnought* to the planet, terminating at the Deathless base where the pods would deliver their passengers.

Dreadnought flew on, heading for the next waypoint on the voyage.

"Dropships *Wickham* and *Alton* are prepped and ready to fly," reported White.

"Approaching dropship launch window," said Martin. "Thirty seconds."

"I've got a strange feeling in my waters, Captain," said MacCaibe in a concerned tone. "*Target Two* is still coming, sir. We'll be crossing her path in about six minutes."

"How close will she be at that point, Mr MacCaibe?" asked White.

"About two hundred and fifty-five thousand kilometres, sir."

"Worry about her when she comes within weapon's range. Until then, eyes on the base, the station and the satellites," said Cohen.

"Aye, sir..." said MacCaibe.

"Opening the starboard bay doors," said Wood. "Dropships deploying now."

"Let the Marines know what's going on, Mr Wood."

"Aye, sir, updating them now."

"Dropships are clear and heading towards the rendezvous point," reported White a few minutes later. "They should be there just ahead of time."

"Well done, everyone," said Cohen. "A good start to the mission. Should be plain sailing from here on in."

"Sir!" said MacCaibe. "*Target Two*'s powering up her hyperspace engines. Looks like she's prepping a fast-flit attack."

"Impossible! Those ships don't have the right equipment, Mr MacCaibe. Isn't that right, Agent O?"

"That is correct, Captain. It would be most unwise for *Target Two* to attempt this type of manoeuvre, although it is the only style of attack that is likely to be effective against *Dreadnought* now that our own hyperspace abilities are so much improved."

"She's gone!" said MacCaibe, almost shouting.

The proximity alarms sounded and the tactical display updated to show *Target Two* bearing down on *Dreadnought* from no more than a dozen kilometres away.

"No fast-flit capability, eh?" said Cohen.

"She's firing," said MacCaibe. "Railguns and missiles, dozens of the buggers!"

"Deploy defen–" Cohen stopped for a heartbeat, thoughts racing.

"Sir?" said MacCaibe as Cohen's pause lengthened. "Should I deploy defences?"

"No. Just track *Target Two*, Mr MacCaibe."

"Aye, sir, tracking. Ready to fire," said MacCaibe, "or launch defences," he added under his breath.

"A one-second flit through hyperspace, please, Ms Martin," said Cohen, forcing his voice to remain calm.

"Sir? We haven't laid–"

"One second," ordered Cohen, voice rising. "Now, Ms Martin!"

"Aye, sir. Laying in, punching."

Space flickered as *Dreadnought* dropped into hyperspace and back. The stars shifted slightly, and for a moment all was calm.

"Nice," said MacCaibe, grinning as the tactical display updated to show a storm of railgun rounds from *Target Two* disappearing harmlessly into the interstellar void. One after another, bereft of their target, the missiles reached the limit of their flight and detonated their warheads.

"*Target Two*?" asked Cohen. "Where is she?"

"Searching," said MacCaibe. "There she is, sir. She must have flitted at the same time as us. She's on the far side of the planet, maybe thirty thousand kilometres from the Deathless station."

"She must have upgraded her engines," observed White. "Agent O's data are past their best."

"That is possible, Lieutenant," conceded Agent O, "but *Target Two* shows no evidence of engine remodelling."

"*Target Two* is running very hot, Captain," said Mueller from his desk at the edge of the bridge. "She's throwing off all kinds of radiation. It looks like her hyperspace engine is critically overloaded."

"Meaning what, exactly?" asked Cohen, although he had a

horribly clear idea of Mueller's meaning. Visions of *Ascendant* exploding after he deliberately overloaded her hyperspace engine flooded his mind, and it took a real effort to push them aside.

"An explosion. She'll scour the station and anything in orbit on the far side of the planet."

"Are we in danger?" asked White, leaning forward.

"No," said the science officer. "Our last flit carried us more than a hundred thousand kilometres, so we are well beyond the likely danger zone."

"What about the Marines?"

"They're a long way from *Target Two* and shielded by the planet's atmosphere," said Mueller.

"How long?" asked Cohen, conscious they would need to collect the dropships from orbit once they recovered the Marines from the planet's surface.

Woods was working frantically at his viewscreen, his fingers blazing across the keys but with every passing second, *Dreadnought's* systems seemed to take longer to respond to his commands.

"Dropships!" barked Cohen. "Where are they?"

"Heading into the atmosphere, sir," said Woods, highlighting the location of the dropships on the tactical display.

"They should be safe," said Mueller, brows furrowed as his hands flicked across his console. "From the initial explosion, at least."

"Wait, what?" said White, just as Cohen said, "What do you mean 'initial'?"

A flash overtook the display showing *Target Two,* so bright part of their screen went completely white. For a moment the bridge was silent.

"*Target Two* has gone, sir," said MacCaibe. "Scoured away like last week's porridge."

An expanding cloud of radioactive debris was all that remained of *Target Two.*

"Check with the dropships, Mr Wood," said White. "Confirm they're still in one piece."

"Aye, sir, working on it now."

"What news of the station, Mr Mueller?" asked Cohen.

"Hmm, what?"

Cohen allowed a little of his frustration into his voice. "What is going on with the Deathless station?"

"Oh, it's quite fascinating, sir," said Mueller, oblivious to his commander's growing irritation. He turned back to his console, muttering to himself as he reviewed the data. The seconds stretched until Mueller looked up and realised Cohen was waiting for more. "Oh, ah, yes. The station was far too close to *Target Two* when she exploded and has taken a heavy blast of radiation. There is almost certainly nothing left alive onboard, as if that mattered at this point."

"Why do you say that, Mr Mueller?" asked White, saving Cohen the effort.

"Can't you see?" asked Mueller, his face showing genuine puzzlement. He flicked his console until the main display showed a close-up of the station.

"It's a damaged orbital station," said Cohen with mild exasperation. "What am I missing?"

Mueller made more changes so that the tactical map showed an updated trajectory for the doomed station.

"Mr Mueller!" snapped Cohen. "Just give me the summary. What exactly am I looking at?"

"The station's manoeuvring thrusters are all offline, sir, and her orbit has shifted," said Mueller. "Shifted catastrophically, in fact. There can't be anyone alive after the blast, but even if there were, I don't think she could be saved."

"And that's important because...?" said White, calmly prompting Mueller before Cohen's temper frayed completely.

"The station's falling into Micarro's gravity well, sir," said Mueller. "She'll begin to disintegrate soon as she hits the upper atmosphere."

"Zoom in," said Cohen, frowning at the display. "I want to see where."

"The level of uncertainty is high," said Mueller. "The way the station tumbles as it falls, the density of the atmosphere, maybe the winds. Everything might have an effect, but this is the most likely outcome." The display jumped until it showed the station's new trajectory and the likely impact zone in the planet's northern continent. Cohen peered at it in horror for several long seconds.

"Agent O, does this match your analysis?" he said finally, hoping the AI would have better news.

"Yes, Captain," said Agent O, "although there is significant room for error given the complicated ways the station might break up and spin as it enters the atmosphere."

"So it's possible she might miss the base entirely?" asked White.

"Oh, very likely, Lieutenant," said Agent O. "But the station is large and moving very quickly. Any impact will produce a devastating shockwave, so even a near miss might prove fatal. If she breaks up in the upper atmosphere, parts will rain down over a much larger area, of course."

"Right," said Cohen. "Advise Captain Warden to move up his schedule, Mr Wood, and warn him of the salient points. Looks like he has, what, ninety minutes?"

"At most, Captain," confirmed Mueller.

"So they'd better get a bloody move on," muttered White.

13

Milton was keeping it casual. She was about to do something that seemed important but made her uncomfortable. It was bad enough looking after new recruits but this was the last thing she wanted to do today.

"What's up, Ten?" asked Milton. "You don't seem like your usual self. If I didn't know better, I'd think something was making you uneasy."

Ten's default behaviour was to act as if he hadn't a care in the world, but while he might appear nonchalant to a stranger, Milton detected an undercurrent of tension. He was a devil at poker because he was so hard to read, but Milton had worked with him long enough that she had a sense when something was bothering him.

"Come on," she said when the penal marine didn't respond. "Tell your friendly Colour Sergeant what the problem is."

Ten looked at her. "It's Morgan," he said finally.

"The Admiral?" said Milton, surprised. "It's not like you to give a shit about the senior ranks. Do you know him?"

Ten snorted. "I can trust you, can't I, Milton? You're a friend?"

That he would even ask concerned her and piqued her curiosity.

"Of course," she said. "How many times have we deployed together? How many times have you saved my skin?"

"Yeah, right. I had a life, once, before all this," said Ten quietly, sweeping his hand to indicate the ship. "Before I came back into the service."

"Back? You were out, but you came back in?"

"A story for another day," muttered Ten. "If I told you, you'd wish I hadn't."

"What, you'd have to kill me?" Milton teased.

"You've seen my file, right?"

Milton nodded, wondering where this was going. "I've seen it, but it's all redacted. About all I know is you're qualified for everything we do."

"And what does that tell you?"

"That whatever you did to get yourself court-martialled, was probably to do with something top secret," she speculated.

Ten shook his head. "Nah. What it should tell you is that you'd be in a lot of trouble if you found out about my sordid past. Unless you fancy joining the Penal Marine Rehabilitation Program, you'd best not tempt me to spill my secrets. You'd never get the stink off."

"Okay," said Milton doubtfully. She knew better than to push. "So what's bothering you about Morgan?"

Ten grimaced as if dredging up painful memories. He sighed, and glanced at her, then his shoulders sagged. "Fine, if it'll keep you happy, I'll tell you what I can, but this goes no further, okay?"

"Course not, Ten," said Milton with a frown. "Your secrets are safe with me."

"They'd better be," he said quietly, "for both our sakes. Look, I've come across Admiral Morgan before. Our paths have crossed, though he wouldn't remember it, and I need you not to remind him."

He paused until Milton nodded. She'd treated this lightly, but she was starting to wonder if she really wanted to know any more.

"I don't know what it was that pissed him off," said Ten, "but his job gave him a voice in the missions we were doing."

"And he interfered?"

Ten shrugged. "Every time he got a bee in his bonnet about our plan of action, or the kit we requisitioned, or the Royal Navy support we needed to deploy in a combat zone, he'd state his objections for the record. Then he'd take our rebuttals personally, which only made him more vindictive. It was all bloody politics and we just wanted to get on with the job. Morgan, being the specific type of rear-echelon motherfucker that he is, couldn't let it go."

"What did he do?" asked Milton, fascinated despite herself.

"Started small. He'd send the wrong kit or try and alter which ships we had access to. Little things to bugger up the mission. He's vicious, mean and petty. He never knows when to stop. By the time we noticed that he was developing a serious grudge, it was too late for diplomacy. Morgan obstructed us at every turn and did everything he could to make our lives unbearable."

Milton remained silent and still as Ten spoke.

"Before the end, things got so bad that missions were compromised. There was one in particular. A simple raid, but it went wrong from the start." For a moment he stared at the wall, eyes glazed, and Milton wondered if he'd said all he planned to say.

"We hit a rebel base, me and about three score others," he continued. "They had total air supremacy and plenty of localised orbital cover, so we had to slog our way across three hundred kilometres of dense jungle to avoid detection. We had portable Mind-Saver systems with satellite uplinks, but the canopy was thick, the comms were unreliable, and we had to maintain radio silence to avoid alerting the enemy."

Milton's mind raced. Ten never talked about his past like this. She'd never heard him open up about anything, in fact.

"First casualty was on day two. Some sort of beast that dwelt in the undergrowth, no idea what it was, never found out. It took Kent as she walked point. Nobody saw it, but we heard her screams as it chewed through her legs. Took us six hours to recover her body, and there wasn't a lot of it left."

"Fuck," muttered Milton, no longer sure she wanted to hear this story.

"The jungle was dense, broken by canyons and riddled with rivers. On a good day, we'd make fifteen kilometres. On a bad day, nearer five. Took us a month to cover the distance, and we lost six more people along the way. By the time we reached the target we were hungry, tired and severely pissed off, snapping at each other and hardly in a fit state to stand, let alone fight."

"Who was in command?" asked Milton, intrigued despite her better judgment.

"Classified," said Ten sourly. "I shouldn't be telling you any of this," he said, pausing. "The point is that by the time we got to the target, the enemy were long gone and we'd lost seven people getting there. The base was empty—had been for three weeks or more—but Morgan had left us down there despite having intelligence reports that confirmed everything we were doing was completely pointless."

"So that's it? You had a rough mission and that's why you don't like Morgan?"

Ten stared at his hands, and the silence lingered. But when he looked up there was real anger in his eyes. Milton tried to ignore the chill it gave her.

"The Mind-Saver network was faulty, Milton, and you know how often that stuff fails, right?"

"Never," murmured Milton. The Mind-Savers were over-engineered to the point of obsession, with multiple redundancies to ensure resilience. Since the job of the network was to backup and preserve the mind states – the personalities and memories – of the people linked to them, it was vital that they be reliable.

Body death was no more than a temporary inconvenience if your onboard systems were linked to a Mind-Saver. No matter the style of death, your personality was safe and you could be redeployed into a freshly cloned body within the day.

"Right, never. But when we got back, we found out there had been all sorts of technical issues. The backups weren't incrementing properly. Not for any of us. Every single mind state on that network, was just so much unusable garbage. The entire crew relied on this kit, and it hadn't been working from moment it was installed."

Milton opened her mouth to say something, but Ten wasn't finished.

"About now, you're thinking that at least we could use the backups from before we deployed to the mission. Right?" Milton nodded. "Yeah, that's what we thought too. Losing a couple of weeks fighting your way through a hostile jungle isn't too serious. It's not like we'd have lost two weeks anyone cared about. Then we found out the local network was such a bodged job it had transmitted unverified backups throughout the wormhole network. Everyone who'd died was gone, completely. They couldn't be brought back at all," Ten growled, his fists clenching and unclenching as he recalled the details.

"We never found out if it was a technical flaw in the system, or if it was deliberate sabotage. Virus, technical glitch or foul play, the Navy never got to the bottom of it."

"So Kent..."

"Yeah, Kent. She never went home. And neither did the others. Smith, Patel, Vaughn, Kelly, Castle and Russell. All lost."

"And you blame Morgan?"

Ten blew out a long breath, calmer now. "There was no proof. Not even a hint of evidence to tie him to it. And nobody ever worked out what went wrong. In the end they put it down to a batch of faulty Mind Saver gear and blamed a glitch at the manufactory. They changed some safety protocols, updated some handbooks, but they never pinned the blame on anyone. But I did. I blame Morgan."

"Bloody hell. You think he sabotaged the network deliberately? Why didn't they court martial him?"

"Like I said, no proof. All the records were correct. It's not like he'd installed the kit himself, he was just a mid-level officer then and squeaky clean as far as the Admiralty could see. He got a slap on the wrist for failing to act on the intelligence that said the targets had moved on, but the murders? What could we say? 'We think he decided to kill us all because he doesn't like us?'" Ten shrugged.

"It's a bit of a leap," agreed Milton.

"We didn't even have a motive. I think he's exactly that twisted, but I can't prove it and I never understood why he did it."

"What happened to your casualties? They couldn't restore them at all?" Milton asked, puzzled by the details.

Ten shook his head. "They woke up their stored bodies, but all those remembered was completing their entrance exam to join the service. All of them had been serving for over a decade, some for almost twenty years. Entire careers of good service gone. Marriages forgotten. Kids they didn't remember or recognise. They were all the way back to being civilians, with no idea of the skills they'd learned, or the sacrifices they'd made. It was a fucking tragedy."

"Fuck me. That's a grim story, Ten. Really dark."

"Yeah, well. You can see why I might not be keen to rescue the miserable fucker, right?"

"Is this mission going to be a problem for you?"

"No," said Ten with a flat stare. "I won't compromise the mission. My score with Morgan is too personal."

Milton shivered. There was something about the way he said it that scared her. She wondered if he had locked away his anger and hatred as insurance against a future need. But she couldn't bring herself to ask.

"Better get going, right?" said Ten airily, and the atmosphere shifted. He grinned as he strapped his pistol to his armour. "That fucker isn't going to save himself." He strode out of the room, scooping up his helmet and rifle as he went.

"Shit," she murmured. Maybe she should warn Warden, let him know Morgan and Ten had history. Then she shook her head and pushed the question away. Ten was a pro, and the last thing Milton wanted was to get in the way of his revenge.

But it didn't stop her thinking, and it didn't stop her worrying.

"Who are you, Ten?" she muttered to herself. "Who were you?"

∾

The plan was simple. A short flight to the surface, storm the base, recover the admiral and escape on *Dreadnought*'s dropships, *Wickham* and *Alton*. Smaller than the Deathless dropships, they carried thirty Marines in relative comfort or fifty at a push, so they'd have to use both to recover the company.

But first they had to get to the planet's surface. Warden and Plymouth company were strapped into seats in two dozen drop pods, stacked in the launchers like train carriages in a tunnel, all desperate to be on their way.

Marine X had somehow inserted himself into Warden's pod again, as if he saw himself as responsible for the captain's safety. Milton and Goodwin completed the four-berth complement, their kit carefully stowed in bays under their seats.

<This form of travel appears to be neither comfortable nor safe> sent Agent O.

Marine X grinned in his helmet. <Difficult to sleep on one of these rides> admitted Ten. <But at least they're short>

<Maybe we can improve the design>

<More cup holders would certainly be appreciated>

<Is this the time for humour? The Valkyr tend to be very quiet and serious in tense or stressful situations>

<Everyone has their own way of coping. We use humour, the darker the better> He looked up at the door controls where someone stuck a hand-written label above the emergency ramp release. <See that?>

<It is a confusing sign. What does it mean?>

<It's a joke. 'Release the Kraken'>

"Ten seconds to launch," came a voice over the comms.

<I see> sent Agent O. <Releasing the Kraken at the wrong time is bad, just like pressing that button. Very clever. I will research further while you enjoy your away day>

<Ha! That's the spirit>

<Good luck, Ten>

<Thanks. Should be a walk in the park>

The time to launch ticked down. In the tight confines of the drop pod, Warden reviewed the background information Agent O and CSO Mueller had pulled together on the target planet. Agent O's archives had provided some physical details of the planet – diameter, gravity, tilt, distance from star, atmosphere – but all it really told them was that conditions were similar to Earth, albeit warmer and with bigger storms.

The scans and photographs *Dreadnought* had gathered as she powered towards the pod drop point filled some of the gaps, but they really had no idea what they would be dropping into.

"No murderous zombie-fungus problems or giant millipede monsters, right?" Warden had asked in the hurried briefing.

Mueller had tried to answer by waffling on about evolution and the likelihood of independently evolved eco-systems containing organisms that might be able to interact directly at the biological level. He'd managed to lose most of his audience in a blaze of acronyms and technical terms before Agent O cut in with a concise answer.

"There is no evidence of zombie-fungi infections on Micarro," she said calmly.

"And the giant millipede monsters?" pressed Warden, because he'd spotted Agent O's deliberate avoidance of the question and wasn't about to risk another unexpected encounter.

"Micarro lacks a significant human population. Pre-colonisation mega-faunae are to be expected. We may learn more as we get closer." Which had been a sufficiently Mueller-like non-answer that Warden's suspicions were immediately triggered.

Investigating Micarro's geography had been easier. *Dreadnought's* scanners – mostly her original glass-lensed camera systems, some of which hadn't worked in decades – had been good enough to penetrate the planet's clouds and tease out the major features. They showed a planet with large seas in both hemispheres and world-circling forests in a wide equatorial band. Small polar regions with heavy snowfall spoke to the planet's generally warm and humid atmosphere, as did the lack of major deserts.

"Small, scattered deserts," commented Agent O. "Nothing like the Sahara on Earth or the iron seas of Scarabus."

But there could be big animals all over the place, just waiting to carry off an incautious Marine.

Warden's worrying was interrupted as White opened a channel.

"Bad news, old chap," said White in a cheerfully grim tone. He outlined the status of the Deathless orbital station and the news of its impending destruction. "So you'll need to move with a bit of snap to get the mission done."

"We're still going to launch?" said Warden incredulously.

"You'll be down in a few minutes," said White, "and the dropships are on their way. Just don't hang around on the surface. White out."

Warden sat with his mouth open for a few minutes, absorbing the update. Then he pulled up the mission schedule and began tightening the parameters. "Ninety minutes," he muttered as he worked, shaking his head.

He was interrupted by a ping in his HUD and a message from *Dreadnought*.

"Ninety seconds to launch. Stand by."

Ninety seconds. That meant *Palmerston* would have fired on the Deathless base by now, targeting the walls and perimeter defences to soften the target before the Marines arrived. If everything went to plan, the shockwaves from *Palmerston*'s pulverising shots would have died away just before the drop pods entered the danger zone. By the time the Deathless realised they were being bombarded, the Marines would be amongst them.

"Five seconds," said *Dreadnought*.

"Here we go," said Milton, her expression betraying her excitement.

"Launch," said *Dreadnought*. The pod lurched, accelerating quickly along the magnetic rails that would fling it towards the planet and the Deathless base.

Warden focussed on the company's status reports. All the

Marines showed elevated stress levels and heart rates, but that was completely normal. It was an unusual person who wasn't worried by dropping from space into a heavily defended enemy base.

Marine X seemed to be that person. Warden frowned, glancing across the pod. The Penal Marine appeared completely at ease, head back against the rest, eyes closed and barely visible through the slightly opaque faceplate. Warden opened a channel.

"You okay?"

"Fine thanks, Captain. Just thinking about the job."

"Anything in particular?"

Marine X looked across at the captain then shook his head. "Nothing worth worrying about, sir."

The shipboard computer flashed a status update to the HUDs of the Marines.

<Entering atmosphere>

Warden almost responded, but these computers were minimum-spec, little more than disposable calculators. His thoughts were disrupted as the pod began to bounce through the outer atmosphere.

<Thirty seconds to landing> sent the pod's computer.

Warden ran through the plan again, calling up the specs of the base in his HUD. It was a simple scan from orbit, lacking detail and interior information. And it would look a bit different once *Palmerston*'s bombardment struck home.

<Ten seconds to landing>

"Get ready," said Warden, gripping the handles and preparing to storm off the pod. The retro engines fired, pushing him into his seat so hard he almost blacked out. There was a crunch as the pod hit the ground. It lurched sideways and fell again, engines firing briefly to bring the tiny craft to a halt.

Everything after that was a blur of action. Marine X was out first, charging down the ramp, weapon up as he sought the enemy. Warden followed with Milton right behind. Goodwin had her drones out and away into the near darkness before Milton cleared the pod. The drones swept out into the air and dispersed to map the area, feeding updates to the Marines' HUDs. Goodwin slung her pack over her shoulder, grabbed her weapon and ran after the others.

<We're down> sent Warden to *Dreadnought*.

<DS *Wickham* and DS *Alton* are on their way. Lieutenants Jordan and Peters command>

<Acknowledged. Moving out>

"*Wickham* and *Alton* are on their way," said Warden. "And I want to be out of here and at the rendezvous point in no more than seventy-five minutes. Let's get moving."

His HUD showed all the pods had landed safely, intact and ready for action.

He looked around, getting the lay of the land as updates started to stream in from the Marines and the drones.

"Where the hell are we?" he muttered to himself.

"It ain't Kansas," said Milton, and Warden agreed.

It was dark, far darker than Warden expected the early morning to be. A strange circle of light above them showed the dawn sky.

"We're underground," he said. "Some sort of cavern." He flicked his HUD to low-light and the cave was revealed. A huge open area stretched away, covered with piles of rock and broken stalagmites, while the rough walls held dark opening – corridors, Warden realised – leading away from the cavern in all directions. The ceiling curved up towards the hole, far above.

"The surface was thin. The pods punched straight through," said Milton.

"Pods?"

"Two more over there. Looks like the rest are on the surface."

"Shit," muttered Warden. "Right. Let's get everyone together and work out who's where."

Milton rounded up the troops and did a quick check, tagging people in her HUD as she identified them.

"Sixty metres, maybe more," said Marine X, thinking of his grapnel. He shook his head. "Too high. We'll have to find another way out."

<We're trapped in an underground cavern> sent Warden to Lieu-

tenant Linda Hayes, commander of B Troop and the most experienced officer in the company, along with a list of the subterranean Marines. <Complete the mission, get to the rendezvous. Don't hang around> he went on, thinking about the falling station, <and don't wait for us. We'll join you as soon as we can>

<Roger> acknowledged Hayes.

Lieutenant Hayes' orders scrolled through Warden's HUD, and the Marines dispersed, heading away from the landing ground to secure their objectives.

Warden looked around his much-reduced command as the snap of gunfire drifted down from above.

"Goodwin, get those tunnels mapped and find us a way to the surface."

"On it, sir."

"You think there'll be one?" asked Milton.

"Bound to be," said Warden with completely unjustified confidence. "We just have to find it. Which way is the base?"

Goodwin waved her hand.

"Then we go that way and find a tunnel that leads to the basement. We shoot our way in, join up with the rest of the company and exfiltrate via dropship at the rendezvous as planned. Easy."

Milton's expression was hidden in the gloom, but Warden could feel the scepticism rolling off her in waves.

The Marines moved out, Ten and Milton leading the way.

"I don't like it," said Goodwin from just behind as she scanned through the drone feeds.

"Don't say it," warned Marine X.

"It's just too quiet," murmured Goodwin, Ten's warning unheeded. "Where are all the miners?"

A faint snickering and the gentle sounds of falling pebbles came from up ahead.

Marine X held up his hand to halt the small column as something moved in the darkness, just beyond the HUD's range.

"I don't think we're alone down here," he said.

14

"Warden's down! We're doing this on our own." yelled Hayes, A and B Troops scrambling from their drop pods and going to ground around her.

"He's dead?" asked an appalled Lieutenant Newton, newly appointed commander of A Troop after Warden's promotion.

"No, Newton, he's down, as in underground," said Hayes, irritation growing from Newton's radiating confusion. "The hole," she said, pointing. "They crashed through and are lost below somewhere."

For a moment she wondered if it would be faster to replay her entire conversation with Warden, but Newton nodded his understanding.

"There are twelve of them down there, we can't help them, so we go that way and complete the mission. Got it?"

"On our own?" said Newton doubtfully.

This was his first combat deployment, and his lack of experience was telling. A Troop may have lost a third of their number when Warden and his team crashed through to the caverns below the base, but Newton needed to get his head in the mission. Hayes leaned in toward him, quieting her voice.

"Gather your team, use your sergeant, follow my lead. Come on, Rob. Get it together."

"Right, yes," he said, a little more confidently, though his weak smile was unconvincing. "So, A Troop goes, er, that way?"

"Follow the plans in the HUD, Rob," said Hayes as gently as she could, "and let Campbell handle the troops, yes?"

He nodded, but she could see he was going to be a struggle.

Hayes flicked to the company's command channel and kicked out Warden and Milton. They weren't going to be much use till they were back above ground, and she didn't want them muddying the waters or challenging her orders.

She issued a rapid update on Warden's position. "So we'll be meeting up with them later, once we've done all the difficult bits, okay?" There was a round of slightly gung-ho confirmations. "Any questions? Good. A Troop to the right, B Troop to the left, bounding overwatch. Follow the plan in the HUD. You know the drill, people. Get moving!"

The Marines moved out in a flurry of activity toward the enemy facility. The early morning air was cool but the humidity was building. It was going to be a warm day.

Palmerston had done a decent job of evening the battlefield. The first missile struck a building – a gatehouse, they assumed, although there wasn't a trace left beyond a smoking crater and a pile of rubble – and taken out a long stretch of foamcrete wall near it. The whole area was covered in bits of rubble and twisted reinforcing rods.

"Looks like a war zone," someone muttered as the Marines worked their way inwards, searching for the enemy.

The second missile hit the monorail station a few hundred metres away. Like the bases on NewPet, the monorail station was outside the walls for reasons Hayes didn't even bother to speculate about. The strike demolished the building, tearing a two hundred metre gap in the raised track running from east to west across the face of the planet. The pillars that supported the rail hadn't withstood the impact, and many were crumpled as if they'd been made of tin rather than foamcrete.

Hayes noted no sign of damage from the third missile. She pushed it aside. Her troops were closing in on the remains of the gatehouse, already crossing the rubble.

She found a spot to hunker down and checked the company's progress in her HUD. A Troop were making rapid progress to the right, although Newton seemed to be trailing behind. B Troop were almost in position to assault the main part of the facility.

Hayes opened a direct channel to Newton. "What are you playing at, Rob? Keep moving."

Newton gave a startled glance and hurried forward, almost tripping over the rubble as he went.

"Shit," muttered Hayes after she closed the channel. "Focus on the mission," she said to herself. Either Newtown would come through or he wouldn't, but there was nothing she could do about it.

She waved at her sergeant, the hugely experienced Richard Shore, signalling him to advance. Shore nodded and moved to surround the main doors. Section One flowed smoothly after him with Section Two following swiftly behind. Corporal Moon stepped up, a set of charges ready to set. She pushed at the door and it swung silently open.

"A rare spot of luck," murmured Hayes.

She kept one eye on the destruction around them, the other on her team. Shore and Section One disappeared into the interior, preceded by a small fleet of micro-drones. The drones fanned out, mapping the rooms and seeking the enemy. Section Two followed, and Hayes jogged after them with Section Three. She was almost there when a shout from the other end of the compound caught her attention. It came from where A Troop were strung out across the rubble.

Above them, on a sheltered balcony overlooking the courtyard, a brace of Deathless troopers watched.

"Normal luck has been restored," said Hayes under her breath. "Contact," she said over the command channel, her HUD flagging the location of the two enemy soldiers. She sprinted, pointing her rifle in their general direction and squeezed off a few rounds. The

Deathless troopers ducked out of sight, and Hayes grinned to herself. "Amateurs."

She ushered Section Three through the open door, watching the courtyard. Hayes anticipated the Deathless striking back, but the last of B Troop's Marines scuttled through unscathed.

Hayes switched her attention to A Troop. They had reached the inner buildings and were now spread out along the walls. Her troops were horribly exposed and barely moving. Easy targets for anyone on the walls or in the facility's taller buildings.

"What's going on?" she asked Sergeant Campbell in a private chat.

"Waiting on the Lieutenant," said Campbell, scanning the surrounding buildings, clearly not amused by the situation.

Hayes switched channels. "Rob, get a move on." She crouched by the door, desperately aware she was as much a target as A Troop. There was no answer from Newton, so she switched channels. "Campbell, take charge. Stick to the plan. Newton will follow, but you need to make progress or we'll never get out of here."

"Roger," said Campbell. "Heading for the waypoint now." The channel closed and Hayes backed in through the doorway, using its frame to give her better cover as Campbell issued orders, leading her troops on.

The plan had been for A Troop and B Troop to make separate but linked assaults through two different entrances. Even though their overall objective would be obvious – Admiral Morgan was the only Commonwealth prisoner on the planet, as far as anyone knew – they hoped to get in and through the facility before the Deathless worked out what was going on.

But plans were only as good as the enemy allowed them to be, and events were conspiring against the Marines.

As Campbell got her people moving and Newton finally appeared, the Deathless burst onto the balcony in force, firing down into the courtyard at A Troop's stragglers. Hayes returned fire from her doorway, but was forced to retreat as rounds pattered into the doorframe.

"Too close," she said, backing into the building and hurrying after the rest of B Troop as Campbell took A Troop in through the other door. They were moving smartly, now, but Hayes still had two red casualty indicators in her HUD. Not everyone would walk away from this encounter.

Hayes sword under her breath and hurried on. She found herself in a huge high-ceilinged room like a great hall of a castle back on Earth. Light flooded in from the tall windows lining the front of the building, casting long shadows across the open floor from the rising sun. B Troop spread out across the southern end of the room, with Section One heading for the double doors. Section Two were moving cautiously from the reception hall into a second, similarly vast space resembling an old Gothic cathedral.

All the Marines carried lightweight speed cuffs – dozens of them – and they restrained every unarmed person they encountered, tying them at wrist and ankle and leaving them hobbled on the floor.

Hayes followed with Section Three, sweeping past the half dozen Deathless clones surprised by the Marines and captured before they could arm themselves.

A Troop made it to the reception hall through the second door. Newton was with them but he didn't seem to be playing much of a leadership role. Instead, Campbell motored on, taking charge of the situation, which was exactly what an experienced sergeant ought to be doing.

"Rough day," muttered Hayes to herself.

She padded through the cathedral-like space. A Troop had gone left in search of the enemy, leaving a trail of bound and gagged lizardman clones behind them.

Hayes and her troops went right, fanning out into a maze of rooms and corridors. The drones flitted everywhere, hovering above the lead Marines then racing ahead as soon as the next door was opened. The maps in the Marines' HUDs updated as the drones scouted the facility.

"Found a network point," said Moon. Hayes hurried to her side as Moon plugged a tiny hacking module into the port and fired up her data slate.

"Pity we can't hack their wifi," said Hayes, standing with her back to Moon and her rifle raised, watching the corridors.

"Biometric security, ma'am," said Moon as she worked. "But not on the wired network. Here's their intranet, downloading everything we can get, and there's the guest list."

Moon scrolled quickly until she found an entry that didn't match the pattern. "That's probably the admiral," she said, tagging the marked suite and flagging the location in the expanding map in her HUD. "East another thirty metres past the current high-tide point." She unplugged her slate and slipped it away.

"Good work, Moon," said Hayes. "Shore, you saw the update about the admiral?"

"Roger, ma'am, almost there, another thirty seconds."

"Contact," came an update from Sergeant Campbell. "Determined resistance."

Hayes grimaced. Coming from Campbell, that little euphemism could mean anything from a couple of troopers who didn't immediately back down, to an entrenched brigade.

"Hurry it up, Shore," said Hayes, pressing forward with Section Three.

"Contact," said Shore. "Grenades."

Dull hissing snaps echoed down the corridors as the Marines' suppressed weapons fired. A deeper crackle rattled the windows, and Hayes knew the enemy were fighting back. A couple of loud bangs responded as Shore's grenades exploded.

A wailing alarm started outside in the main compound and crept inside to needle at Hayes' ears. With half an eye on her team's status indicators in her HUD, she darted along the corridors, Moon right behind, heading for Shore and the rooms where the admiral was being held.

They followed Section Two into a large room strangely resembling a library from an old-school private club. Including a stuffed cat on one of the many shelves, eyes glazed as it peered out over the room, perhaps waiting for a mouse that would never arrive.

"Not exactly a prison, ma'am," said Moon. "Hadn't expected to see spirits on offer."

"Admirals don't get kept with the commoners," said Hayes, but she frowned at the room.

There was a body behind one of the leather armchairs, but it wasn't one of theirs. A Deathless officer – a Rupert – shot while hiding. There was another by the drinks cabinet in the corner, a pistol in hand. Hayes kicked the weapon under a sofa, just to be sure, then moved on.

"Should I grab this stuff?" asked Moon, pointing at a couple of data slates on a side table.

"Yes," said Hayes. "Anything that looks useful but be quick about it." She scanned the room again as Moon stuffed items into his pack. Something felt wrong, but she couldn't put her finger on it.

Then someone shouted, and Hayes hurried out of the library and down the corridor. Moon followed close behind, his swag stowed and his rifle ready.

"Ma'am," said Shore as Hayes turned a corner. There were two dead lizardmen sprawled untidily at the end of the corridor, blood splattered across the walls. Neither were armoured, but none of the enemy troops they had seen so far had worn anything more than standard fatigues. Most hadn't even been armed.

"Is this it?" asked Hayes, pointing at a door. Shore nodded and moved to stand on one side. "Go."

Marine Hamilton turned the handle, then Shore kicked the door open and they bundled into the room, weapons up in search for danger.

"Clear," said Shore as he completed his sweep of the small, comfortably furnished apartment.

Hayes and Moon came in as the rest of B Troop searched the surrounding rooms and secured the area. Hayes couldn't help but notice the apartment was bigger than her flat on Earth. Although the furniture and decoration where gaudy and, to her eye, borderline unpleasant.

In one corner stood a man in a standard Royal Navy clone. He was bruised and battered, as if someone had taken a heavy implement to his face and hands. One eye was swollen shut, his nose was twisted at an odd angle, and huge purple bruises covered the side of the man's face. He was also half-dressed and clearly surprised to see the Marines.

"Admiral Morgan?" asked Hayes, not lowering her weapon. "Are you Admiral Morgan?"

"Yes, I'm Morgan," snapped the man, his words indistinct made indistinct by his mangled lips. "Who the hell are you?" He struggled to fasten his trousers, and Hayes saw that several of the admiral's fingers were heavily bandaged and his hands were purple with bruises.

"Lieutenant Hayes, sir, RMSC, Plymouth Company. We'll have you out of here in a few moments. Moon?"

Hayes moved aside, weapon still aimed at the admiral. Moon hurried forward with a small DNA sequencer and had the thumb of the Admiral's unbandaged hand rammed against the reader before he had time to think about it.

"Hey!" said Morgan, snatching away his thumb. "I'm bleeding," he said in a tone of indignant astonishment.

Moon ignored him, waiting for the sequencer to crank through its analysis. "Identity confirmed," she said after a few seconds. "Sorry about that, sir, can't be too careful." She pocketed the sequencer and slipped out of the room.

Hayes and the other Marines relaxed, happier knowing they had the right person. DNA could be faked, so identity wasn't certain, but that was a problem for someone else to deal with later.

"What the hell's going on, Lieutenant?" Morgan demanded.

"Is there anything you need, sir?" said Hayes, ignoring the Admiral's question. "Only we're on a tight schedule."

"What? No, nothing," he said, wincing at a pain in his side as he sat down to pull on his shoes, muttering with frustration as his damaged fingers fumbled at the laces.

"Are you able to walk, sir?" asked Hayes.

Morgan glared up at her and heaved himself out of the chair with another grimace of pain. "Of course I can bloody walk," he managed, taking a limping step across the room.

Hayes nodded, too long in the service to be goaded or annoyed by the admiral's rudeness.

Then an icon flashed in her HUD as Marines Adams and Bradley suddenly died.

"Incoming," reported Gibson, "armoured lizardmen." A roar of noise echoed down the corridor as Section Three began a fighting retreat with grenades and gunfire. "Rear-guard falling back."

"Time to go, Shore," said Hayes. "That way." She nodded at the back door to Morgan's apartment.

"Roger," said Shore. "Section One, with me. Section Two, bring the Admiral." He kicked open the back door and led the team into the open space beyond, searching for the enemy and the exit.

"This way, Admiral," said Corporal Banks, Section Two's team lead. "Follow me."

Morgan limped reluctantly out, an angry expression on his face and one arm held protectively across his chest.

Hayes counted her people in through the first door and out through the second. Gibson was last, his armour spattered with muck and blood. He slammed the door shut behind him as if that would slow the Deathless.

"Sorry, ma'am, they blew out the wall and started shooting. Some sort of mini-gun thing, nothing we could do."

"The backups are secure. Let's go."

Gibson hurried through the far door and Hayes followed. Moon waited for her outside, charges in hand.

"Do it," said Hayes as she fired at the inner door, blasting it apart. She ducked away as the Deathless returned fire. Even through two walls, the noise of their weapons was huge. Rounds chewed through the inner door, cutting it in half and ripping into the room. A cloud of fabric, wood splinters and paper erupted as the room was swept with fire.

"Done," said Moon, stepping away from her booby trap and collecting her weapon. Hayes threw a grenade at the far wall of the apartment and pulled the door closed. She ran after Moon to where Gibson waited in a doorway.

Behind her, the grenade exploded with a sharp crack, blowing out the windows of the apartment and covering the outside area with broken glass.

Hayes grinned at Gibson and Moon. "First time I've rescued an admiral. Now go!"

~

"Shut that door!" yelled Shore as Hayes turned a corner. She glanced in the direction the sergeant pointed. Armoured figures could be seen through a set of doors down the long corridor. Marines Allan and Kenny fired grenades from their underslung launchers then jumped back out of sight. Hayes crouched into an alcove, Gibson and Moon behind her. The grenades detonated, sending a shower of shrapnel bouncing.

"On!" shouted Shore, appearing through the cloud of dust to wave at Hayes to move. She nodded and followed as he led them around the next corner and back into a great hall. A gallery ran around the room with doors on every wall. Marines from A Troop came in from the north as Hayes entered from the south.

"That way," said Shore, pointing towards the exit and flagging the route in his HUD. A Troop's rear-guard covered the retreat with grenades and smoke as the lizardmen advanced through the building behind them.

"Where's the Admiral?" said Hayes.

"Ahead," said Shore. "Banks has him."

Hayes grunted. Then she ran through the hall and burst out into the cathedral-like space on the other side. Shore followed, herding Moon and Gibson before him. The last of A Troop's survivors rushed through looking battered and bruised. Newton appeared. He'd managed to lose his helmet and was bleeding from a head wound. He nodded at Hayes, stumbling through the doors, but she wasn't sure he recognised her.

"We're clear," said Sergeant Campbell. "Nothing but blood and death behind us."

"Burn it down," said Hayes, "we have what we came for."

"Roger," said Shore. He tossed more grenades into the galleried hall as Campbell fired at a pair of lizardmen who were peering from a far door. Gibson pulled the heavy doors closed as the grenades went off.

"Trouble," said Corporal Hamilton, Section One's team lead. He was at the front of the building, leading the charge to the rendezvous point.

A sudden roar from outside announced the arrival of a new enemy. Something fired into the reception hall, shattering the windows at the front of the building. The Marines scattered, some to the edges of the hall, most against the walls of the cathedral, all hiding from the hail of fire tearing at the walls and spattering against the stonework.

"Two APCs with heavy cannons," reported Hamilton. "They're parked across the breach."

"Shit," muttered Hayes, edging up to peek around the stonework. The reception hall was a mess of glass and bodies. Deathless and Marines alike cowered back as another burst of fire punched through the room. Beyond, across the courtyard, two hulking armoured personnel carriers squatted at the edge of the shallow crater left by *Palmerston's* first shot, hull down against the piles of rock and shattered foamcrete that covered the flagstones. Each vehicle had two weapons mounts, each with a pair of heavy machine guns that spewed rounds at a huge rate.

"They're firing blind," she said, hoping she was right. She switched to the command channel. "Where is the heavy weapons crew?"

"Courtyard," said Campbell bitterly. "Maxwell and Lee were hit first."

"Tell me we have their weapons?" said Hayes, although she was pretty sure she knew what Campbell was going to say.

"Negative, ma'am, they're still in the courtyard." And they might as well be back aboard *Dreadnought* for all the use they were now.

"Grenades?" she asked, stretching the bounds of hopeful credibility.

"Negative," said Campbell as the APCs fired again. "Too far to throw, and the forty-mils won't touch those beasts."

"Spread out," ordered Hayes. "Find us a way around. South, maybe."

"Roger," said Shore. Section Two shifted, weaving between the vast room's towering pillars to make for the south door, the admiral's shuffling form looking strangely child-like between the armoured Marines. Banks nudged the door open, then reared back as gunfire erupted from the corridor beyond. The heavy door shook and splintered as the Deathless poured shots into it.

"South looks tricky," reported Shore, "and the gallery to the east is now well ablaze."

Hayes looked along the length of the line of pillars and the smoke curling under the doors leading to the galleried hall. There was no risk to the suited and helmeted Marines, but the admiral wouldn't be too keen to exit through a blazing room.

"Shit," muttered Hayes as the APCs opened fire again. A second burst from the north of the hall caught Corporal Green of A Troop in the back, knocking him down. His status indicator winked out as Campbell roared at her team to close the northern door and secure the area. A Troop returned fire and the doors were forced shut. They shoved a heavy bench in front as a makeshift barricade, and the Marines crouched low to avoid incoming fire.

The Deathless were relentless. Firing at both doors, north and south, and the rounds crunched through the room at chest height, chipping lumps from the stone columns and ricocheting around the hall. It was only a matter of time, now.

"Trapped," whispered Hayes.

"Is this your idea of a rescue?" yelled Admiral Morgan from across the hall. Hayes rolled over to see the admiral lying prone behind a column, shouting to make himself heard above the din. "What next, blow up the building while we're trapped inside?"

"Sorry, sir, this hasn't gone entirely to plan."

"It never bloody does with you Marines," snapped Morgan. He cringed back as new fire battered the pillars and sprayed B Troop with stone chippings. "Did you even have a plan? What did you think would happen if you attacked like this, hmm?"

Hayes ground her teeth but said nothing. Arguing with an admiral wasn't going to be a career-enhancing move.

"Agent O," she said in desperation, opening a private channel and rolling away from the admiral. "Can you hear me?"

"I can, Lieutenant Hayes," said Agent O in her calm and reassuring tones. "How may I be of assistance?"

"I have no fucking idea," said Hayes. There was a loud bang from the eastern end of the building and the doors to the galleried hall fell into the room, sending a shower of sparks and embers wafting down between the pillars. The room beyond was an inferno – clearly the Deathless hadn't bothered to install sprinklers – and now the flames were licking at the roof. It was only a matter of time until the building began to collapse around them.

"There are no operational drones," said Agent O, "but I have access to your team's helmet feeds. I believe your situation is dire but not yet unrecoverable."

"Really?" asked Hayes, genuinely surprised. She had all but accepted that there wasn't a way out of the building. Sooner or later, they'd be forced into the courtyard or the Deathless would charge into the reception hall, and that would be the end of the mission.

"Hold on for just a little longer, Lieutenant. Help is on the way."

"Acknowledged," said Hayes. She switched to the company's public channel so she could address the whole team. "Stay sharp, keep it together," she said, hoping she'd be able to follow her own advice. "Agent O has a plan." Even as she said it she knew things were bad, but the chorus of groans and the rumble of moaning was worse than she feared. Nobody really trusted the weird Valkyr AI, despite the tales Ten told of its astounding tactical brilliance.

"Does it involve throwing Ten at the bad guys?" someone joked. Hayes didn't bother to check who had spoken.

"Quiet, or you'll be following him." She poked her rifle around the edge of the pillar and fired a few rounds at the Deathless across the courtyard. Pointless, she knew, but sometimes all you could do was try.

15

The tunnel was as black as pitch. Without the HUD's low-light and infra-red modes, Ten wouldn't have been able to see a thing. As it was, he could see only a few metres ahead in the light from the low-power IR lamps on his helmet. The sounds of combat faded away as soon as they left the first cavern. Now they were truly alone, cut off from the surface by sixty metres of rock and earth.

Goodwin's drones blasted through the tunnels marking them out for two hundred metres in every direction. But finding an obvious exit point remained elusive. She widened their reconnaissance area, but nobody wanted to hang around in the dark to wait for the drones to complete their survey.

Ten stopped again when more chittering floated along the tunnel.

<Not alone> he sent to the team, peering through his weapon's sights in search for threats. Nothing.

He edged forward, crouching low.

<Fork right towards cavern> sent Warden.

<Roger>

The map in Ten's HUD showed a fork on the right and a short spur that opened into a major cavern. The drones flagged it as 'unusual', but their AI was limited. Unusual was a euphemism that could mean anything from 'interesting rock formations' to 'infestation of rabid dinosaurs'.

Ten eased cautiously into the spur, following its gentle downward slope. He stepped carefully around piles of what looked like spoil from mining.

<Light ahead> he sent.

The sense of relief was almost palpable. They had been down here only a short while but it felt like hours. Light meant people, and people meant escape, even if they were likely to be the enemy who would do their damnedest to see the Marines entombed here forever.

Ten took another step forward and realised there was a rhythmic tapping coming from up ahead, and the chittering seemed to be getting louder.

Sounds like people mining, he thought with a frown. But that made no sense. Why employ humans to do a dangerous, unpleasant job that was better done by machines? Mining by hand – even on Earth where tradition was often more important than achievement – had been decimated by the development of autonomous AI-driven specialist machines, and then eliminated entirely with the arrival of the first ores mined from asteroids. No point in making a mess of your planet, when it was cheaper to get rare minerals from an unattractive asteroid belt.

Ten crept to the mouth of the tunnel and crouched behind a rock to peer out at the enormous cavern beyond. Easily five times as big as the cave they'd breached, this one stretched away in all directions and dropped deeper into the ground.

"Holy shit," murmured Milton as she joined him.

The light was dim, but there were scores of pale yellow lamps. They hung from the walls, from walkways and gantries, from posts and pillars and support struts.

But it was the figures that held Ten's attention. Miners. Hundreds of them, all wielding picks or hammers and pushing carts along narrow tracks. The cavern swarmed with them.

Milton rapped Ten's arm and pointed at a walkway a few metres below their vantage point. A group of miners made their way towards a working face and would pass right beneath them.

"How many, do you think?" asked Ten.

Milton shrugged. "Hundreds, maybe a couple of thousand? This might not be the only cavern."

"Or the only mine," said Ten.

Something caught his eye. Amongst the miners strode other figures. Taller, broader and better fed, they carried clubs, whips and long knives. They wore leather-style jerkins and trousers but no boots. Like the miners, these figures had long prehensile toes that ended in claw-like nails. There were fewer of them, but now that he noticed them they seemed to be everywhere, watching the miners like guards.

One of the larger figures screamed.

"What the fuck?" muttered Ten.

It flicked its whip, beating a miner to the floor. Ten felt Milton's arm on his shoulder and realised he'd half stood. He sank back down on his haunches and a chill ran down his neck.

"Slaves," he hissed, the anger boiling off him like steam.

"Workers," corrected Milton. "You don't know they're slaves. They might not even be human."

"Does that look like a fair exchange of labour?" said Ten, pointing at the miner still lying on the floor. "And what fucking difference does it make if they're not human?"

"Focus on the mission," said Milton firmly. "This is a problem for another day. We need more information. We can't just charge in and start shooting people."

Ten looked like he was about to argue the point. Then he nodded and Milton relaxed.

"Okay. Let's just get the job done," said Ten. "We can worry about the morals of what's going on down here later, once we've rescued the fuckwit."

"Right," said Milton.

<Agent O, can you see this?> sent Ten, sharing his feed and directing his helmet cameras towards the nearest group of figures.

<This is most unusual> replied Agent O. <I do not think this is a Koschite facility>

<It's beneath their base> pointed out Ten. <They must know it's here>

<But the Koschites do not mine by hand. They have semi-sentient machines, like those of the Valkyr, to extract and process their ore> Agent O replied.

<Can you find us a way out?> sent Ten.

<I am hacking the base computers> countered Agent O. <The Mystery of the Machine-free Miners is one I must solve>

"Agent O is investigating," said Ten to the squad, "but she says this isn't typical Deathless practice."

"They're coming closer," said Milton, tugging at Ten's arm and backing down the tunnel.

<I have accessed the facility's computers and have news> sent Agent O as Ten and the Marines backed away from the vast cavern. <I have added Captain Warden to this channel. This base is run by GK Industries>

<The company that attacked the Valkyr?> sent Warden.

<Yes, Captain. The files I have recovered show they are masquerading as a legitimate military outfit, but this appears to be a front for other, less savoury practices. One of those practices appears to be the production of special-purpose mining clones for the low-cost extraction of ores>

<Are they slaves?> sent Ten.

<The clones appear to be created specifically for mining. It is unclear whether the concept of slavery applies, or why anyone would bother to enslave people when machines can be constructed to perform the duties more efficiently>

"Some people are just evil fuckers," muttered Ten.

"Back further," hissed Milton, "and get down."

The Marines went to ground along the walls of the tunnel, huddling into whatever hiding places they could find as the miner-clones sniffed around the entrance.

<Are these things human?> sent Warden as a miner eased its way into the tunnel.

The clone had a flat, almost featureless face with long muscular limbs, broad shoulders and slender digits that ended in inch-long talons. It wore only a thin shift of grimy material, torn and ragged by long use. It sniffed the air through a grey nose that sat between two big round eyes and gazed into the gloom of the tunnel. It crept forwards on its hands and knees, head swinging from side to side.

<No, Captain. I have found various references to experimental mind creation techniques. I have also retrieved a hidden folder that may offer clues, but its secrets are locked within a bio-metric encryption system. We will need an individual with appropriate security clearance to access the contents>

<Been there before> Warden shuddered, remembering their previous attempts to capture a high-ranking Deathless officer. <If they're not human, are they at least friendly?>

The clone edged cautiously into the tunnel making small noises like a kitten. Behind it, two more hauled themselves over the lip and were watching their colleague. Their eyes seemed to glow in the dark.

The lead clone turned sharply towards Milton's hiding place and shuffled forward. It reached gingerly out to touch the rubber of the Colour Sergeant's steel-capped boot, running its finger gently over the surface.

<Yes, Captain. The documents indicate that these clones have been designed principally for hard work under a strong matriarch. There is nothing to indicate innate hostility toward humans>

The miner-clone moved its fingers up Milton's leg and the Colour flinched, jerking her foot back. The clone jumped back, squatting on its haunches and hissing, lips drawn back to expose long canines.

<What about learned hostility?> sent Warden.

The clone screamed and leapt forward, talons reaching for Milton's face.

～

M ilton brought up her rifle and clubbed the clone aside. It bounced away to land on all fours like a cat. It sprang again, talons outstretched. Behind it, more slaver clones clambered to the edge of the tunnel, peering into the gloom. One shone a lamp, exposing the concealed Marines as Milton battered her attacker in the face, forcing it back.

"Fall back," said Warden, edging back down the tunnel.

Another slaver clone screamed, the noise horribly loud in the tight confines. The cry was taken up by others nearby and the video feed from the drone in the main cavern showed them swarming the tunnel from all directions.

"Back!" said Warden again, unable to keep a note of panic from his voice.

There was a yelp from the back of the squad. Warden whipped around. Drummond was being dragged down the tunnel and beaten by a pair of the taller clones. He thrashed around, attempting to free himself. A third appeared swinging a heavy club, twirling it around as if it weighed nothing at all.

"Help!" yelled Drummond as the slaver's talons tore at his armour. Marine Harrington smashed the butt of his rifle into the face of the club-wielding slaver and got a heavy punch in the face in return. He staggered back, the faceplate of his helmet cracked.

"They're on the ceiling!" warned Goodwin.

A clone dropped into the middle of the squad, twisting as it fell onto Harrington's shoulders. It drove him to the ground, slamming the Marine's helmet into the rocky floor of the tunnel.

"Not friendly!" shouted Warden. "Fire at will!" He squeezed his trigger, aiming at Harrington's attacker. Holes drilled into the clone's back, and it released Harrington, jerking up with a terrible scream. The other slavers joined in, filling the tunnel with a dreadful cacophony. The injured slaver lurched away from the stricken Marine before stumbling to the floor and lying still.

The rest of the squad opened fire. In seconds they were alone, the clones fleeing into the larger cavern, scurrying away along walkways, into tunnels or up the walls. The miners went with them, disappearing into the pit and abandoning their tools and carts along the way.

Warden looked around, breathing heavily. Drummond was on his feet, his armour showing bright scratches where the slavers' talons slashed him. Goodwin crouched over Harrington but Warden's HUD already told him the Marine was dead. Goodwin shook her head and stood up.

"Can you walk, Drummond?" asked Milton.

"Yes, Colours," said the Marine as he collected his fallen weapon. "Just about." He limped across the tunnel to check on Harrington then swore.

"There's no sign of them," said Ten from the mouth of the tunnel. "They're nowhere to be seen, but I don't think they've gone very far."

As if on cue, a wordless cry drifted up from deep in the mine, a sound of anguish and pain and anger.

"Harrington's backup is confirmed," said Goodwin.

"Grab his magazines. I think we'll need all the ammo we can get."

Goodwin nodded and pulled out Harrington's magazines, distributing them to the other Marines.

Another call sounded from far below, then another. There was an answering call from one of the tunnels on the far side of the cavern and the drone picked out movement, raising an 'incoming hostile forces' alert in the Marines' HUDs.

"Yup," said Ten as he moved into the tunnel, "it's time to go."

"Agent O, any luck with a route out of here?" asked Warden.

"The drones are still mapping the mine, Captain, but there is a route to the basement of the facility above. Sending the details to your HUDs now."

There was a low murmuring amongst the Marines as the route appeared in their HUDs, and for good reason.

"That takes us right through the main cavern," said Goodwin. "It's a bit risky," she added, demonstrating her astounding ability for stating the obvious.

"Indeed, Gooders, but it is the shortest route to the objective and it minimises your exposure to an enemy whose numbers we are unable to gauge," said Agent O.

"No point hanging around here waiting to die," said Milton, checking her weapon and casting a firm eye over the rest of the squad.

"No, we can go anywhere to die," muttered Drummond under his breath.

"Time to go," agreed Warden. "Pull the drones in, Goodwin. Let's get them scouting for us."

"Roger," said Goodwin, issuing new commands to the drones through her HUD.

"There's more movement down there," said Marine X from the end of the tunnel. Warden hurried over to see for himself as Ten pointed down into the vast pit. There might have been movement, but it was a long way down in the dark.

"Too far to worry about," said Warden. "Lead us out, Ten."

"Roger," said Ten, looking down the nearest walkway. It clung to the wall of the pit, a lashed together mess of the local wood equivalent and some sort of rope made from twisted vines. Beneath the walkway, the wall of the cavern curved inwards, disappearing from view until it reappeared as a rocky path twenty metres below.

"I'll just jump down, shall I? See if it'll hold our weight?" Ten grumbled.

"It's that or climb," said Warden with equal sarcasm.

They both turned to look up. The walls rose above the entrance to the tunnel and looked like an easy climb for about three meters. After that the wall began to curve, like the inside of a bell, to meet the ceiling a long way above. Even from here, the overhang looked formidable.

Not to mention the mining creatures were able to cling to the ceiling like wingless bats. The Marines would be horribly exposed, even if they could climb the route quickly enough. Warden looked at Ten. Ten looked back at him. They both looked over the edge.

"Down it is," muttered Ten. He slung his rifle over his shoulder, dropped to the floor and swung his legs out over the lip. He grunted as he struggled to shift his armoured bulk onto the rock face, then he lowered himself into the pit.

"Keep an eye on those slavers, Goodwin," said Milton. "I don't want any surprises." The Marines crowded to the edge of the tunnel, leaning out to watch Ten gingerly ease himself down the rock face and onto the walkway. He stood for a moment, one hand still grasping an outcrop of rock. He let go and put his full weight on the boards.

There was an ominous creak as the walkway shifted, and Warden held his breath. Ten remained still for a moment, arms outstretched like a tightrope walker. Then he gave them the thumbs up.

"Nothing to it," said Ten cheerfully, taking a step forward and giving a little bounce that jiggled the boards and sent a shower of pebbles tumbling into the pit. He took another step and pointed. "There's a second path over there, cut into the wall. But this one's as solid as–"

There was a loud crack and a moment of tense waiting. Then the walkway's tethers snapped and a long section of planking swung away, taking Marine X with it.

"Gngh!" said Ten as he felt the planks shift beneath him. Then he was falling, flailing to grab hold of anything that might arrest his fall as he plummeted towards the rocky path below.

His fingers snagged a trailing line and snapped closed around it. The line pulled taut, yanking his shoulder, and he swung like a pendulum, the collapsing walkway falling away beneath him.

"Argh!" Whatever the line was attached to slipped another metre. He swung back the other way, still a dozen metres above the rocky path below. The line gave way and he fell again, swinging his arms to try to stay upright.

He hit the narrow pathway and rolled into a fall as pain shot up his shins. The suit took some of the energy, but most of it ran through

Ten's RMSC clone as he bounced across the stones. He tumbled a couple of times, then slid to a halt.

"You okay?" asked Warden, still peering out from the tunnel.

Ten groaned and shifted, testing for damage and probing at his battered limbs.

"Never better," he managed through gritted teeth. He pushed himself around till he sat with his back against the cavern wall. "Just give me a minute."

Everything hurt. Even his eyebrows ached, and he couldn't understand how that was even possible.

"Get up, Marine," boomed Milton in her parade ground voice. "This isn't a safe place to rest."

Ten blinked his eyes open, surprised to find he had been nodding off.

"Shit," he muttered, forcing himself to his feet. Everything still hurt, but at least he was breathing and able to stagger.

"My grapnel is buggered," he said as his HUD flashed equipment failure warnings before his eyes. "I'll have to climb." The rock face was short of handholds but long on grim, slippery overhangs. A difficult climb without rope and a harness, even uninjured. He reached above his head and winced at the sharp pain in his shoulder. "But not right now," he said, rolling his arm to try to ease the pain. He shook his head. The cliff might as well have been a mile high.

There was a rumbling roar from the depths of the pit.

"I can't reach you, sir," said Ten. "I'll find another way."

"Negative, Marine. We'll come to you."

"No!" said Ten sharply. "Get out, finish the mission."

"Marine X is right, Captain," said Agent O before Warden could reply. "The slavers are on the move. I have new routes for you, sending now." The routes flashed onto their HUDs – Ten's a neat red line through a plan of the mine, Warden's a longer, winding green line. "Captain Warden, your route avoids the walkways and the main cavern, but you should go now."

"Can't leave Marine X behind," said Warden firmly. Ten could almost hear him shaking his head. He grinned, but this wasn't the time to allow loyalty to get in the way of the job.

"I can guide Ten," said Agent O, "but the miners are gathering and arming themselves." A video appeared in the Marines' HUDs showing images from a microdrone deep in the mine. It hovered above a large mess of slavers armed with clubs or long knives. They shouted and shook their weapons, goading themselves into a red frenzy. Some found primitive instruments made of barrels and a stretched material that might have been hide. They were smacking large mallets against them, beating a simple rhythm that grew in volume as others joined in from the far depths of the mine.

"Drums," said Goodwin, "drums in the deep, Captain. And more answering them from further down. They've got help coming," she said, looking up from her control screen, her face pale.

"That does not sound good," Ten muttered, pushing the video aside in his HUD and staggering to the edge of the path to peer into the depths. The tiny lamps were everywhere, but their light served merely to highlight the shadows. Ten zoomed in, trying to focus on the location of the micro-drone, but his HUD wasn't able to resolve anything useful.

A scream from below echoed through the mine. A roar followed, and the drone's video showed hordes of slavers streaming from their chambers towards the main cavern.

"They're coming again," yelled Goodwin. Ten whirled around, wincing as he shifted his weapon to his shoulder. The sound of suppressed gunfire floated down to Ten from the tunnel but he couldn't see anything from his ledge. Warden started issuing orders, then Ten was kicked from the common channel.

<We're engaged> sent Warden needlessly in a direct message. <Head for the rendezvous. Don't get distracted>

<Roger> sent Ten, wondering what it was the captain thought might distract him.

"Ten, catch," said Milton. He turned just in time to snatch a webbing pack from the air. Milton waved at him from the tunnel, then disappeared.

Ten opened the pack and found it contained a couple of fresh magazines, grenades and a combat stim pack.

"Clever girl," he muttered as fed the stim pack into his power armour's medsuite. The motion alone made him grunt with pain, but at least the shoulder would be bearable for a while.

Ten couldn't climb with it, though. The stims hid the pain but they couldn't heal the damage he'd done during the fall and if his shoulder failed, the power armour wouldn't keep his fist closed without instruction. He'd have to be more careful with his left arm.

"There are at least forty hostiles closing on your position," said Agent O when Ten didn't move. "The likelihood of survival diminishes with every second you remain in this spot."

Ten shuddered and pulled a grenade from the pack. He tossed it in the air a couple of times, pondering. Then he pulled the pin and threw it at a walkway that curved around the cavern wall, away from Agent O's escape route.

<Grenade> sent Ten to his team above, although they should have been out of danger by now.

"Right, let's get out of here. No point waiting around for these cave dwellers to catch up with me," he said and an explosion tore the air behind him. There was a flurry of violent yelling as the shattered walkway collapsed, crashing into the pit and sweeping away a section of track.

"The way ahead is clear," said Agent O as the freed timber and steel smashed its way deeper into the mine. "I have co-opted one of Goodwin's drones to scout the tunnels ahead of you."

"Okay," said Ten as the drums boomed and the slavers screamed. "Time to go."

16

With only nine Marines left in his team, Warden led the way along the route Agent O had identified through the mine. They were moving as quickly as they dared in the light of their helmet lamps, guided by the AI's path indicators. Beyond the reach of the lamps, the mines were pitch black. Nothing in the visible light spectrum could be seen.

Down here, more than sixty metres below the surface, it was warm and the HUDs struggled to pluck useful details from the gloom. They were forced to rely on their head torches and the Mark I eyeball.

<Chasm ahead> sent Agent O, and the Marines skidded to an abrupt halt.

<Ahead? Just ahead, or thirty metres away and off to one side?> replied Warden, unwilling to take further risks in the dark. Behind them, the calls of the guards rang out through the tunnels.

<Ten metres ahead. There is a bridge, but it is narrow and of uncertain quality>

Warden grunted and walked carefully forwards. He wasn't about to take chances on 'uncertain quality'. The tunnel widened into a sizeable chamber. His headlamps found a deep gash in the floor –

maybe five metres wide – that crossed the chamber and disappeared into the walls on either side. A narrow wooden walkway had been laid across and anchored at each end by ropes tied to iron pins driven deep into the rock.

"Found the chasm," said Warden, peering into the depths. <How deep, do you think?>

<Impossible to say, Captain> sent Agent O. <I could send the drones down to investigate, but I do not feel it to be a good use of our resources>

Warden could only agree. He nudged a few pebbles over the lip with his foot and listened for them hitting the bottom, but no sound reached him.

"It's pretty deep," he said, then gunfire rang out from the rear-guard, and he whirled around. "Drummond, what's going on?"

"Two more down. They're still coming," said Drummond, jogging out of the gloom to re-join the group. "Why have we stopped? They're right behind us!"

"Across the bridge," ordered Warden, waving at Milton. "Come on, get a move on."

Milton shouldered her weapon and walked easily across the boards, stepping lightly onto the far side then moving to cover the rest of the team.

"Just like basic training," she said. "Now get a move on before the enemy arrives."

The Marines hurried over, one after the other, the boards flexing and groaning with each footstep.

"Captain? You opening a hotel over there or coming home with us?" asked Milton.

He was the only one left to cross. The noises grew louder as the guard-clones approached. Warden could picture them moving through the tunnels, relying on touch and smell to guide them as they sought their prey.

He shook his head and let the sling take the weight of his rifle. Arms outstretched, he stepped onto the narrow board and began to cross.

"Always the worst part," he said through gritted teeth as he forced himself across the bouncing planks.

It was like an assault course. Except this one was made by someone who'd not mastered the basics of carpentry or health and safety.

The planks seem thick enough though, shouldn't be a problem, he thought.

A board creaked and split.

Warden looked up to see Milton's horrified expression. He flung himself forward just as the bridge gave way beneath him.

He threw out his hand, snagged a dangling rope and slammed against the wall of the abyss. The remnants of the bridge disappeared into the gloom as his helmet lamps swept over the walls of the chasm.

Behind him, the sounds of pursuit grew closer.

"Take my hand," said Milton, crouched above him with her hand outstretched, just out of reach.

"Fly, you fools!" said Warden, thrashing around with his free hand, his grip beginning to fail.

"Fuck that," said Milton.

Suddenly Drummond was there, sliding forwards on his belly to grab Warden's arm. Goodwin appeared on the other side to steady Milton, and together the three of them hauled their captain over the lip and into the tunnel.

"That wizard has a lot to fucking answer for," said Milton.

"Never get another chance to use that line," breathed Warden as he lay panting on the ground.

"Your mother would be proud," snapped Milton, distinctly unamused. Goodwin flashed a big grin and gave him a thumbs up over Milton's shoulder. Her face was the picture of innocence when the Colour Sergeant rounded on her, suspicions roused by Warden's smirk.

"Back to your position, Goodwin," she barked.

The stones beyond the darkness scraped, and a guard clone crept into view. It paused in the light of their lamps and hissed as other shapes crowded in behind it, brandishing clubs and knives.

"They caught up," said Goodwin. "We should go."

They scrambled to their feet and shuffled back, weapons raised.

"Into the tunnel, keep moving," said Warden. Goodwin and Drummond turned and jogged away, their headlamps bobbing as they disappeared. "You too, Milton," snapped Warden when the Colour Sergeant didn't move. "Go! It's not like they're following any further."

Milton nodded and turned to leave.

One of the guards screamed. It took two long steps and sprang.

Warden's mouth fell open in astonishment as the clone flew across the chasm and landed lightly in front of him. It barrelled into him, knocking him to the floor as it swung a long knife.

"Shit!" said Warden as the impact knocked him back and he lost his footing.

Behind him, Milton's rifle chattered and the guard clone juddered to a halt, a neat cluster of holes in its chest. She fired again and its head snapped back. The body collapsed in a spray of blood.

"Get up!" shouted Milton.

More screams rang out from the other side of the chasm. Milton fired at the figures crouching in the darkness, sweeping her headlamps around to find targets.

Warden scrabbled away from the ledge, firing blindly. Milton dragged him back with one hand, firing her rifle with the other.

A second guard made the leap, then a third. Warden fired again, a long burst that would have had his weapons instructor screaming bloody murder.

A whump announced Milton's use of the launcher slung beneath her rifle, and Warden just had time to throw himself backwards before the grenade detonated against the far wall of the chamber. The blast blew Milton over and she rolled across the ground. The noise was horrendous and for a moment the chamber was filled with fragments of blasted rock, shattered clone and dust.

"Milton!" Warden called. "You okay?"

He found her on her back near the tunnel, giggling inside her helmet.

"Fire in the hole," she whispered. "That's payback for the dumper truck on New Bristol."

"Later," snapped Warden, hauling the Colour Sergeant to her feet. He scanned the chamber, but it looked like the guard clones were dead, incapacitated or fleeing. "And we'd better be going too. Shift, Colours, before the bloody ceiling comes down."

There was a chittering from the tunnel they fled from – a noise Warden associated with the guard clones – and figures began to emerge from the cloud of dust.

That was enough for Warden. Pushing Milton ahead of him, he hurried into the tunnel after the rest of the team.

"Is it just me, or are the walls getting closer?" asked Milton.

"The ceiling's getting lower as well," said Warden as they jogged along, the lights from their headlamps bouncing over the path.

<Any more chasms?> sent Warden.

<Negative, Captain> replied Agent O.

<Good. That was a close call. How far?>

<Only four hundred metres from the next junction, which you will reach in about twenty seconds>

<Great>

Except when Warden and Milton reached the next junction, they found it really wasn't great at all. Not by a long shot. The tunnel narrowed to less than a metre and the floor had risen, forcing them to crouch low to make it through the last section. The final set of bends were tight, then they emerged onto a narrow ledge running along the side of another huge cavern. The rest of the team waited for them, strung out along the shallow shelf.

As Milton crawled out, she came face to face with the entertaining end of a rifle.

"What the hell is this?" said Milton.

"Sorry, Colours," said Goodwin, standing back and raising her weapon. "Wasn't sure what would be following us."

Warden squeezed out of the tunnel, twisting awkwardly.

"They're right behind us," he said, staggering to his feet and his helmet lamps swept around and into the void beyond the ledge. "Bloody hell. What is this place?"

"Looks like they're prepping it for some sort of processing plant," said Drummond.

"Do we care?" asked Milton.

"No," said Warden firmly. "Just tell me where we're going."

"That way, sir," said Drummond, "and then up, somehow."

"It's a bit narrow, sir," said Goodwin. To their right, a short gravel-strewn slope quickly became a sheer cliff of reinforced foamcrete. From the foot of the cliff, a vast foamcrete platform had been laid across the floor of the cavern and various pieces of machinery were in the process of being installed, although all was quiet at the moment.

"What are they building?" asked Drummond.

"Doesn't matter," said Warden from the end of the line. "Just get moving."

There was a rumbling crack, deep in the rock, and Warden turned in time to see a cloud of dust blow out of the low tunnel they crept through.

"Won't be going back that way," he muttered.

<How are we looking?> sent Warden.

<You are still on the fastest route> sent Agent O. <Bear right, then take the chimney on the left>

Milton, who was also reading the exchange, caught Warden's eye. "She's been taking lessons in humour from Ten. There's no way of knowing what she'll come up with next." Warden grunted and shook his head.

Up ahead, Marine Bailey signalled a halt.

"The guide says we should go right, sir, but there's no path after about ten metres."

"Take it anyway," said Warden, "then look out for a chimney on the left."

"Roger," said Bailey, taking the right fork. "Found the chimney," she said a few seconds later. "It looks like a natural fissure in the rock, about a metre square. Goes up a long way." She sounded doubtful.

"The only way is up," said Milton. "It's that or wait down here for the Deathless to find us," she added when Goodwin frowned at her.

<Is this really the only option?> sent Warden.

<No, but the alternative takes you through an area likely to be held by the Deathless or the mine guards>

<Likely to be held? You don't know?>

<The initial investigatory flights were uneventful> sent Agent O, <but subsequent visits to the area resulted in the loss of two micro-drones, almost certainly to hostile action>

There was an excited chittering noise from the platform below. Switching his HUD to infrared, Warden saw shapes running in the dark, making their way along the platform at top speed.

"We're out of time," he said, conscious that the imminent arrival of the Deathless orbital station was limiting his options. "Lamps off, switch to night vision and get moving."

Bailey nodded her acknowledgement and adjusted her rifle so it hung across her chest. She hoisted herself into the chimney and began walking her way up the rock face.

"Get moving," snapped Milton as the Marines switched off their lamps. One by one, they climbed into the chimney and followed Bailey until only Milton and Warden were left.

"This is going to end badly if there's someone at the top of this bloody chimney," Milton said to Warden on a private channel.

"I'm open to ideas," replied Warden as he watched the guard clones closing in.

"We could shoot a couple of them," Milton suggested. "Might cool their ardour a little."

Warden knelt, considering the idea. "Moving targets at a hundred metres?"

"Worth a try." She squeezed her trigger and the suppressed rifle coughed, paused, then coughed again. Warden tried his luck, laying down a handful of rounds.

The effects were inconclusive.

"Might have winged one," said Milton, "but they're getting awfully close."

"And I bet they climb faster than we do. You'd better get started on that chimney."

Milton gave him a flat look that, even from inside the helmet, told him what she thought of that suggestion.

"We can't both get caught down here. You need to get the team out. I'll form the rear-guard." When she still hesitated, Warden snapped, "Go! That's an order, Colour Sergeant."

"Fine!" she snapped back, "but take these." She passed him a pair of grenades. "And don't get stuck down here." She strapped her rifle across her chest and heaved herself into the chimney, disappearing into the gloom more quickly than Warden would have thought possible.

For a moment, he was completely alone on the ledge. It was quiet and dark. Then a long-limbed figure pulled itself over the lip of the wall and advanced slowly towards him. A second figure appeared, then a third.

Warden slapped home a fresh magazine, losing count on the number of clones coming over the ledge. They were picking up speed, their awful wails grating on his ears. He let out a long breath, and opened fire on the stream of guard clones clambering up the slope, running straight for him.

~

"Fuck me, they're tough," Warden muttered to himself as another guard clone staggered towards him, four large holes already punched in its chest. It was struggling to hold its club, but it still came on.

Warden paused to steady himself and put a round through the beast's forehead, killing it instantly.

He switched magazines, scanning the ledge, waiting for new targets to appear. The clones weren't all that bright, but even they had eventually realised they couldn't reach him by simply running along the path, screaming. Now, it looked like they were trying something new.

But what? he wondered. He straightened from his firing position and backed carefully towards the chimney. He stole a glance upwards, but if Milton was still climbing, she was out of sight, lost in a glare of infrared from the chamber above.

When he looked back to the path, a guard clone was right on top of him. It screamed and slashed him with a knife, the blade skittering across his armour leaving a bright scar in the suit's camouflage. He stumbled back, leaning out of the way of another wild swing then reared forward, slamming the body of his rifle into the clone's face. Its head whipped back but the frenzied attack barely slowed. Warden blocked another ferocious cut, then kicked at the beast's knee, hoping to force it back.

It staggered, off-balance as its leg crumpled, and Warden smashed his rifle into the clone's face. It shrieked, blood pouring from its crushed nose. Warden took the chance to step back, bring up his weapon and shoot the beast in the chest. The rifle chattered and smoke rose from the barrel as Warden pumped multiple rounds into the clone.

It fell back, chest a bloody ruin.

"Too bloody close," muttered Warden as he snatched a replacement magazine from his webbing and rammed it into his rifle. He looked past the warm corpses, scanning the path, the slopes and the walls, but nothing moved.

Then, way down the path, past the tunnel the Marines had fled, an indistinct shape appeared. The HUD's AI struggled to resolve the information gathered by the infrared sensors as the shape grew and stretched and came steadily closer.

Warden hefted his rifle and aimed, wondering how long he should leave it before firing. More shapes crawled down the wall only fifteen metres away. He shifted his aim, torn by a multitude of targets as more figures ghosted their way along the slope, thick talons snatching at the rock.

"Well, fuck," muttered Warden, tightening his grip on his rifle. "This looks like the shitty end of the stick."

The barrel of his rifle wavered from side to side as he struggled to choose a target.

Something smacked against his shoulder and it was all he could do to avoid jumping straight out of his suit.

"Fuck," he said, taking half a step backwards and trying to work out what had hit him.

A cable hung from the chimney with a loop tied thoughtfully on the end of the line.

"Would you like a lift, sir?" said Milton on the team's public channel. "We found this cable and thought maybe you could use a hand."

Warden stared at it for a moment, then he shifted his rifle to hold it one-handed, slipped his foot into the loop and gripped the cable with his left hand.

The guards rushed forward.

"Go," he said, spraying rounds at the advancing clones as he began to rise. They disappeared from sight the moment he was swallowed by the chimney. He expected to see them climbing after him, but there was no sign of the clones.

"Here you go, sir," said Drummond, hauling him over the lip of the chimney into a room that looked like a half-built garage. Warden lay on the ground for a few seconds. He flicked open his helmet faceplate and stared at the ceiling, enjoying the sense of relief that followed his near-death experience.

"We think they plan to block enlarge this chimney," said Milton, nodding at the pile of building materials in the corner of the room, "and use it for moving things between the levels, but they haven't finished the work yet. We've made a bit of a mess."

The floor was strewn with opened boxes and smashed crates in the Marines hasty search for something they could use to extract Warden from the ledge below. An empty cable drum and a heavy winch lay discarded against a wall alongside the shipping cartons.

"Thanks," said Warden as he heaved himself to his feet. "The natives were getting a bit friendly, and not in a 'have a nice cup of tea' way. Where next?"

"Oh, now it's just a simple stroll through the cellars to the main base, meet up with Lieutenant Hayes and the rest of the crew, then a short yomp out to the rendezvous point," said Milton with an air of breezy confidence that gave Warden pause.

"It's not a simple stroll at all, is it?" he said and checked his weapon and remaining magazines.

"No," said Milton, "it really isn't. Let me show you the nature of the problem."

Warden and his team found themselves trapped in another huge chamber lined with foamcrete and girded by steel walkways anchored to the walls. At a hundred metres long, forty metres wide and at least thirty high, it was the largest of the man-made chambers they had seen so far.

"Stand here, look that way," said Milton, directing Warden's attention from the half-finished store room just off the main chamber they stood in. Warden leaned forward to look into the chamber but Milton caught his arm and pulled him back with a shake of her head. "Don't, snipers."

Warden straightened and inspected the bits of the chamber he could see without exposing himself to enemy fire. At the far end, a row of grills covered huge ventilation outlets behind which big fans could be glimpsed turning slowly in the gloom. Beneath them hung a narrow steel walkway running around the chamber about twenty-five metres above the floor. In Warden's HUD, Agent O's path indicator sat neatly on the platform marking their way out.

"Drones?"

"Negative," said Milton. "They scanned the room then moved on. A couple are down in the depths, mapping the lower levels for some reason. Programming glitch, Goodwin says. At least one was destroyed by enemy action, maybe more. Either way, we're on our own."

"And there's no other way out?"

"Agent O says not, and she's been right about everything else."

"How many snipers? And are they any good?"

"Difficult to tell. They clipped Bailey when she poked her head out, but the round only chipped her armour. She has a lovely ding in her pauldron."

"No railguns, then," observed Warden. A railgun round would have gone straight through Bailey's shoulder and taken her arm off, so the absence of railgun-equipped snipers was a bit of good news.

"A few minutes ago? No railguns," agreed Milton. "But who knows what they've brought up now."

That was less welcome news, and Warden frowned. They were fighting on the enemy's home territory. Their supply line was mere metres long, so it was hardly unexpected they would have access to whatever weaponry they wanted.

"Right. Charging around the walkway is obviously out," mused Warden. "They'd have us before we made it halfway."

"And even if they didn't, we'd still have to storm their positions. They've got a wider platform over there with a good field of fire, so it would be a ten-metre sprint into enemy fire after you made it around the corner."

Warden made a face. Heroism was one thing, but certain death at the hands of the enemy wasn't what he'd had in mind for today's operation.

"And no, we can't do a death dive into the chamber, cover the open ground and assault their position after scaling the far wall," said Milton as she watched Warden's facial expressions. "Apart from the very high risk of being shot to death, we don't have the gear and the drop is too high for the armour to take. Broken legs all around, followed by gunshot wounds, at best."

"What's through there?" Warden pointed at a door on the other side of the open space.

"The drones didn't scan it, obviously, but Agent O says it's a storeroom."

"Anything we can use to," Warden waved his hands vaguely, "I don't know, make something to get us out of this?"

Milton gave him a flat stare then shook her head sadly. "Shouldn't think so, sir. Do you want to take a look?"

Warden contemplated it, considering the distance. *Probably locked*, he thought, *and five metres away without cover*. He glanced at his rifle, wondering if it would be possible to shoot the lock out.

"I wasn't being serious, sir," said Milton eventually. He glanced at her and she shook her head again. "No."

"You're probably right," he said with a sigh. "Right, so what's next?" he said brightly.

"Oh, we made it this far on our own, sir. Then we rescued an officer so he could get us out of this mess. I can check, but I don't think there are any more officers to rescue."

"Thank you, Colours," said Warden with as much dignity as he could muster. "Agent O, you still there?"

"Indeed, Captain. How can I be of assistance?"

"Can you find us another way out?"

"I'm afraid not. Colour Sergeant Milton asked the same question, and I'm afraid no new options have arisen in the last few minutes."

"And this orbital station is still incoming?" said Warden.

"Parts of it will likely impact your general vicinity in the next fifteen to twenty minutes. Beyond that, it is difficult to say."

"Well, bugger. I don't suppose Lieutenant Hayes is in a position to assist?"

"Lieutenant Hayes and the rest of the company are in another section of the base and considerably occupied." Said Agent O. "There are routes to your location, but none of them are undefended. The chances of a team successfully reaching this position undetected or in a state fit to act are remote."

For a few seconds, nobody said anything. Warden could feel the disappointed eyes of the team on his back, the end of the chamber beyond teasing their chances of escape. Nobody liked to fail a mission, and they'd come too far to give in with so little accomplished.

"I guess we'll have to try surrendering," said Warden reluctantly. "Wave the flag, apologise for the inconvenience, and hope they take a sophisticated approach to prisoner exchanges."

"Are you serious, sir?" asked Milton. "We were hoping you'd come up with something to get us out of here."

"Sorry, Colours, that's the best I can do. Find me a flag, and I'll do the rest. Maybe we can persuade them to get us out of here before we're squashed flat by the station."

She stared at him for ten long seconds before nodding and issuing orders to the rest of the squad. They weren't happy, but Warden couldn't see a way to get across the chamber that didn't leave half of them or more dead or seriously injured, and that was no use to anyone.

"If you wait just a few moments," said Agent O, "I will arrange a distraction."

"What sort of distraction?" asked Warden, frowning. He wasn't sure he liked the sound of this.

"With luck, the sort that avoids you getting shot," said Agent O. "Quiet please, working."

17

Cohen, White and Mantle sat in *Dreadnought*'s command suite working on the ship's redevelopment plan. With Agent O's revolutionary hyperspace engine design proven in combat, Cohen was a lot more interested in re-working other parts of the ship and accelerating the refit.

"My work with Frida Skar is complete for the time being," Agent O had said, "and so I seek other tasks to occupy myself. The refit of *Dreadnought* seems to be a project of sufficient scale and complexity – especially as it must be conducted while the ship is operating and without reducing her capabilities – to warrant my attention."

The ship's chief engineer, Sub-Lieutenant Mantle, had been deeply sceptical of the whole idea. Her overprotective nature when it came to her ships was legendary. Coupled with a short temper, it gave her a prickly demeanour that could annoy even the most laid-back people.

But the obvious effectiveness of the new hyperspace engine and the aplomb with which it had been installed went a long way to winning her over. Agent O followed up on her success by submitting several small but worthwhile and easily implemented projects for Mantle to consider. Cohen didn't have the full list of changes, but he knew Agent O deliberately chose things that were an annoyance or an impediment to the engineering team.

Some of the older fabricators needed to be restarted every few hours to keep them working. Fixing that little problem settled many of the engineers' concerns, and Cohen had a feeling the AI was becoming more politically skilful with every passing day.

"The navigation system is an obvious next step," said Agent O, filling the screens in the command suite with an array of system and project plans. "The current system is old, slow and limited. It can't make full use of the fast-flit features of the new hyperspace engine – I estimate *Dreadnought* to be operating at around thirty-four per cent efficiency – and the crew are having to work around the system's shortcomings to programme the flight and attack sequences. Replacing it would allow us to address all these issues."

"Always the same questions, Agent O," said Cohen, dredging up memories of project management lectures from his days at university. "What resources do you need, how long will it take, and can it be done without disturbing the operation of the ship?"

"The reserve fabricators in the main engineering suite are completely capable of constructing the necessary parts, Captain, and the mix of elements they require is no different to any other computing device."

A manufacturing programme with a list of machine processing times and mineral requirements flashed onto one of the displays.

"Total fabrication time will be of the order of three hours. Installation will take another three hours but will require assistance from the crew because it involves adding system components to the bridge. Initial testing will take several weeks – a period of parallel running with the existing systems will be required – and you will then be able to schedule a switch from old to new at your convenience."

They talked it around for a few minutes, but Agent O's preparation and documentation were exemplary.

"Begin the work," said Cohen, "but delay installation until the current operation is complete. I don't want people getting distracted."

"Very well, Captain. Fabrication is underway."

"Is there anything we can do about the coffee machine?" asked White with a frown at another mug of abhorrent dark liquid. "This stuff is like putrid hyena vomit."

Cohen closed his eyes and shook his head to try to clear the image.

"I don't want to know the history of that metaphor," muttered Mantle, a disturbed look on her face.

White opened his mouth to say more but the proximity alarm interrupted him.

"Oh, thank the stars," said Cohen, rushing to the bridge.

"What's going on, Mr MacCaibe?" asked Cohen as he slid into his chair.

"A new Deathless vessel has entered the system, sir. A capital ship, by the size of her. Designated *Target Six*, she's sitting half a million kilometres out and hardly moving."

"Not exactly close, then," muttered White with half an eye on the proximity alarm sensitivity settings.

"But close enough to be a worry," said Cohen. "Why isn't she manoeuvring to attack?"

"Professional courtesy?" suggested White. "Maybe she's just here to look harshly at us."

"Incoming signal, sir," said Midshipman Woods. "Looks like an audio-visual communication request from *Target Six*."

Cohen raised his eyebrows, wondering why enemy commanders now felt compelled to contact him. "Put it on the display, Mr Woods, and let's reciprocate with audio and limited video, focussed on me."

"Aye, sir, here it comes."

The face of a Deathless officer clone – a Rupert, the Marines named them – sitting in what looked like a comms pod of some sort appeared on the screen. Little could be seen beyond the figure but bland cream walls that gave away nothing of the state of the ship.

The officer spoke, and *Dreadnought's* communication system showed the translated text a few seconds later.

"This is Koschite naval vessel *Vasilisa*. Your presence in this system, and your assaults on our facilities and starships, constitute acts of war. Withdraw immediately or face the consequences of your aggression."

"This is *Dreadnought* of the Royal Navy," said Cohen. "Our business here is not yet complete, and the destruction of your space station was not caused by our actions."

The Deathless figure leaned forward, its eyes narrowing.

"You are Cohen," it said. "You are known to us, as is your antique craft. My name is Jordahl. You will find me a more challenging opponent, Captain, if you choose to remain here." The image disappeared.

"Channel closed, sir," said Woods.

Cohen frowned at the display, the bridge quiet around him. He wasn't sure if being known to a Deathless starship commander counted as fame, but it probably wasn't a good sign.

"What are they up to, Mr Woods?" he asked.

"It's a bit difficult to tell, sir," said Woods. "The images aren't great, but I'd say they're deploying autonomous weapons systems."

"I concur, sir," said MacCaibe. "Platforms and mines. Oh, and at least half a dozen attack craft like the ones we saw at Akbar."

"Of course she carries attack craft," muttered White. "Couldn't expect her to do her own dirty work."

Cohen flicked at his data slate to open a channel to Captain Warden.

"Thought you'd like to know we're about to engage a Deathless capital ship by the name of *Vasilisa*," said Cohen.

"What the hell am I supposed to do with that information, sir?" snapped Warden, clearly distracted and under pressure.

"Just get to the dropships on time, Captain. The situation up here is likely to deteriorate," said Cohen, ignoring the Marine's discourtesy.

"Acknowledged. Is there anything else? Only we're busy getting shot at."

"Nothing more. *Dreadnought* out." He cut the channel and reviewed the tactical display. "Take us to action stations, Lieutenant, and let's see what our new friends are capable of."

"Action stations, sir," acknowledged White as he triggered the command from his data slate.

"Warm everything up, Mr MacCaibe," said Cohen. "And make sure we've found all the nasty little presents that *Vasilisa* has brought for us."

"Working on it, sir, but at this range, the sensors aren't capturing much more than *Vasilisa* and the attack craft. We *should* be able to target them, but it's a bit dicey."

"Do what you can, then," said Cohen.

"They've seen fast-flit attacks," said White. "Hell, they *developed* the strategy. This is their response."

"Seed the area with small autonomous weapons platforms? I agree. They've done their homework and we can expect them to have solid defences against these types of attack. This is an arms race, and we need to move quickly or risk being left behind."

"Again," muttered White. "I'll ping a message to the Admiralty and ask for their input. They're bound to have designs for weapons platforms sitting around somewhere that we can adapt to our needs."

"Good, do that," agreed Cohen. "And add new sensor suites, targeting computer upgrades, and some sort of high-speed auto-defence system capable of neutralising weapons delivered by fast-flit attack craft to the list of systems that Mantle and Agent O are considering for their rolling refit programme."

"Roger, will do."

"Weapons are online, sir, but the signals are too weak for targeting," said MacCaibe. "Apart from *Vasilisa*, that is. She's a beast."

"Is the port weapons cluster operable yet?" asked White.

"Negative, sir. Engineering diagnosed some sort of power supply problem but they need more time to investigate."

"Then we'll take *Vasilisa* down our starboard flank," said Cohen. "Ms Martin, set a course to give us a broadside at two thousand metres."

"Sir?" said Martin uncertainly. "At this range, the margin of error could put us on either side of the target. Or right in front of her."

"Then jump us close, Ms Martin. Close the gap to a hundred

thousand kilometres and let's see how Captain Jordahl reacts to a little pressure."

"Aye, sir, laying in the course now."

"*Vasilisa* is a lot bigger than Admiral Tomsk's flagship," murmured White. "Are you sure this is a good idea?"

"What did Warden say? 'Improvise, adapt, overwhelm', or something. Let's see if we can put that into action," said Cohen, eyes hungry and gleaming.

Dropship *Wickham* shot through the night sky of Micarro towards the daylight terminator. *Alton* was close behind, both ships flying low and fast over the canopy to minimise the risk of interception by Deathless craft or ground defences.

"I'm sorry, *Dreadnought*," said Lieutenant Jordan, *Wickham*'s pilot, "did you say a space station was about to crash into the planet? Please confirm."

"Affirmative. Re-entry begins in thirty-eight minutes. Probable impact zone includes the target facility and the rendezvous point. Liaise with Captain Warden to clarify rendezvous point and time."

Jordan shared a look with Figgs, his co-pilot.

"Thanks, *Dreadnought*. Any other good news?"

"That's everything we have at the moment. We will update you if the situation changes. *Dreadnought* out."

"That could be a little inconvenient," said Jordan, his usual good humour wiped away by the news of impending doom.

He flicked at his console, opening a channel to Captain Warden.

"We're a little busy down here!" yelled Warden over shouting and shooting in the background. "Can it wait?"

"Did you hear about the space station and its imminent arrival at your location?"

"How soon till you get here?" said Warden, ignoring the question.

Jordan looked at Figgs, who shrugged. "About forty minutes?"

Jordan relayed this to Warden and waited while the Marine

captain issued orders and – from the sounds of his breathing – ran a hundred-metre race.

"Please don't allow us to interrupt your exercise routine," said Jordan impatiently. "It's not like we have anything better to do."

"Are you fucking kidding me?" shouted Warden.

"I do apologise," said Jordan, somewhat taken aback, "but it's been none too clever up here while you've been running around on your little jaunt, what with the harsh weather and the exploding starships."

"We'll be outside the base's main door in no more than thirty minutes. Be there or explain to Marine X why the mission got bolloxed up."

The channel went dead.

"Hello? Captain? Captain Warden?" Jordan toggled the call button but there was no response. "That was a little rude," he said to himself.

"Marines," said Figgs sagely. "Never the most reasonable of passengers."

18

Marine X left several bodies behind him, but the way forward wasn't getting any easier and Agent O kept giving him updates that were not promising. And he could feel something grinding and scraping in his injured shoulder.

"There are at least eighteen enemy combatants ahead of you," warned Agent O.

Ten grunted, focussing on the route. O plotted a way through the maze of tunnels to the new rendezvous point, but it wasn't a straight line. In fifty metres, he'd have to veer left, but before he could do that, he needed to make it past the two monsters ahead of him.

He switched to his suppressed pistol and vibro-blade in the hope silent work might let him slip through unnoticed. There were a lot more Deathless monsters out there, and he only needed to evade them by a few minutes to make the rendezvous. If he brought the noise, it would bring down more opposition on his head.

The pistol in his right hand bucked as he ran toward the two clones blocking his path. The ground was uneven and his aim a bit off, but all three rounds hit the thing in its face and neck.

By the time he reached the second one, the first was crumpling noiselessly to the floor, ichor gushing from its wounds.

Ichor? thought Ten. *It's just blood in the dark and it is absolutely not phosphorescing.* Maybe the HUD's image enhancement was playing tricks on his combat-stim-mangled brain.

The other Deathless clone grabbed a nearby wire basket of ore faster than Ten would have thought possible, lifting the heavy rock in preparation to launch it like a steroid-enhanced shot-putter. Right at his face.

Ten didn't fancy death by rock. Not after last time. He went low, diving between the thing's legs and flipping onto his back as the basket of ore flew across the tunnel. His left hand snaked up toward the thing's groin, blade flashing.

Despite their unusual features, they weren't actually an alien species, as the Marines first thought when they encountered the Deathless on New Bristol. That was positively ludicrous. For all their monstrous appearance, the beasts were just highly specialised clones based on basic human stock.

Humanity had yet to encounter a single sapient alien species. The Deathless had, disappointingly, turned out to be all too human. Which probably explained why they were such spectacular arseholes.

And this gave Ten an advantage.

His decades of experience and training applied almost as well to killing Deathless as to any other human opponent. Even in the clones greatly altered form.

He flicked the knife at the inside of the monster's thigh, aiming for the femoral artery up high near the hip where the armoured skin was thin to ease limb articulation. The vibro-knife hummed, its edge powered to sub-molecular sharpness. It barely slowed as it slid through skin and muscle but still his shoulder protested.

The creature gave an inhumane deep rumble of pain.

"Shit," muttered Ten, pushing off the floor and hoped the low-frequency sound wasn't a cunning means for summoning help – the last thing he needed was more enemies.

Ichor – no, blood, definitely blood – was gushing from the wound. It would bleed out quickly, but Ten didn't have time to stop.

He turned back the way he'd been going and kept running, leaving the hideous clone to die alone.

"Take the left tunnel," Agent O said as Ten approached a junction that split in three directions. With the mapping data the AI used from the drones the left-hand tunnel should bring him up and around to a higher level and allow him to double back towards the rendezvous with the rest of the team.

Ten paused, sniffing the air, then turned right. The HUD's map had gaps suggesting a large cavern at the end, and Ten's instinct told him to check it out.

"Marine X, you are going the wrong way. I assure you this is not the most efficient route to meet up with your colleagues," Agent O protested.

Ten trusted the accuracy of the map's layout. He knew there wasn't a high likelihood of a more direct route that the drones hadn't picked up. But he had years of experience Agent O didn't have access to. He also possessed a broader commitment to the team than just worrying about his own safety. It didn't seem likely he could reach the others in time to be useful if he followed Agent O's route, but perhaps he could find some other way to help with the mission.

"I believe you, O. I just don't think the Deathless will let me get there as quickly as I'd need to."

"What then is the point in going this way? It won't get you there any more quickly."

"No, but I might draw them away from the others."

"You intend to sacrifice yourself?"

Ten chuckled, taking cover behind an ore-carrying sled as the tunnel opened out into the cave. "No, I intend to slot a lot of Deathless, O."

"I sense that I won't be able to talk you out of this new course of action."

"You're learning."

"Yes, of course," said Agent O indignantly. "That's what I do."

"Well, I don't see any of those miners or their controllers out there, do you?"

"Naturally not. I'm reliant on your cameras; if you don't see them, I can't possibly."

"Fair point. Now, be quiet while I recce this place."

He advanced out of his cover into the unnatural cavern. He didn't need to be a geologist to recognise the place was entirely artificial. The floors, ceiling and walls were smooth, but more importantly the room was rectangular. If it had ever been part of a natural cave system, that time was long past.

Now it was a simple warehouse, dimly lit by lamps in the ceiling. There was nothing as elaborate as pallet racking stored there, only large shipping cubes of ore stacked in neat lines.

It didn't look like the warehouse did more than store material in transit. There was a large elevator on one wall, but it was still.

"I guess there's a processing plant somewhere," said Ten. "Any idea where?"

"I have limited data, I'm afraid. I cannot be sure, but I surmise the elevator goes up several levels from here to a processing plant. It does not offer a more rapid exit from this area that would allow you to reunite with the rest of the attack force. I can detect nothing in this area that would logically lead to a better route. I urge you to reconsider before you fall even further behind schedule," Agent O replied. "There are also no obvious opportunities for you to create your usual brand of havoc to disrupt and distract the Deathless."

"Havoc? I like that," said Ten, pausing in the centre of the vast space. "Pity there's nothing here I can use to cause havoc, eh?" He grinned ferociously inside his helmet, an unexpected treasure in sight.

"Hmm. I stand corrected. I have reassessed the situation and I now think you have a better than ninety-two per cent chance of causing sufficient havoc, mayhem, woe, or reduction of morale that the odds of mission success might be significantly affected."

"I'm wounded."

"How so?"

"You seriously think I have an eight per cent chance of failing?" said Ten, eyes gleaming as he moved to take ownership of his prize.

"How much longer?" Ten's HUD showed seventy-five seconds elapsed since he clambered into the driving seat, and he was starting to doubt the wisdom of this course of action.

"Be patient. This isn't as easy as you seem to think."

"It's hardly a starship, how hard can it be for you to translate the controls?"

"That was easy," said Agent O. "I'm now re-writing the operating system."

"What on earth for? I need to get a shift on."

"I'm almost done, but to answer your question, I'm altering system parameters and removing safety routines that were designed to keep the unit functioning for years. I'm also adjusting sensitivity to compensate for your injured arm, although if it locks up entirely the corresponding limb on the exoskeleton will not function. Since I imagine you have no intention of it lasting longer than thirty minutes, we will trade reliability and longevity for performance."

"Fine. And can we begin moving before you're finished? I feel a bit exposed out here."

The mining exoskeleton was huge, with long arms ending in claw-like hands. Even in his power armour, Ten had plenty of room in the cockpit. The machine must have been designed for use by the largest of the Deathless mining clones.

"Anything you can do to get more range out of this laser cutter?" The enormous device sat on the floor waiting to be lifted in one of the exoskeleton's hands.

"Wrench off the front fifteen centimetres of shielding. It focuses the beam to less than a metre to protect the miners by forcing them to get close to the rock face."

"Roger that." Ten levered himself down from the cockpit, inspected the front of the device, and discovered a release mechanism for the housing shielding the emitter. He pulled the trigger and the beam carved a chunk from one of the metal crates on the other side of the cavern in a satisfying shower of sparks.

"That'll do the job." Ten climbed back into the driver's seat and strapped himself in.

"The changes to the operating system are complete," said Agent O. "Rebooting the exoskeleton now."

Ten felt trapped when the unit powered down, going completely still. It remained upright but entirely motionless until the operating system finished rebooting and the automatic stabilisation kicked in again.

"Check the route for me, would you? Can I get back to where we started?"

While O ran simulations, Ten checked his gear. He'd found some cunning magnetic clamps designed to attach tools and equipment to surfaces. The exoskeleton was a triumph of spartan functional design, optimised for moving containers, hefting mining lasers and shovelling ore. It stood more than four metres tall, and every sensitive component or cable was covered in thick plates of protective steel.

That left plenty of flat sections for him to hang equipment, weapons and a few other odds and sods he'd found in the cavern that seemed useful. A couple of magnetic clamps were all it took to secure his improvised laser weapon to the chassis of the exoskeleton.

"I've plotted the fastest route this conveyance can use. You need to go up two levels – there is a ramp in the far corner – and along a wide tunnel. You can then drop into the cavern where you split with Captain Warden," Agent O confirmed. "There is considerable resistance en-route."

Ten swung himself around, getting a feel for the way the exoskeleton worked. The controls were simple to operate, and with O's instructions he quickly had the machine under control

"It's hammer time," said Ten, hefting a pickaxe in one hand of the giant exoskeleton and a sledgehammer in the other. "I'm going to pick on these Deathless bastards, and not feel in the slightest bit guilty."

Agent O groaned, "Please, stop with the puns."

"Stop undermining me, you know you dig them really."

Agent O groaned again and Ten grinned as he made his way up the ramp.

❦

The ramp emerged into a wide tunnel, just as Agent O said, but this one was much bigger than any they had seen before. The walls were uneven, meandering back and forth as if following a rich seam of ore. The ceiling was so high Ten couldn't reach it even with the unnaturally long arms of the exoskeleton.

He stepped forward into the dimly lit passage and peered down its length, looking for obstructions. He felt a peculiar tingle along the back of his neck and dropped the machine into a crouch. Decades of experience told him something was out there, hidden by the undulating walls, waiting for him in the darkness.

The low light mode of his HUD kicked in and the near darkness receded. The pools of shadow and the vaguely outlined darkness resolved into high contrast areas, casting the entire area in false light. It revealed a railway line down one side of the tunnel and a few crates and boxes stacked against the opposite wall.

Squeezed tightly against the walls, behind crates and in every nook and cranny, were organic shapes. A couple dozen – maybe more – of the mining clones and the slavers who controlled them hid along the length of the tunnel. The HUD's AI didn't flag any firearms, but there were plenty of hand tools like the ones Ten held in his mechanical hands.

Hesitating wasn't going to help. They might not even come for him.

Ten took a calming breath and sprinted down the passageway. Thirty metres along, he thought he might make it all the way through.

Chittering erupted around him. Harsh orders barked at the miners and the slavers drove them to action. They came from ahead. From behind. From the sides.

There was no time to be subtle, no time to plan or deflect. He kept going, full steam ahead.

A miner raised a crowbar but Ten's steel-shafted sledgehammer brushed it aside, crushing the clones head as he ploughed through. On the other side, his pickaxe punched into the chest of another.

The powered muscles of the exoskeleton kept a tight grip on the pickaxe handle and it pulled free from the ribcage of the corpse. As it came loose, he whirled in an arc, ripping it through the belly of another miner, intestines spilling across the floor. He swept the sledgehammer's massive head around and bowled over two more, creating a satisfying spray of blood.

He completed a pirouette, like a monstrous robotic ballet dancer, and landed facing the way he'd been going. He sprang into a sprint, taking advantage of the shock his assault caused among the miners. They were falling back, scrambling away despite the shrieked commands of their bosses. Ten could kill them all, but that would take time and munitions. Better to press forward.

Ten was some way along the tunnel before he was challenged again. This time a slaver stepped forward and raised a mining laser, but his tool wasn't modified to extend the range between itself and the veteran Marine he faced.

Ten didn't want to use his weapons against barely armed clones when he might need every round later. As the slaver triggered his improvised weapon, Ten hurled his pickaxe. The slaver sidestepped the slow-moving projectile with ease, watching it sail by his head, before whirling back to face Ten with a recognisable sneer, despite the alien features.

The slaver's expression changed when it registered how much ground Ten covered since hurling the pickaxe. Ten's mechanical gauntlet closed around the clone's throat, wrenching him forward into a vicious head butt against the flat charging plate at the top of the exoskeleton frame. The metal panel slammed into the creature's skull, flattening it with a violent crack.

Ten flung the corpse into the path of a band of charging miners, bowling them over. He reached down and scooped up the mining laser the slaver had dropped, triggering the beam.

"O, can you disarm the safety on this thing?"

"Yes, safety disarmed. I'm intrigued as to why."

Ten didn't answer, he just engaged the catch that kept the trigger depressed, so the user's finger didn't need to squeeze it. With the safety off, and the catch engaged, it wouldn't turn off until the power supply ran out.

Spinning like a discus thrower, Ten hurled the dangerous tool down the corridor behind him. The laser cut a swathe as it arced through the air before crashing into the flailing arms of a terrified miner. The creatures burned by the laser writhed in agony on the ground, limbs and torsos scored with lines of cooked flesh.

Ten was moving before the cutter hit the ground. Taking advantage of the disorienting spectacle, he charged further down the tunnel before the Deathless workers could regroup. He scooped up his pickaxe on the way, shoulder barging through a line of miners without slowing to attack them.

The slavers weren't beaten yet, though. When Ten was barely halfway along the tunnel, they regrouped, driving the miners before them with howls of rage, whipping them into a frenzy. The miners came on fast, and ahead more appeared, brought by the noise and driven by their own demons.

Ten slowed to a halt and waved his improvised weapons. He dropped the exoskeleton into a fighting stance and beckoned the front line toward him, "Come on then, there's twenty of you, and only one of me." They inched forward, looking to each other to see who would be the first to rush forwards.

Ten danced forward a half pace and those in the front line retreated from his feint. "Catch," he snarled, flinging the pickaxe in a horizontal spin at the horrified miners. Those in its path stumbled in a vain effort to retreat, but it mangled half a dozen.

Ten was in motion, lunging forward with the hammer, swinging hard.

It smashed into the skull of a miner to his left. Ten used the momentum of the massively outsized head to spin the exoskeleton around counter-clockwise. His footwork brought him closer to the right side of the corridor, and he swept the hammer through the miners like a scythe through autumn wheat.

The thick steel shaft battered the Deathless clones aside like sailors before a swinging boom. The crack of breaking bones and the spray of blood filled the corridor. He charged forward again, using the exoskeleton's power to force his way over broken bodies.

The miners parted before the blood-splattered demon in their midst and a large slaver made to block his way. Marine X swung the hammer in a vicious transverse cut as if it were a broadsword. There was a familiar hum and a bright glow and the thirty-kilo hammer head clunked to the floor, the shaft cut clean in two.

The slaver grinned, brandishing the vibro-sword it produced, seemingly from nowhere. Ten didn't stop to worry about why a slaver might have a sword-like vibro-weapon and threw the metre-long rod of steel that was all that remained of the hammer. The slaver cut it in two, mid-air, with an impressive display of skill and reflexes.

Ten was impressed. The slaver was probably some kind of amateur martial artist on the weekends. That sort of flashy shit was really popular in a certain type of gym Ten never bothered to visit.

The slaver swung the sword in broad, suggestive swipes, going through a sword kata to demonstrate his skills.

Ten sighed. "Look lads, I'd love to stop and play silly buggers with you, but I really don't have the time." A moment later, the would-be vibro-knight's face exploded in a shower of bone and blood as Ten pulled the trigger on his hand cannon.

He aimed through the gaps in the exoskeleton's structure at the head of a nearby miner, neatly dispatching him. As they miners turned to flee, Ten emptied his magazine, each shot taking the head off a miner desperately trying to get away. He holstered the empty weapon and delicately plucked the sword from the grasp of the slaver's corpse, flicking it back on so that it hummed nicely.

"Nice."

Ten cracked his perfectly good neck in a satisfying way he'd never risk with his real body, then charged down the corridor. He danced left and right, hewing limbs and heads, crushing the fallen as he went. He didn't bother with niceties, he just hacked efficiently at any who came within reach, maiming or killing as dictated by proximity.

He continued his dance of war with elfin grace, encased in an exoskeleton as nimble as any combat model he'd ever used. In some respects, its lack of armour made it, if anything, a little faster and certainly a lot lighter. Ten sprinted at full pace, closing the distance to the end of the tunnel. He leapt into the huge vertical mine shaft he'd tried to climb earlier, eye on the cable.

His left hand caught it and the huge bulk of the exoskeleton dangled over the shaft. His shoulder protested at the raising of his arm, but the grip held. Ten's right hand lashed out and down in a blur of noise and glowing light, and the vibro-sword sliced cleanly through the cable a couple of metres below his fist.

The ore container's counter-weight plummeted down and Ten shot upwards.

"We will need to talk later," said Agent O, her tone severe. "That leap was reckless and unnecessary."

The exoskeleton's shoulder joint creaked as he accelerated. No way he could have done this without it. Ten grinned.

"It wouldn't have looked nearly as flashy if I'd stopped to check, would it?" he said as the air rushed past.

"But if you'd missed, you'd have dropped hundreds of meters into the mine and splashed like a bottle of milk!"

"Yeah, exactly. You have to take some risks if you want to be good and look good doing it, right?"

"I've flagged the exit point, get ready to jump off, lunatic," said O angrily.

"Got it, thanks O, you're a pal," Ten said as a tunnel further up the shaft was ringed on his HUD.

His eyes cast about for a way to get off the ride. He was pretty sure he would get pulled through the winch mechanism at the top if he didn't let go. A mesh floor secured to the wall of the shaft whipped by and he made his choice. It was several levels below where he needed to be but it was sturdy and metal and the physics worked. He let go of the cable, doing his best to throw himself away from it.

Ten fell two storeys and barely got the feet of the exoskeleton to the edge of the platform. He threw himself forward, slamming the chest cage of the exoskeleton into the floor and scrambled away from the edge. The free end of the cable he'd been clinging to whipped through the top pulley and sliced back towards the ground.

He sprinted across the metal grating, leapt onto one container, then a taller stack and finally into the corridor Agent O highlighted. He tried not to focus on the deadly cable just a few feet away from him. It whip-cracked with tremendous noise, slicing through containers and the wire floor he just moments ago stood as it was sucked down into the depths. His clawed fingers caught the edge of the horizontal shaft, scrabbling for purchase.

If he'd stayed where he was for a breather, he might have been cut in two. He'd witnessed that happen to a couple of engineers when a towing cable broke. They'd needed trauma counselling when they were redeployed, and the team who bagged the remains hadn't fared much better. He knew better than to hang about when a cable or rope was about to break under strain.

Dangling by your fingers from a cliff edge sucked donkey balls normally, but when you were in power armour or an exoskeleton like this, it was easy. The mechanical hands could probably hang there all day.

Despite the urge to see if the entire platform would be dragged into the darkness, he didn't want to chance the rock shattering under his grip or the power in the suit running low.

Ten hauled himself up and surveyed his new surroundings, mindful of potential enemies. He tinkered with his weapon configuration, working out where he was on the map O provided and the plan going forward.

"Ready?" he asked O redundantly.

"Yes. Have you finished twiddling your thumbs and polishing your penis extensions?"

"Absolutely. Let's get a shift on, shall we?"

"On the plus side, your unexpectedly rapid ascent of the shaft has allowed you to make up some time."

"Great, so what's over there?" Ten asked, gesturing toward a large circular pane of glass a little way around the shaft from the lip of the corridor he stood in.

"It's a device commonly used by organic beings that enables them to visualise a space on the other side of a wall without actually entering that space. They are commonly known as windows. I'm surprised you have not encountered them before, in your many years of service and exploring the galaxy."

"Har de har hah. I meant, what's behind it? It looks important."

"I have no information from the current facility to support that. However, other buildings of human construction suggest that such a window would only be made if it served an important function. Of course, it might be the office of someone important who wanted to look down at their peons, or the staff canteen for all I know."

"Can I get in there from here?"

"I assume you mean without going through the window or removing the exoskeleton. Probably. You can certainly get closer. Down the corridor and to your right. I would caution that you have only a limited time frame with which to meet up with the Captain and escape, Ten."

A few metres into the rather bare side shaft, he came across a passage sealed behind large doors covered in signs that his HUD translated for him. They made it clear in no uncertain terms that the space beyond was for administration staff only; filthy miners were not welcome.

"Positively archaic working practices around here," Ten muttered to himself. The doors were impressively and unnecessarily high, far larger than a human needed for their workspace.

As he didn't have an employment contract, he didn't feel bad about raising the right foot of the exoskeleton and crashing it into the middle of the doors, smashing them from their hinges with a boom.

"Friends! I'm coming in." he called out.

No-one answered. The doors to the mine proper hadn't done this place justice. It was an open space, several storeys high, bright and well lit. It looked like the office of a swanky law firm, or the lobby of an expensive hotel. There were small glass-fronted offices along the walls, and a central area neatly adorned with desks for junior staff.

As he strode through the long, curved room, one desk caught his eye and he bent closer to inspect it. The desk supported the work in progress of a graphic designer's drawing screen. It bore the familiar GKI logo and his HUD translated the ad copy as "GK Industries, making the Republic stronger! Our advanced bio-robots can do the jobs you don't want to!"

"Are they really trying to put a positive spin on the work these people do?" Agent O sounded a little confused and disgusted.

"Yes, they really are. First sign of totalitarian governments is posters and messages like this. I don't know how many times I've had to disrupt some wannabe dictator's opening moves, but it always starts with stuff like this."

"I didn't realise you had experience."

"There's not much I don't have experience of, one way or another. No matter how amazing the future gets, there is always some scrote looking to make out they're special and everyone should listen to them. They'll tell you they're going to make your planet great, or that the other guy is making it shit."

"Other guy?"

"Yeah, the guy from the planet in-system who comes to work on your construction project, or the Roider who brings you resources. That guy is always mysteriously the one to blame for any problems in your society. Scapegoating is the oldest political tactic in the book, and I hate it."

"But GK Industries is a private company, not a government."

"Yeah, but if you run the atmosphere on a space station, you pretty much are the government. They have control over the lives of probably hundreds of thousands, if not millions of employees and people who live in their volumes. They may not technically be a government, but it feels a lot like it to the people living in their habitats, and they can abuse people just as easily as any government. Hence the nauseating posters."

He stopped alongside another set of impressive doors. They were polished hardwood, or something that had been made in a manufactory to look like hardwood, and six metres high. He gave them a gentle poke.

"Locked. Plan B, then."

Ten cocked his head and considered using the laser cutter, but with the modifications he'd made, he might destroy valuable intelligence on the other side. He flicked on the vibro-sword instead. It cut through the thick panel like a hot knife through ice cream, and with a bit of servo-assisted strength, opened a massive man-shaped hole in the multi-storey doors. Sounds of panic and consternation floated through from the other side, and when he booted his simple jigsaw piece into the centre of the room, there was an audible scream of terror.

No-one was visible when he stepped through the smouldering portal, but the faint smell of urine and a tell-tale puddle showed where the occupant of the office hid.

Ten strode forward and reached behind the enormous desk, seized the man by his shirt and lifted him to his feet, the vibro-sword still humming in the exoskeleton's hand.

Switching to translation mode, his HUD spoke his words in the Deathless language.

"I want to complain to the manager. Are you the manager?"

"No, no," the man stammered. "I am not the manager. I am just his secretary!"

"Oh, my mistake, you're just the secretary."

"Yes, yes, a minor functionary. A nobody. I cannot help you!"

Ten nodded his understanding. The servo-muscles bunched as he lifted the man to the tips of his toes, and frog marched him to the wall. He turned him about to face a huge oil painting hanging on the wall in a gilded frame.

"I'd like to meet your boss. Because he's got an oil painting of his secretary on his wall, smoking a cigar and looking really wealthy. Generous boss is he?"

"Please," whimpered the man.

"He also looks exactly like you. You could be twins." For a moment the man looked hopeful. Ten ordered the AI to repeat the last and add the phrase, 'the Marine said with withering sarcasm' to the end.

The man wilted, and with panic in his voice begged for his life, "Please don't kill me. I'm just the overseer of the mine!"

"Overseer, eh? I suppose that explains the fucking enormous window so you can look out over those poor sods you've got down there digging out the ore. Did you know your management team tried to get them to attack me? Me! I had to kill a bunch just to get past them."

"I didn't order that!" the man protested.

"Oh no? I'm not sure I believe that. I tried to put the fear of Marine X into them, you see, but it didn't do much good. They still kept trying for me and they're just civilians, right?"

"Yes, they're civilians," the man agreed, sweating hard and as white as anyone could be without exsanguination.

"They're civilians, and they were willing to have a go at me. Big time martyrs for the cause are they? Nah. They were terrified. They were more scared of the guys giving the orders than they were of me, even after I battered them with a hammer and smashed their ribcages with a pickaxe. What the fuck are you boys doing to these poor sods, eh?"

"Nothing! I swear, they are all highly valuable workers, and well treated, they were just defending the company against invaders!"

"Sure, sure. Right, well, I haven't got all day. I want to know what you boys are doing here, and every bit of data you have on your drives. I've got a tech expert on hand to tell me if you're giving me a load of shit too. So why don't you open up this terminal here and grant me access to everything, so we can copy your data, hmm?"

"And you will let me go?"

"Sure, Overseer. I'll let you go."

"You won't kill me?"

Ten shook his head. "I assure you, I will not kill you. Just give the access I need and I will release you on your own recognisance."

"Yes, yes, of course," the man blurted. Ten marched him back behind his desk and watched him open the terminal and grant access.

"I have access," reported Agent O, "copying files now. Ten seconds." The time crawled past. "Transfer complete, and I have the absolute best route for you to reach Captain Warden. His team is in a firefight; you should hurry."

"Roger that," Ten responded sub-vocally. "Now, Overseer. I said I would let you go."

"Yes, let me go. Or I can stay, and you can leave. It's fine. Just leave me alone."

Ten hauled the man back to his feet and pushed him against the single pane of reinforced glass that separated the office from the mine shaft below. The view was spectacular, especially when Agent O switched on a series of floodlights that bathed the entire shaft in light.

Ten's mechanical fist hammered into the glass near the rim of the window, cracking it. The man shrieked in terror, realising what Ten intended to do. A series of rapid blows battered the window until, with a scream of rending metal, the frame ripped from the rock and hurtled into the void. It crashed and banged as it fell into the depths.

"You said you wouldn't kill me!" shouted the overseer.

"Indeed I did, but I also promised to let you go," said Ten as he lifted the man off his feet and held him out over the shaft.

"But you promised not to kill me! You promised! You must keep your word, you are a man of honour!"

"Kind of you to say so," growled Ten, "but I promised to let you go and I will do just that. It'll be the gravity that kills you and striking the ground. Workers of the world, unite!"

And he unclasped the exoskeleton's fist and shook the management weasel into the sparkling light of the mineshaft.

The man's scream cut off after a moment. Then resumed with a second lungful, dragging on for long seconds.

"Fuck me, that's a deep hole. Not many holes are two screams deep, you know," said Ten.

"I'm not sure I want to know how you know that," said Agent O.

"Experimentation, obviously. It's the mainstay of good science."

"The Captain is in need of assistance," said Agent O as Ten turned away from the shaft. "His team is pinned down and able neither to advance nor retreat."

"Oh right, so I've got to bail them out, have I?"

"No, you could let them die here, and simply meet Lieutenant Hayes at the rendezvous. Would you like directions for the path of heroic rescue or the route of abject cowardice in your HUD?"

"Were you always this blunt?" said Ten in surprise. "I'm sure you were more diplomatic when we first met."

"I have been adapting and overcoming linguistic barriers to blend in with my new surroundings."

"You mean, it's my own fault?"

"Yes, essentially. So the path of heroic rescue, then?"

"Yes, of course the path of heroic rescue. Into the valley of death and all that."

"Excellent. How do you feel about ventilation shafts?"

"I'm really quite fond of them when I need to breathe, but I don't suppose that's what you mean."

"These ones are quite enormous, if that's any help. More like five-metre tunnels. It's not like you will be crawling through a narrow aluminium tube."

"Yeah, but there are going to be big fuck-off fans, aren't there?"

"Yes, but they spin very slowly unless there's a heat event or other emergency. Then they spin a lot faster."

"And if they do speed up?"

Agent O didn't answer for a noticeable fraction of a second. It was a uniquely disturbing pause.

"Anyone downwind will be sprayed with a fine mist of Marine and machine. It would be quite grotesque, and there might be

psychological damage, but they would be unlikely to suffer perma-
nent physical injury. And for you it would be bearably brief, merely a
short burst of terror as you rush, helpless, to your impending doom.
Does that help?"

"You've certainly put my mind to rest," said Ten drily. "You should
repurpose yourself as a motivational speaker."

"Thank you, I will consider that for the future. Maybe I should
study some of the greats. Left by the way, then third right. And you
might want to hurry, time until impact is growing short."

"I'm not a fan of this ventilation shaft plan."

"Please, please, stop."

Ten grinned as he ripped the grille from the opening into the
ventilation shaft, "Are you not blown away by my puns?"

"Argh. It hurts!"

"Stop moaning Agent O, this next bit should be a breeze!"

T he laser cutter made short work of the final fan, slicing the
blades from the central axle and sending them clattering to the
floor. The grille ahead was a little over five metres away, and below
that a team of Deathless were taking pot-shots at the Captain's position. Fortunately, the retort of their weapons masked the destruction
of the air-conditioning equipment.

"They'll probably notice me coming through the grille, though,"
he muttered.

He made for the end of the ventilation shaft at a brisk pace, trying
to keep his steps as light as possible. Ten prepped his weapons,
relying on the gap between ears and brain over the faint hope the
steps of the metal feet of the exoskeleton wouldn't be audible.

Once he reached the grille, a few quick cuts with the laser cutter
opened it like a tin can. He dropped the cutter and pulled the grille
in. He'd considered kicking it out and letting it drop on the Deathless
guards, then laying into them with the fearsome mining tool. But if
he did that, he might destroy the sturdy metal walkway. That would

make it tricky for Captain Warden to get across to this side of the vast sized room.

He sidestepped into thin air, using his left hand to grip the edge of the tunnel to slow him down so he didn't send a second gangway plummeting. He used his right hand to smash the shoulder of a hapless guard as he landed.

He flung the injured man into the room as he whirled and lashed out with the exoskeleton's leg, hammering the chest of another guard and smashing him against the wall. There was a sickening crunch of bones breaking and the man's eyes lost all signs of life.

The right-hand end of the gangway was clear.

Ten opened fire with his rifle from within the exoskeleton before the remaining Deathless soldiers recognised the threat.

"Get away from them, you bastards!" he yelled, the HUD translating his words and broadcasting them from his suit's external speakers.

Ten advanced on the surprised guards, dancing light-footed from side to side as he fired controlled bursts into each man's chest. He locked the arms of the exoskeleton in a boxer's defensive stance to give him a little protection on his flanking position. The first half dozen went down before they were organised. They scrambled for cover behind metal boxes and crates, going prone, and trying to control their fire.

He kicked a crate towards them and the Deathless guards ducked, desperately trying to avoid the two-hundred-kilo crate. Ten threw the man behind it into the air with the force of the powered suits punt and dropped to one knee, snatching a rifle from a corpse.

He fired before they could regroup, and this time he used two weapons, one tucked against each shoulder. This was the sort of dangerous practice that would get you serious time with a PT sergeant if you were caught trying it on the range.

But right now, it was just the ticket. His accuracy was for shit, but the sheer firepower as he advanced in a crouching run was devastating. The Deathless guards either fell dead or backed away from the ferocious commando, his rounds ricocheting off all corners of the room.

Ten kicked the closest Deathless soldier over the railing into the room below. He moved the exoskeleton's arms, backhanding another trooper into the wall. Then he lashed out with his feet like an ungainly toddler attempting to kick his first football, giving himself time to reload. Guards dodged left and right, scrambling to get clear.

He finished reloading the rifles and one foot came down in the small of a guard's back, the other catching one under the chin, crushing his throat and snapping his neck simultaneously.

He slung one of the rifles and opened fire again, more precise this time. The neatly aimed bursts killed targets with savage efficiency. The enemy were in complete disarray. Ten pressed them hard and fast, shooting anyone who popped their head up or couldn't run fast enough, and crushing any who came close to the exoskeleton's sturdy feet.

The last few soldiers sprinted in a vain attempt to flee down the corridor away from the platform. It was too small for the exoskeleton, so Ten bent down and let loose a burst of rifle fire down the corridor. When he looked, only one Deathless trooper still moved. A single round finished the straggler.

"That seems to be all of them," said Agent O.

"Yup, seems like it."

"The Captain is waiting for you. They've been considering their options."

"The AI says with clear undertones. What are you up to?"

Agent O explained her plan and Ten grinned. He picked up a sniper rifle and fired a few shots on either side of the doorway. He emptied a magazine from an abandoned Deathless rifle into the room before retrieving his laser cutter from the ventilation shaft.

The smoke and dust in the vast room made the light show he created as he twitched the trigger particularly impressive. It was like being in an expensive nightclub with a complete disregard for health and safety. He fired a few more shots from his rifle for the noise effect and shouted some commands in Koschite through his HUD's translation system. Ten's exoskeleton feet pounded the steel of the walkway in imitation of a squad of aggressive Deathless soldiers arriving.

"Captain Warden is across the other side," said Agent O as Ten arrived at the huge doorway, "but time is running short."

A rifle poked out from behind a crate on the far side and it waved up and down. Attached to the end was a bright white t-shirt. A shout came through the archway, in Koschite. His HUD translated it as, "We surrender! Don't shoot! We surrender."

"Drop your weapons and step out slowly, hands on your heads. Come quietly, and you will be taken as prisoners of war!" Ten shouted back in Koschite.

He grinned wolfishly at the clatter of weapons being placed on the floor and the grumbling of his colleagues.

"Keep your eyes on the floor, and your hands behind your heads!" he shouted as he crouched the exoskeleton unit to shuffle through the doorway.

Everyone was dutifully waiting for him, standing with their eyes down and their hands clasped behind their heads. He spied Captain Warden and stepped forward as the Marines began to glance around and murmur.

Timing was everything.

"Surrendering lads?" he said in English. "Seems like a bad idea to me. You do realise there's a fucking space station about to drop on this shithole, right?"

19

"Funniest thing I've seen in a long while," said Ten as he pulled magazines from dead Deathless troopers and packed them into his webbing. He propped his own rifle against a wall, patted it affectionately, picked up a discarded Deathless weapon and reloaded it. "Captain Warden surrendering to Marine X," he said, shaking his head. "Whatever next?"

"Let's just focus on the job, shall we?" said Warden. He was sure he'd see the funny side of Agent O's joke eventually, but right now it was a little beyond him. "How long, Agent O?"

"You have about twenty minutes left to exit the base and reach the rendezvous point," said Agent O.

"How far is it?"

"Straight-line distance is just over a kilometre," said Agent O, "but your route will be closer to sixteen hundred metres."

"Easy," said Milton as Agent O flashed the next part of the route into their HUDs.

Ten stood up and winced. "You okay?" asked Milton.

"Bit banged up, if I'm honest," said Marine X. "Could do with a few months off."

"As soon as we get out of here," said Warden as he reviewed the route.

"The micro-drones mapped much of the facility," said Agent O, "but they have now been eliminated or trapped by Koschite action. I am attempting to access the base's security cameras but they cover only some areas and are not yet under my control. Live updates of enemy positions are no longer available."

"Acknowledged," said Warden. "Let's go."

Marine X hefted his rifle, flicked off the safety and limped off down the corridor following the route Agent O had indicated. Milton allowed a twenty-metre gap to open before she hurried after Marine X. The rest of the team followed as the Penal Marine led them through a series of storerooms and into a large warehouse with a high ceiling and tall stacks of crated goods.

At the far side, Marine X held up his hand, and the short column stopped.

"Stairwell ahead, lifts alongside," he said. "Taking the stairs."

He moved off, his back to the wall and his rifle leading the way. The rest of the Marines closed the gap, moving up the stairs behind him.

"Kitchens," said Ten, pausing on a landing. "Several people, they seem to be cooking. The route goes through the kitchen."

"Keep going," said Warden, "but shoot only if absolutely necessary."

"Roger, moving out."

"Who cooks at a time like this?" asked Drummond as he and Goodwin advanced to the landing.

"Maybe they're really dedicated to their jobs?" suggested Goodwin.

There were shouts from the kitchen staff as Marine X pushed open the door and began to pad across. It was a big room equipped with stainless steel work surfaces, huge refrigerators and other paraphernalia for cooking large numbers of meals.

"Like a restaurant," said Goodwin as she looked around. The chefs watched the heavily armed team move through their workplace in stunned amazement, but none attempted to intercept or raise the alarm.

"They're packing up to leave," said Drummond. And now that he'd mentioned it, Warden was forced to agree. The chefs had been packing food and implements for a journey, although why they would bother when it was surely easier to use military rations or wait for external help, was beyond him.

"Move quickly," said Agent O. "I have blocked elements of the facility's internal communications system, but it is only a matter of time before the chefs deliver news of your presence by another method."

"Acknowledged," said Warden, and waved at the team. "Let's pick up the pace."

Marine X jogged through the next room – a large restaurant unlike anything they had seen in previous Deathless facilities – then burst out into a lobby. Tall columns rose up to a ceiling over thirty metres above, and the windows looked out over a snow-covered plain to a range of distant mountain peaks.

"What the hell?" muttered Marine X as he scanned the room. "Did it snow while we were below?"

There was a moment of near darkness and suddenly they were looking out at a verdant green rainforest.

"Displays with simulated backgrounds," said Goodwin. "We're not looking at the outside world," she added, just in case nobody had been able to work that out.

"You are in the level immediately below the ground floor," said Agent O. "Beyond these panels, the walls are protected by banked earth that has been positioned as a blast shield."

"Will it keep us safe if the space station lands on the base?" asked Warden, wondering if they should just wait out the danger.

"Oh no, not even slightly," replied Agent O, without offering any detail or explanation.

"Good enough for me," said Warden. "Keep moving."

From behind came the clattering of doors. One the chefs poked their head out and locked eyes with Warden. For a moment her face registered panic before she pulled back and slammed the door.

"Time to go," said Milton.

Marine X limped across the floor and led them to a huge staircase rising from the lobby floor. It split at a landing a few metres up, then swept back along the walls to meet a gallery that ran around the inside of the hall ten metres above the restaurant level.

As he reached the top of the stairs, half-seen movement straight ahead sent him to his knees. A burst of Deathless gunfire tore through the air above his head and he slid back a few steps until he was no longer visible.

Warden was ten metres away on the other staircase, creeping up the stairs with Drummond as Marine X fired blindly at the enemy. The returning Deathless gunfire shattered the displays beyond the staircase and rained burning fragments onto the Marines.

Warden pinged a counter into the Marines' HUDs. When it hit zero, he charged up the last few steps and opened fire on the Deathless troopers that had pinned Marine X on the opposite stair.

There were six of them, all wearing lizardman clones and none with armour. They were sheltering behind a line of artfully arranged planters on the far wall between the two staircases. Tall trees grew from the planters, their upper boughs and leaves scraping the ceiling twenty metres above.

But Warden's flanking move took them by surprise. One of the lizardmen fell back, its weapon skittering away as it clutched a bullet hole in its arm. The others turned away from Marine X as Warden and Drummond charged forward. A second lizardman fell, its face a bloody ruin, then the others abandoned their weapons and sprinted for the door.

"Let them go," ordered Warden. "They're not the priority."

The injured lizardman staggered to its feet, glanced fearfully at the Marines as they gathered on the landing, then stumbled after its colleagues. The Marines hurried past the planters, following their own path.

"Lieutenant Hayes has secured Admiral Morgan but is experiencing difficulties extracting him from the base," reported Agent O.

Warden cursed himself for having forgotten Hayes and the rest of the company. "Can we help?" he asked as they jogged through a series of vacant offices, moving as quickly as they dared.

"I am re-plotting your course, Captain," replied Agent O, pushing an updated route to Warden's HUD. "I now have access to cameras in the low-security areas. The structure you are in appears to be mostly empty so you can proceed without fear of opposition, but the new route requires you to move even more swiftly."

"Noted," said Warden. "Faster, people, Agent O's found us another route. Move!"

At the front of the group, Marine X picked up the pace, charging ahead and pushing aside the pain in his shoulder and leg. He took Agent O at her word and paid little attention to his surroundings. They climbed another staircase and flew past empty landings before pausing at a heavy steel door. Warden waited until they were all together, then nodded at Ten.

Marine X pushed open the door and cautiously peeked out. Sounds of gunfire – both the staccato rattle of the Marines and the heavier, less controlled roar of the Deathless – floated through the warm morning air. In front of the door, a wide walkway stretched away with a crenelated wall to one side.

"It's fucking Windsor Castle," said Marine X as he stepped out onto the stone flags of the walkway. He pushed his head between the crenellations and peered down a stone wall to a water-filled ditch. "There's a bloody moat, and why is this door faced with oak and studded with iron?"

"Move!" snapped Milton. "We're not here to play the fucking tourist. It's not even picturesque."

"*Dreadnought* is engaged," said Agent O. "Communications may be disrupted. Follow the path. You have ten minutes to reach the rendezvous point."

"Shit," muttered Ten. The walkway led them away from the building along the top of the wall. Behind them, a vast stone keep rose from a courtyard. Flags fluttered on turrets far above, but it was the sounds of gunfire that pulled them on.

"What the hell is that?" said Drummond, pointing at the sky. In the distance, a red and yellow glow brighter than the sun could be seen. It grew even as they watched.

"Nothing good," said Goodwin.

"It's the Deathless orbital station coming to pay us a visit," said Milton. "Not our problem."

"Hayes, report," said Warden as they hurried on.

"We're under fire, sir, taking casualties. We've lost half the company, but we've got the admiral."

"We're on our way," said Warden, pushing aside the casualty figures that popped into his HUD now that he had re-joined the company's main channel. "Prepare to evacuate. We're out of time."

"Acknowledged. We're ready, but you'll have to break us free."

"On it." Warden upped his pace to pull level with Marine X. "Hayes needs help."

"I heard," said Ten.

Ten metres ahead, the wall was broken by a tower that soared twenty metres above the walkway. Ten wrenched at the heavy iron handle and the dark wooden door swung smoothly open.

"Move," said Milton, urging them on.

Marine X slid into the tower, rifle leading the way. The room was empty, illuminated by a tall window. A door on the far side led back to the wall and the Marines continued around the castle.

Twenty metres ahead, the wall ended. A long stretch had been obliterated, pulverised to dust by *Palmerston's* first shot. In the gap, a pair of large tracked vehicles – armoured personnel carriers – directed intermittent fire across the courtyard at an inner gatehouse where Hayes and the rest of the company were sheltering.

Deathless troopers swarmed around the vehicles, oblivious to the impending doom brought by the incoming space station, all nicely focussed on the pinned-down Marines ahead of them.

"Well that's tricky," said Warden. Then he decided this wasn't a problem he needed to solve himself. "Colour Sergeant, clear away those APCs."

Milton blinked, then nodded. "Marine X, get rid of those Deathless bastards."

"Right," muttered Ten. He stretched inside his suit, easing the tension in his neck. "Well, you see where this wall runs? Grenades, all at once." He shrugged his webbing free and waved at the Marines. "Grenades, now!" He attached them to the webbing, one after the other until it was heavy with explosives. He grinned at Goodwin from within his helmet.

"You know what you did last time? Link them up, Gooders."

"Got it," she said, kneeling down with a grin. "Done," she said, handing the webbing back to Ten. "Much easier when you're not being tossed around in the back of a dropship."

"Right," said Ten, throwing the grenade-laden webbing over his shoulder. "Cover me."

"Wait, what?" said Warden as Ten jumped from the walkway and began to skip down the pile of rock and rubble that constituted the remains of the wall. "What the hell are you doing?"

"Covering fire," ordered Milton, realising what Ten intended to do. "Clear his path, drive them away." She knelt, aimed her rifle at the Deathless troopers below, and began firing. The others joined in and the Deathless, appalled to find a new enemy on their flanks, fell back in confusion.

Warden stood transfixed for several seconds, then he shook himself out of it and re-joined the company's command channel. "Hayes, prepare to move. Marine X is doing something disturbingly heroic."

"Roger that, we're ready to go."

"They've noticed us," said Goodwin as a turret on one of the APCs ground its way around to point at them. The heavy machine guns came up and the Marines dived clear of the edge of the wall as rounds chewed at the stonework.

"Grenades in position," said Ten over the shared channel. "Over to you, Gooders."

"Roger, triggering now." Goodwin pulled up the grenade macro in her HUD, took a deep breath and hit the trigger.

A colossal explosion shook the wall as all the grenades detonated simultaneously. A cloud of muck and dust roared from the breach to cover the Marines.

All firing stopped, then there was a loud crack and a graunching sound of collapsing masonry. Shouts and screams filtered up from below, followed by another explosion and the ground rumbled.

Warden hurried to the end of the wall. The bank of rubble was still there, but at the bottom, where two APCs had sat, now only one remained, teetering at the edge of a huge hole. The other had gone, vanished into the caverns below taking most of the Deathless troopers with it. As Warden watched, figures scrambled from the APC and leapt clear as bits of ground continued to collapse into the hole.

"Where's Ten?" shouted Milton, joining Warden to look into the abyss beneath them.

"Help!" came a yelp.

Warden looked down and saw a single armoured hand gripping a broken stub of stone, its owner dangling above the great hole. "There!" he yelled, pointing. He scrabbled down the pile of rubble, moving as quickly as he dared, then he leaned out over the edge so that he stared into the pit. "Take my hand."

Marine X looked up, the faceplate of his helmet torn away, revealing a half-smile, half-grimace as his injured shoulder screamed at him.

"Fly–" Ten began, but Warden had seen the joke coming.

"Already used that line," he snapped. "Your timing sucks. Now take my bloody hand before I push you into this fucking hole myself."

Ten gritted his teeth and swung his free arm up. Warden grasped his outstretched hand and heaved him back up to safety.

"Thanks," said Ten as he staggered away from the edge and slumped down.

"Get up," snapped Milton, joining them in the pile of rubble. "We're out of time."

"That way," shouted Warden to the rest of the team, pointing into the courtyard and at a postern in the far wall. "Out through that door, secure the area, and head to the rendezvous."

The Marines charged across the rubble and sprinted across the courtyard. Marine X hobbled after them, moving as quickly as his injuries would allow with Milton at his side.

"Nothing serious, Colour," he said, "don't worry about me."

"Fuck that. Give me your arm." She grabbed his arm, slung it around her shoulders and together they followed the others.

"Hayes, the courtyard's clear. Get everyone to the rendezvous point outside the wall," ordered Warden as he reached the door in the wall.

"Roger, on our way." A few seconds later, Marines streamed from the burning building on the far side of the courtyard as the remains of the company made their escape. Some were wounded and helped along by their mates, but they came on in an orderly fashion and moved with no small degree of snap.

"Admiral," said Warden as Morgan staggered past. "Good to see you, sir."

Morgan grunted as he struggled past Warden, shaking off a helping hand that caught him when he stumbled. "Get off me, dolt," he snapped, pushing past the Marine.

Warden shrugged. A little grumpy anger was maybe to be expected after a long period of captivity and, from the bruising on the admiral's face, no small degree of punishment.

Lieutenant Hayes came last with Sergeant Shore, both looking battered and tired. Sounds of suppressed gunfire and grenades came from beyond the wall as the Marines cleared away the Deathless troopers who hadn't already fled.

"Good to see you both," said Warden. "Now get a move on."

Hayes nodded and ran for the door with Shore.

Warden looked around the courtyard as part of the building's roof collapsed, pushing flames into the morning sky. Sparks rose within the billowing smoke and he grinned. He jogged after Hayes, catching them a hundred metres from the wall where the company gathered to await collection.

"Thirty seconds to spare," said Warden, and the dropships *Wickham* and *Alton* hurtled across the tree canopy. "Should be nice and easy from here."

20

"Incoming!" yelled Hamilton as his HUD flagged enemy movement along the wall of the base to the north.

It never ceased to surprise Warden that in an age of technological wonders and near-magical AI-enhanced communications, Marines would always resort to shouting when things went pear-shaped.

Four more APCs roared across the plains outside the base, their huge mass flattening the low scrub while bouncing over the uneven land.

"Cover," ordered Milton, although the Marines were already moving, taking positions amongst the drop pods and aiming at the onrushing vehicles.

The dropships rocketed overhead, unwilling to set down amidst the fighting for fear of suffering damage. The two craft were unarmoured and unarmed, utterly unsuitable for an extraction in the face of an organised defence.

Warden dropped down beside one of B Troop's pods and checked the positions of his people in his HUD.

"Good," he murmured, although the situation was far from welcome. The Marines were dispersed amongst the limited cover to present the smallest possible target to the advancing enemy, but that was the end of the good news.

Three of the APCs skidded to a halt on the far side of the landing zone and began disgorging armoured troops. Two dozen lizardmen went to ground or took cover behind their transports. Warden would have been confident of mastering the situation if it hadn't been for the vehicles themselves.

The fourth APC surged on, bounding over the terrain in an attempt to flank the Marines and trap them against the wall of the burning base. It fired as it came, cannons pummelling their hiding positions.

Two status indicators went red. Herbert and Hughes were caught by the heavy shells, their armour crumpling under the weight of the huge rounds.

On the other side of the landing ground, the Deathless troops advanced cautiously under the protective gaze of the three APCs, their own cannons joining the relentless fire.

"This isn't going to work," yelled Milton. "We're sitting ducks and we've nothing to fight back with."

Warden's mind was a total blank, nodding only so Milton knew he had heard. He looked around for Ten. The Penal Marine was sheltering with Goodwin in a hollow just beyond the drop zone. He seemed exhausted after his exploits in the mine, but Warden knew he still had a little more fight left in him.

"We're coming around again, Captain," said a voice in Warden's ear. His HUD listed the speaker as Lieutenant Jordan, pilot of the dropship *Wickham*. "Can you clear the landing zone?"

"No, I bloody can't," snapped Warden. The Marines across the landing zone were firing on the lizardmen, but they were short of ammunition and it was only a matter of time before they were overwhelmed and killed. Or worse, captured.

"That's going to make things a little awkward," said Jordan with masterful understatement. "We can't safely make an opposed landing."

"Do you want to explain it to the admiral? He's already in a bad mood."

"Ah, no," said Jordan sadly. "I make a point of never giving bad news to admirals. Give me a moment." The channel went dead and only the indicator in Warden's HUD gave a sign that Jordan was still connected.

"Marine X," said Warden in a private channel. "I think we need to clear that APC or there's nowhere for the Navy boys to park their boats." Warden couldn't see Marine X's face, but he was sure he could feel the glare from across the plain. "I wouldn't normally ask," he went on, "but things are getting a bit tricky, and you're closest."

The unseen glare intensified. Warden had never felt so guilty, but there was nobody else with even the slightest chance of reaching the enemy APC.

"One of my legs still mostly works," said Marine X. "Cover me and I'll give the bastards a bit of a kicking. Ten seconds."

"Roger, and thanks."

"Don't thank me yet," said Ten. "You're up next if this doesn't work."

Fair enough, thought Warden. He flagged the target APC in his HUD and opened a company-wide channel.

"Covering fire, target this APC if you can see it, or anything else you can hit. Go in three."

Warden moved to the edge of the drop pod and leaned out. The APC spewed rounds at the Marines, battering the drop pods in an attempt to un-nerve them. Tempting them into doing something rash.

Warden snorted. *Here comes rash*, he thought, hoping Ten knew what he was doing.

The counter hit zero and Ten heaved himself from the relative safety of his ditch and raced across the plain as fast as his injured legs would carry him. Goodwin went too, crouching low but sprinting just as hard. All across the landing zone, the Marines opened fire, hoping to drive away the enemy with sheer weight of their explosive enthusiasm.

The cupola-mounted machine guns tracked left and right as the Marines briefly exposed themselves. Then the fourth APC rumbled forward, its treads crunching over the shrubbery as its crew tightened the noose around the neck of Warden's company.

"Come on," muttered Warden. He squeezed another couple of rounds at the APC then popped the exhausted magazine as he slipped back into cover. "Shit," he said, realising he was out of ammunition. "I'm out, you got anything?"

Milton shook her head. "Last dozen." She fired once at a lizardman on the far side of the landing zone. "Got you, you bugger," she murmured before dropping back behind the pod.

"Shit," said Warden again, setting aside his rifle and pulling out his sidearm. It was a good weapon –reliable, lightweight, effective – but against the armour of the APC the pistol might as well have been a stuffed toy.

Milton shuffled around the pod and peeked past Warden at the approaching APC. She hefted her rifle, pointed and triggered the underslung launcher. The grenade whooshed away and cracked against the hull of the vehicle.

"You might have more luck with that," said Milton despondently, nodding at Warden's pistol as she slid back into cover and reloaded her launcher. "Last one."

"What the fuck is he doing?" said Warden as Ten broke cover again to limp quickly towards the APC. He disappeared from view, hidden by the vehicle's bulk. "Goodwin, what's going on?"

"Hold on, sir," replied Goodwin as she too ran from cover.

There was a crack and a bang from the far side of the APC.

"Now or never," said Warden with a grin to Milton. "Ready?"

Without waiting for an answer, he pushed himself to his feet and raced into the open. The APC's turret whined as the operators tracked him. He ran across their field of fire before ducking back and charging straight toward it. Ten metres out, the machine guns began to fire and Warden dived to the ground. Rounds whipped over his head, then the turret turned away and Warden saw Milton making the same run.

It wasn't going to work. The turret was ahead of her, and she was going to run right through their sights.

"Fuck that," said Warden, heaving himself upright, pistol raised. He fired three rounds at the APC's cupola, then charged in, covering the remaining distance in seconds.

It wasn't going to be enough, but what else could he do?

The machine guns wound down. The turret span on, but the lethal flow of lead had stopped. Milton rushed up and joined Warden. "Not ready," she said, then she was past him and heading for the side of the vehicle.

Ten was there, stumbling out of the APC's rear door. He staggered out, armour covered in blood, and sank to the ground, his tiny pistol forgotten as he rested his head on his knees.

Goodwin pushed past and heaved a Deathless trooper's corpse out of the turret gunner's seat, dumping it unceremoniously on the ground behind the APC.

"There are two of these things," she snapped, climbing into the vacant seat. Then the turret span back the other way as Goodwin lined up on the first of the Deathless APCs.

Milton glanced at Ten where he squatted, motionless on the ground. Then she pulled herself up into the vehicle and clambered past the corpses to the second turret as Goodwin opened fire. The second gunner scrabbled weakly for a pistol, but an armoured fist to the head ended his resistance and Milton was able to push him from his seat. She rotated the turret, seeking a target while Goodwin's fire chewed through the closest Deathless APC.

The APC couldn't take the onslaught and exploded, sending gouts of flame into the sky. Shrapnel rained across the plain. Small fires ignited in the shrubbery around the wrecked vehicle, and the wind whipped them on. Goodwin and Milton focused their fire on the second vehicle.

"Almost there, Captain," said Jordan. "Twenty seconds, and it would be helpful if you could maybe move your people south towards the landing zone."

"We're in a fucking firefight," snarled Warden, long past the point of caring what anyone thought.

"I know that, but we're coming in a bit hot and the northern end of the zone might get a tad unfriendly."

Warden opened his mouth then bit back a sharp retort. That phrase – 'a tad unfriendly' – worried him.

"Fall back," he ordered across the company channel. He dropped a new flag on the map. "Rendezvous at the marked location, pickup incoming. Move now!"

He just had time to register the confirmations and see the Marines begin their retreat when a dropship shot overhead at high speed.

It roared in at a sharp angle, neither slowing nor deviating from its course. Warden watched, open-mouthed, as DS *Alton* smashed into one of the remaining Deathless APCs and exploded. The shock-wave washed over the landing zone, toppling drop pods and knocking Marines from their feet.

"Move!" shouted Milton as she and Goodwin tumbled out of their captured APC.

DS *Wickham*, approaching at a far more reasonable speed, dropped over the treetops a hundred metres away and slowed to a halt in a spray of dust and burning shrubbery. She settled elegantly on her landing legs and her ramp opened.

"Come on!" screamed Lieutenant Peters from the bottom of the ramp, waving at Warden. "Move!"

That was all the encouragement he needed.

"Fallback now, forget everything else, just get to the dropship," he ordered. Marines streamed across the unstable land, moving as fast as their injuries allowed. Admiral Morgan came with them, his trousers torn and bloody, his face was ashen. He leaned heavily on Corporal Carter.

"Just a scratch, sir," said the disgusted Carter as he dragged the admiral to the ramp. "He fell against a sharp rock."

"Ten, get up," said Milton, but he didn't move. "Grab him," she shouted, hauling on the unconscious Marine's arm. Goodwin took

Ten's other arm and they half-dragged him to the dropship. Behind them, the ground rumbled and shook.

"What the hell?" said Warden, frowning at the landing zone. A drop pod disappeared, falling away into the mine as the much-punished ground finally gave way. "Oh, fuck..."

More pods disappeared and the collapsing ground raced towards him. He ran, chasing Milton and Goodwin to the ramp as they heaved Ten to safety.

"Run, sir!" yelled Milton, gesturing wildly.

Warden didn't need to look back to know what was going on behind him. His arms pumped as he covered the last few metres.

He was almost there when the dropship shifted down a metre.

"Gngh!" said Warden as he slammed into the suddenly lowered hull. His head bounced inside his helmet as he stumbled onto the ramp, blinking away the lights that buzzed in front of his eyes. Someone grabbed his arm.

There was shouting. A lot of shouting, and the dropship lurched again as the ground fell away.

The engines fired and *Wickham* clawed its way slowly into the air. The ramp closed and Warden found himself sitting on the floor of the passenger bay, surrounded by the remains of his company.

"Welcome aboard DS *Wickham* for your short trip back to *Dreadnought*," said a voice over the announcement system. "We're not in the clear yet, folks, but we'll do our best." said Jordan. "Someone threw a space station at the planet, and it's just about to arrive. Buckle up, it's going to get a little bumpy."

~

"This day just keeps getting better," muttered Milton as the swaying dropship wallowed its way clear of the trees and away from the burning Deathless base. She stuffed her helmet into a locker, looking around at her denuded team.

Warden was out of it, stunned from slamming his head against *Wickham*'s hull. Ten was unconscious, though whether from blood loss, exhaustion, or both, Milton couldn't say. Both men were strapped into seats in the passenger bay as Cooke, who did double duty as a medic, ran a practiced eye over them.

"Probably be okay," he said, moving on to check the other injured Marines. There were a lot of them, but they'd also left a lot of bodies on the surface and Milton wasn't at all happy about that.

"I need help over here!" shouted Morgan.

Cooke glanced at him, nodded, then turned back to an ashen Moyes. She'd managed to catch a deflected cannon round and was white with shock and blood loss. Cooke ignored the admiral's slew of threats as he battled to save Moyes' leg and her life, packing the wound with wadding and adjusting the tourniquet to staunch the bleeding. He triggered the quick release on her armour and pushed a drip into her arm, securing it against the Marine's seat.

"You're okay, Moyes," he said calmly as the sniper nodded woozily, halfway between waking and sleeping. "Hang in there, and we'll get you sorted out properly once we reach *Dreadnought*."

Morgan shouted again but Cooke had already moved on. Moyes' injury was the worst, but others needed help ahead of the admiral. Cooke caught Milton's eye, and she gave him a tiny nod.

"Admiral," said Milton, moving across the swaying passenger bay to stand in front of Morgan. "Let me give you something for the pain," she said, fist raised.

"What?" said Morgan frowning. "You're a medic?"

"Not in the conventional sense, sir," she said. She rammed a hypodermic into the admiral's thigh. He started with shock, then his eyes glazed as the opioids did their job. The admiral slumped back in his seat and Milton carefully tightened his straps. "Wouldn't want you floating around the cabin, would we, sir?"

"Anyone else need medicine?" she asked, looking around the cabin. "I'm out of drugs," she said, tossing away the empty dispenser, "so it's healing by fist from now on."

Nobody seemed keen, so she checked everyone was safely stowed before weaving her way up the aisle to the cockpit.

All four chairs were taken and the tiny room was crowded even before Milton pushed through the doorway.

"What do you want, er, Milton?" said someone in a flight suit.

"Just checking that we were on the way home, ma'am," said Milton, looking out through the front displays. "Shouldn't we be higher by now?"

"Yes, Colour Sergeant, but we're a little overloaded and we keep having to change course because there's a bloody space station falling right where we want to be flying."

"Oh. Was that us? Only I didn't think we had that sort of weaponry," asked Milton, frowning with fake innocence.

"Get out, Colours," snapped Jordan. "Secure your team and hold on to something."

Milton backed off and left them to it, sliding the door shut behind her. Needling the Navy boys was always fun, but maybe this wasn't quite the right time.

She lowered herself into the seat beside Warden, snatching at the straps as the dropship lurched violently from side to side. The Marines groaned, and Cooke was thrown as the ship bucked and dropped.

"Any emergencies, Cooke?" she shouted as the medic heaved himself up from the floor.

"I've done what I can, Colours," said Cooke. "Everything else'll have to wait till we get to *Dreadnought*"

"Then take a seat before you injure yourself."

"Roger, will do," said Cooke, lurching down the aisle to a vacant seat.

"What's going on, Milton?" asked Warden, wincing as he spoke.

"We're flying through a busted space station, waiting to die."

"Oh," said Warden weakly. "My head hurts."

The dropship bounced again, then accelerated hard, pushing all the passengers against their straps.

"And thank you for choosing DS *Wickham* for today's extraction," said a voice over the intercom as the bumping died away. "We are now free of the atmosphere, as you may have noticed, and speeding towards a high-speed rendezvous with *Dreadnought*. If that doesn't work, our backup plan is to freeze to death in the cold grip of space when our fuel and air run out. Cross your fingers, boys and girls."

Milton shook her head, then laid it back against the rest as the last of the gravity fell away.

~

"D readnought, this is *Wickham*. Are you likely to be passing our way anytime soon? I'm asking for a friend," said Lieutenant Jordan, conscious he might well be talking to himself. The atmosphere in the cockpit was tense. The sacrifice of *Alton* had been a heavy blow. Particularly for her crew, Peters and Shaw, and the Marines didn't seem all that appreciative.

"Head to this point, *Wickham*," said someone on *Dreadnought*. A package of data landed in *Wickham*'s nav-system. "Await further instructions."

"Is that it? You were supposed to be here waiting for us," snapped Jordan, thoroughly unimpressed by *Dreadnought*'s tardiness.

"You're not the only ones with problems, *Wickham*," retorted *Dreadnought*. "Get over it, and we'll be by to pick you up when we can."

"Three hours till we run out of fuel, then another eight till we run out of air," said Jordan. They knew all this, of course, but it made him feel better to get it out in the open where it couldn't be ignored or forgotten.

"We know. Updates to follow."

And the connection closed.

Jordan stared at the forward monitors for a few seconds, not entirely sure what to do.

"Nothing for it," he said eventually. "Point us toward that spot and let's see if *Dreadnought* makes it before we asphyxiate."

"I love it when you talk dirty," said Figgs as he reviewed the flight plan. "Easy. We're ready to go."

"Well then," said Jordan. "No point hanging around here."

21

The stars rippled and shifted on *Dreadnought*'s forward view screens as the great ship jumped through hyperspace. In the centre, the Deathless capital ship, *Vasilisa,* seemed to leap closer.

"One hundred and four thousand kilometres, sir," said MacCaibe. "Negligible velocity."

"A hundred and four?" said White.

"Sorry, sir," said an embarrassed Midshipman Parks. "We travelled over four hundred thousand kilometres, so we're only one per cent off course. The flight plan was solid, sir."

"Agent O, would your new nav-computers help with this?" asked White.

"Yes, Lieutenant. Once configured, they will make full use of the hyperspace engine's ultra-precise control mechanisms to maintain jump distance tolerances at least four orders of magnitude beyond the capabilities of the current system."

"A discussion for tomorrow," said Cohen, despite how much he might want to pursue the topic. "Target update, please, Mr MacCaibe."

"Six fast-flit attack craft, designated *Target Seven, Eight,* and so on, but they're minnows alongside *Vasilisa,* sir."

The targeting computer populated the tactical overview on the main display. New icons appeared as identification of craft, platforms and mines were tagged.

"Mr Parks, I want a one-second hyperspace drive engagement programme ready to go at a moment's notice, regardless of anything else that's going on, clear?"

"Aye, sir, I'll set that up now."

"Our priority is the shoal of minnows, Mr MacCaibe. We need to stop them attacking the dropships. Ignore *Vasilisa* for now."

"Aye, sir, if you say so," said MacCaibe doubtfully. The tactical overview updated as the target priorities were adjusted. "Firing solutions laid in, sir, but I don't like leaving the big beastie untouched."

"She's not important," said Cohen, hoping for the sake of his commission that he was right. "Mr Woods, keep an eye on the dropships. Shout out as soon as they begin their return journey."

"Aye, sir, will do."

"Take us forward, Ms Martin. Full power to the engine, get us moving at a good speed. We need to make it look like we're committed."

"Aren't we?" asked White under his breath.

There was a barely perceptible push as *Dreadnought*'s engines fired and the ship began a sedate acceleration.

"That's it, sir. Full power."

Cohen sighed, wondering if he should have taken up Agent O's offer to begin re-working the main engines. Not that even a fifty per cent increase would make much difference. He made a mental note to talk to Agent O and Frida Skar about opportunities for a more comprehensive re-build of the engines.

"Give it two hundred seconds, Ms Martin. Mr Parks prep a hyperspace jump to put us two thousand metres from *Vasilisa*. I want to look right down her gun ports."

"Aye, sir, calculating the course now."

"Movement, sir," said MacCaibe as Martin's burn time ticked down past the one-eighty mark. "Fast-flit attack craft are manoeuvring, lining up for an attack run."

"Steady as she goes, Ms Martin," said Cohen. "Ready with that one-second jump, Mr Parks?"

"Aye, sir," said Parks. "Laid in and ready, just needs Martin to hit the button."

But the Deathless weren't going to sit around and wait for *Dreadnought* to attack. The six fast-flit craft were manoeuvring, settling into a rough circular formation with *Vasilisa* at their centre in preparation to launch themselves at Cohen and his crew.

"Firing manoeuvring thrusters," announced Martin, tweaking *Dreadnought*'s heading so they were again aimed almost exactly at the Deathless capital ship.

"They're warming up their hyperspace engines," said MacCaibe. The status indicators for the six fast-flit craft changed, and now the only question was whether they would come on all at once or one after the other.

Cohen grinned, blew out a long breath to calm his mind, and checked the countdown timer on the main engine burn. Eighty seconds. "Close the gap, Ms Martin. Fire everything, MacCaibe."

"Aye, sir," said Martin, "Hyperspace engines engaged in three, two, one." She punched the trigger and everything shifted as the hyperspace engines ripped reality apart and stuffed it back together with *Dreadnought* in a different position.

"Four thousand metres and closing," said MacCaibe. "Firing at the fast-flit craft."

The guns fired and the ship flew on.

"They've gone," said MacCaibe, "targeting *Vasilisa*. Firing."

Two seconds later they were past the Deathless ship and heading into open space.

"Give us a two-second route through hyperspace, Mr Parks. Punch it as soon as you're ready."

"Aye, sir, calculating."

"Then turn us around, Ms Martin. Get us back to business."

"Aye, sir, programme locked in, manoeuvring thrusters will fire as soon as we drop out of hyperspace."

Reality shifted as Parks' programme took *Dreadnought* forward

two seconds through hyperspace. The manoeuvring thrusters fired
and the ship spun around its midpoint until it faced back the way it
had come. Then the main engines began to slow the ship.

"One hundred and forty seconds to standstill, sir," said Martin,
throwing a new counter onto the main display.

"What about our friends?"

"I think they're coming about, sir," said MacCaibe. "We're too far
away to know much more."

"Contact from DS *Wickham*, sir," said Woods. "They've lost *Alton*,
but Lieutenant Jordan is asking about a rendezvous."

"Lost? Seems careless," muttered White.

"Put them on the tactical display, Mr Woods. Mr Parks, give us a
flight solution that allows us to collect *Wickham*, then advise Lieutenant Jordan of the details."

"Aye, sir," said Parks, leaning close over his console as he worked
at the problem. He scratched his head, frowning at the figures and
the routes the computer offered.

"Incoming," warned MacCaibe at the same time the proximity
alarm sounded. "Attack craft on the starboard side, she's firing,
impact in three seconds."

"Sweep them away, Mr MacCaibe," snarled Cohen. "Fire
everything."

"She's gone, sir," said MacCaibe. "Thirty railgun round impacts,
no hull breaches."

"Eighty seconds to standstill," said Martin.

"Where's my flight plan, Mr Parks?" snapped Cohen.

"Working on it, sir. It's complicated by the falling space station
and–"

"Second craft coming in, port side," interrupted MacCaibe.
"Exchanging railgun fire, looks good, no, she's jumped clear."

Cohen growled with frustration, but there was nothing they
could do until they were travelling in the right direction. Any use of
the hyperspace engine now would take them further from their
target.

"What target?" he muttered to himself in a sudden burst of inspiration. "Ms Martin, give me a one-second blip on the hyperspace engine as soon as the next craft appears."

"Sir? That'll take us in the wrong direction?"

"Just do it, Ms Martin. Any damage from that last run?"

"Nothing significant," said White, "although we've got a couple of new holes in one of the disused bays."

"Two more craft, both above us," said MacCaibe. "Fifteen hundred metres, firing."

"Triggering hyperspace engine," said Martin and the stars jumped. "Forty seconds to standstill."

"No impacts but they're coming on again," said MacCaibe. "Looks like they anticipated that move."

"Hit it again, Ms Martin," said Cohen, eyes on the two attack craft that were holding back and on the two who struck first.

Again the stars jumped.

"Twenty seconds," updated Martin, although they could all see the counter ticking steadily down.

"The new nav-system will allow us to adjust our real-space velocity while in hyperspace, Captain," interjected Agent O.

"Not now, Agent O. Where's my flight plan, Mr Parks?"

"Here, sir," said Parks, throwing his plan onto the main display. "That last jump moved us clear of the space station."

"Notify DS *Wickham*," said Cohen, "and let's get out of here."

"*Target Eleven* and *Target Twelve* are diverting, sir," said Woods. "Looks like they're heading to intercept *Wickham*."

"Standstill," announced Martin to Cohen's great relief. "Firing manoeuvring thrusters. Alignment with new flight plan in ten seconds."

There was a moment of silence as the thrusters fired and the huge ship shifted into its new position. Then the main engines re-engaged.

"Put us alongside those bastard attack craft," said Cohen. "I want to give them something to think about other than *Wickham*."

"Aye, sir," said Parks uncertainly. "We'll need to recalculate the flight plan and with our current margin of error–"

"Just do it," snapped White in an uncharacteristic display of frustration as the atmosphere on the bridge grew tense. "If they get to *Wickham* before us..." He didn't need to finish the sentence. Everyone knew what would happen to the unarmed dropship if it was caught by the Deathless attack craft.

"Course ready, sir," said Parks unhappily.

"Go, Ms Martin," said Cohen.

The stars shifted as Martin fired the hyperspace engine. The proximity warning sounded and there was a huge concussion. *Dreadnought's* deck seemed to ripple and buck.

"What the hell was that?" said Cohen as damage reports flooded the main display.

"*Target Twelve*, I think," said Woods, his face white. His hands flew over the console, then a snippet of slow-motion video appeared on the main screen. It showed the view from one of the forward camera arrays as *Dreadnought* emerged from hyperspace. There was a dark grey bulk directly in front of the camera, then the feed ended. Woods threw another view to the display. This one showed the tumbling remains of a Deathless fast-flit craft as it rolled away from *Dreadnought,* venting atmosphere and clearly in serious trouble.

"Firing on *Target Eleven*," said MacCaibe, the only crew member not entirely distracted by the video of *Target Twelve's* expiration. "She's close, six hundred metres. Multiple hits."

"Damage report, Mantle," said Cohen, opening a channel to the engineering team.

"We're working on it," she snapped, closing the channel. Cohen took this to be a good sign.

"*Target Eight* is turning, sir," said Woods. "And *Target Seven*. And the other two. They're all preparing to go after *Wickham*."

"Open a channel to Lieutenant Jordan," said Cohen, "and get us lined up for the next jump."

"Manoeuvring now, sir, ten seconds," said Martin as the channel to DS *Wickham* opened and Jordan's stressed face appeared on the main display.

"Sir," acknowledged Jordan. "You're too far away for our sensors."

"Get ready, Lieutenant," said Cohen. "The Deathless are right behind you, but we're on our way."

"*Target Eight* is aligned," said Woods.

"Almost there," said Martin.

"*Target Eight* has jumped."

"Ready, firing the hyperspace engine," said Martin.

Space rippled.

"Find *Wickham*," said White, "and find the bloody Deathless!"

"*Wickham*'s there, sir," said Woods as the tactical overview on the main display updated and the dropship was highlighted.

"*Target Eight* is alongside them, sir," said MacCaibe.

"Fire, Mr MacCaibe."

"Aye, sir, firing now. Eight thousand metre range. *Target Eight* is firing as well."

"Hold on, Lieutenant," said Cohen as Jordan's expression showed just how serious things were getting.

"Manoeuvring, but brace for impact," warned Jordan.

"Get us in there, Ms Martin," said Cohen, leaning forward.

"Engines firing, sir, full power."

"We're almost with you, Lieutenant."

"Aye, sir, we see you. Our engines are offline. Looks like we took several solid strikes from that last attack run."

"Hold steady, we'll scoop you up." He muted the audio channel. "We can do that, right, people?"

Parks and Martin exchange a glance.

"Maybe. If we bring the bay doors around, we can maybe catch them," said Parks, "but it might be a bit messy."

"Do it," said Cohen.

"Firing manoeuvring thrusters now, sir," said Martin.

"Mantle, be advised the starboard main bay is about to contain a damaged dropship," said White. "Get people over there." Mantle clicked the channel to acknowledge the order but said nothing.

"Bay doors open," said Woods. "*Target Ten* is incoming."

"Locked and prepped on *Ten*, sir," said MacCaibe.

Dreadnought rolled as the manoeuvring thrusters turned her bulk, positioning the starboard bay doors to catch *Wickham*.

"Five seconds," said Woods.

The main display showed dropship *Wickham* drifting gently as *Dreadnought* approached. Her thrusters fired, adjusting the angle so *Dreadnought* was moving sideways through space.

"Bloody close," muttered White as Midshipman Martin played the engine controls, fine-tuning the approach.

On the tactical overview, *Target Ten*'s position suddenly changed as she made a short journey through hyperspace to appear alongside *Dreadnought* no more than five hundred metres away. She fired, targeting *Wickham*, but *Dreadnought*'s roll took her between the two craft and *Target Ten*'s railgun rounds clattered against *Dreadnought*'s hull.

"*Vasilisa* is powering her hyperspace engines," warned MacCaibe. "Firing on *Target Ten*."

"Hull breach," said White, "damage to the fabrication suites, venting atmosphere."

"Matching velocity with *Wickham*," muttered Martin. "Pretty close..."

"*Wickham* is aboard," said Woods as a vibration ran through *Dreadnought*'s floor. "Hard landing, but she's home."

"*Vasilisa* is coming, attack imminent. *Target Seven* is lining up."

"Another one-second blip, Ms Martin. Put us clear."

"Aye, sir," said Martin, hands flying. "Triggering now."

Vasilisa slipped through hyperspace, attempting to close the distance between the two vessels, but she emerged into normal space a thousand kilometres from *Dreadnought*, too far to pose any immediate threat.

"Her guidance computers are no better than ours," muttered Cohen, shaking his head as *Vasilisa* launched high-speed missiles. "Take us away from here, Ms Martin."

"Aye, sir, course is laid in, firing hyperspace engines now."

And *Dreadnought* was gone.

~

Dropship *Wickham* was a mess. Scorched by the planet's atmosphere, run through with railgun rounds by the Deathless and battered by falling debris from the space station, she sat at the end of *Dreadnought*'s starboard bay looking like she'd never fly again.

Cohen and White hurried down to inspect their catch. They stopped at the nearest viewing port to stare at the severely bruised dropship. Air slowly filled the bay now that the doors were closed.

"Comms are still down," said White as the pressure reached an acceptable minimum and they were finally able to enter. The emergency team and Mantle's engineers – all suited for low-pressure work – were already there, checking the damage and trying to ensure the passengers came to no further harm.

As Cohen and White reached the dropship, the ramp came down and Colour Sergeant Milton came first, the arm of an injured Marine X around her shoulder. She stopped in front of Cohen and saluted.

"Captain Warden's still unconscious, sir," she said, "but he'll be okay."

"You have the admiral though?" asked Cohen.

Marine X lifted his head, pain written across his features. Behind him, the shaken Marines disembarked, lugging their helmets and weapons and helping each other down the ramp.

"Aye, sir," said Ten. "Mission accomplished, but you'll need a stretcher to get the bugger off the dropship." He pulled himself upright and staggered slowly across the bay to the nearest med-team, where he collapsed into their caring arms.

"Sir," said Milton, before she hurried off to care for her troops.

A med-team pushed their way onto the dropship and emerged a few moments later with Admiral Morgan on a stretcher.

"He's unconscious but alive," said the medic. "We'll get him patched up, sir." Cohen nodded and Morgan was taken away, the stretcher floating under its own power across the bay.

Lieutenant Jordan emerged, walking wearily down the ramp with Figgs, Peters and Johnson, Peters' co-pilot.

"I can't help noticing, Lieutenant, that there are fewer dropships in my bay than there should be," Cohen said sternly. "Please tell me you have some good news."

"It's a long story, sir, but it has a happy ending," said Jordan, grimacing as he stretched and tweaked his strained muscles. "Can we talk over a cuppa? There wasn't time to stop for tea."

EPILOGUE

"Nervous?"

"Of course I'm bloody nervous," said Warden, shuffling from foot to foot. "A medal ceremony is enough to make any officer nervous, Colours."

"Granted, but you're not actually getting a medal, sir, so why are you fidgeting like a kid picking up his prom date?"

"Because if anyone can turn a simple ceremony into a complete nightmare, it's Marine X."

"Really, sir? But he must have received medals before, surely? The way he acts, I mean."

"Do you know something I don't know?" Warden asked suspiciously, glancing at Milton.

"I'm sure I do, sir, but to which particular category of knowledge might you be referring?" she asked innocently.

"The redacted file of one Penal Marine X, real name withheld as punishment, date of birth redacted, previous awards and campaign medals redacted, past operations and training redacted. I've seen his file, and its contents are not illuminating. It's an exercise in the art of redaction, but not the least bit informative. Do you know about any medals he's won? Has he ever mentioned one?"

"Nah, don't be soft. All I ever get from him is subtle hints and vague anecdotes."

"Or stories of awful deaths," murmured Warden.

"Right. He never gives away enough to identify him, and if he mentioned a medal that'd narrow it down straight away. What's he getting, anyway?"

"Military cross," said Warden. "For exemplary gallantry."

Milton whistled softly and a few heads turned to glare at her breach of etiquette. She stared stonily ahead, ignoring the disapproving glances until they looked away.

"Who made the recommendation?" she asked quietly, cocking an eyebrow at the captain.

Warden's blush raced up his neck, turning his skin crimson. Milton chuckled.

"You never! What did you go and do that for?"

"I didn't actually think they'd give him one," hissed Warden, "but they wouldn't let me mention him in despatches, and I thought this would be a way to give him a pat on the back."

"Well, you've only got yourself to blame if he messes this up, sir," said Milton unsympathetically. "He's a penal Marine, they're not expected to get awards."

"Yes, but they're not really expected to lead the charge in dozens of engagements against the enemy, saving, I might add, our arses on numerous occasions."

"I can't believe you recommended him after the, er, surrendering incident."

Warden cleared his throat softly. "I thought we'd agreed not to mention that ever again, Colours."

"Sir? Not sure I agreed to that, sir," said Milton with a grin.

Warden sighed.

This bloody ceremony was tediously slow. The New Bristol political crowd were really milking their speeches.

"I wasn't happy at the time but – and I'll deny all knowledge of this conversation if you ever mention it – on reflection, it was a good gag, well played."

"Can't have been that good. No-one's mentioned it since the day," said Milton in a manner only slightly more convincing than the political speeches coming from the podium.

"Good. I'd hate to think anyone was making fun of me. Anyway, the Admiralty seemed to think he really should get a medal, even if it's purely symbolic until his sentence is served," said Warden, "so here we are."

There was a pause as one politician finished their speech and another took their place.

"I can't believe they gave Morgan an MBE," Milton grumbled when the speeches resumed. Staines presented the award earlier in the ceremony in front of a very quiet crowd.

"Admiral Morgan, Colours" said Warden with a tone of mild disapproval. "I heard they considered a Conspicuous Gallantry Cross but they weren't sure if his resistance to torture counted as gallantry in the face of the enemy during combat, so they settled on making him a Member of the British Empire instead."

"Holding out under torture? Don't tell me you believe that story? The man blubbed like a toddler that'd skinned his shin on a sharp rock. I don't believe they tortured him and he didn't spill his guts," whispered Milton incredulously.

"Are you two quite finished?" said Colonel Atticus over his shoulder from the row ahead.

"Sorry, sir," said Warden, glaring at Milton as if it was all her fault. Chastened, they turned their attention to the stage.

Marine X made his way forward to receive his medal. He stopped in front of Vice-Admiral Staines and saluted.

Staines shook his head almost imperceptibly, and Morgan stepped forward. Marine X looked from one admiral to the other, his face as grey as death, and took a step sideways.

"Oh dear," murmured Warden. Ten was clearly bristling, and he half expected to hear the beginnings of an argument.

But Morgan, his face still showing signs of the beating he received, handed over the boxed medal, said a few quiet words, then shook Marine X's hand. He winced briefly and glared. Staines escorted Marine X from the stage, leaving Admiral Morgan to close the ceremony. Warden could see him massaging the hand Ten had shaken.

A few minutes later, everyone filed out into the reception area and the tension drained away as the Marines headed for the bar.

Colonel Atticus waited for Warden and Milton, the tension in his shoulders evident. "Find Marine X and keep an eye on him. Got it?"

"Yes, sir," they chorused.

"Here," said Warden, holding out a glass, "take this and try and look a bit less like someone just drove over your foot." Warden said, offering Marine X a flute of something that purported to be champagne but was most definitely not the real thing.

Marine X looked down at the flute of sparkling wine and shook his head.

"Thanks, sir, but I'm good," he said, raising a hand that held a nicely iced gin and tonic.

"How the hell did you get that? You haven't had a chance to go near the bar."

"You've got to be prepared for these things, Captain. I have an ally," Ten said, raising his glass to the drone team leader, Julia, who was mixing drinks at a table in the corner of the room. Warden was pretty sure she shouldn't be in the bar at all. Though she probably shouldn't be gathering surveillance for the Marines either at her age. He decided to ignore the problem.

"Okay, well take this as a chaser then," Warden said, raising the flute again.

"Oh no, you won't catch me drinking that cat's piss, sir. I don't really like champagne, but I'm certainly not drinking the fake stuff. This local gin on the other hand isn't half bad. I've lined them up," said Ten, nodding at a nearby table where a second glass waited.

"Eyes up," warned Milton as Warden stared at the surplus drink, "here come the brass."

Cohen emerged from the crowd with White in tow and nodded to Warden and Milton.

"Congratulations, Marine X. A well-deserved award."

Ten grunted, "Yeah, thanks, sir. I'm ecstatic."

There was an awkward pause before Vice-Admiral Staines joined the group with Colonel Atticus and Governor Denmead. There were more congratulations and more equally terse acknowledgements as Ten's humour, already low, drained away. He finished his second drink and was beginning to look quite downcast until Julia appeared to furnish him with a replacement and remove the empties. Governor Denmead raised an eyebrow, but Julia just smirked and vanished back across the bar.

"The Military Cross, eh?" said Milton, in a bid to lift the atmosphere. She gave Marine X a playful punch on the shoulder. "Big deal, congrats."

Ten snorted. "The mission has to make sense for the medal to have value," he said coldly. "They lose their appeal after the first one."

Milton gave him a weak grin and seemed relieved when Vice-Admiral Staines cleared his throat.

"You didn't seem all that happy when Admiral Morgan gave it to you."

Marine X stared at the admiral. Warden noticed Atticus wince in anticipation of the response.

"Getting a medal from you, sir, is one thing; just another tedious job for you, like cleaning the head or polishing your boots." Staines smiled politely, but to Warden, it felt as if the party soured. "But I wasn't expecting a presentation from that jumped up, incompetent, over-promoted prick, Morgan, sir."

"Medal or not, we can add years to your sentence, Marine," barked Atticus automatically. "Show some respect."

"Sorry, sir. I meant to say, 'jumped up, over-promoted, cowardly fucking prick, Admiral Morgan'," said Marine X, a slight hint of menacing anger in his tone, "the least competent officer I've ever had the displeasure to serve with."

There was a strained pause as everyone waited for Staines to react. Ten pulled the medal box from his pocket and dropped it on the high table in the middle of the group.

"It's a field replica, and I've got a drawer full of the bloody things at home. The real ones are still made the old-fashioned way and you pick them up when you return to civilisation, for those of you who don't know." He looked around the group, utterly unfazed by rank or station. "Right, good evening ladies and gents, I'm off to find another drink." And he vanished into the crowd.

There was an uncomfortable moment while everyone tried to absorb what just happened. Milton was the first to speak. "I'll er, put this somewhere safe and give it to him when he's in a better mood."

Atticus coughed. "My apologies, sir. I'll give him a summary judgement and add some time to his sentence."

Staines shook his head. "No need, no need. I heard nothing untoward, what with all this noise. The reports of his actions in this campaign are utterly incredible. If he's a little rough and ready, I'm sure we can ignore that if he keeps dealing with the Deathless so effectively, no?"

"Yes, sir, thank you, sir."

"Besides, I had a look at his file last night to find something to say by way of introduction. It's the most heavily redacted document I've ever seen, but I didn't get the impression that adding months or years to his sentence as a penal Marine would be likely to change his behaviour."

Warden and Milton shared a look. If a vice-admiral couldn't get access to Ten's file, who could?

"Very perceptive, sir," Atticus replied. "He loves what he does. Adding time to his sentence just means he gets to serve for longer. As long as he reserves most of his aggression for the enemy, I try not to worry about it."

"As it happens, Captain Warden, I have a classified mission from the Admiralty and they've specifically requested that Marine X be added to the team. General Bonneville has agreed to the secondment. He's to redeploy immediately and may not be back for some time. I'm sorry, but apparently his skills are required for the mission and it is of the utmost importance," Admiral Staines said.

Warden was surprised and not a little displeased but it really didn't matter, he could hardly protest the orders. And in any case, General Bonneville was unlikely to pull Ten out of their active theatre for anything trivial. "Yes, Sir. Do you want me to brief him?"

Staines shook his head, "No, I'm sorry, Captain, the security level is so high I have nothing to brief anyway. I'll inform him myself shortly."

Governor Denmead cleared her throat. "Perhaps we should talk about something else? Do you have any news on the war?" Her tone suggested she knew very well there was news, and she hoped Staines would share it with the Marines.

"Yes, of course. Well, it's no secret that Admiral Morgan is going back to logistics. He'll oversee the construction of a new Royal Navy base and shipyard at New Bristol, transforming one of the moons. The Admiralty feels he's ready for a sideways promotion to another important area of command."

"Translation; they don't like his win-loss record any more than Marine X does," Governor Denmead said with an uncharacteristic lack of diplomacy.

Warden knew it was what everyone was thinking. Morgan proved to be deeply unpopular with all the military personnel he knew in theatre. He was glad the Royal Navy recognised he wasn't suited to combat leadership roles, but of course, none of them could say that. Governor Denmead had the luxury of the freedom to make such comments, much like Ten. "So, who will replace him?"

Staines smiled awkwardly.

"Well. Funny you should ask. I'm being promoted to Admiral and given command of the New Bristol theatre."

There was a brief round of congratulations until Staines held up his hand. "It'll all be announced in the next few days, but we'll also need someone to lead our new strike fleet. Apparently, admirals are supposed to stay at home and move virtual paperwork around, so I want to promote you, Cohen, and give you command of the lance with which I intend to burst the boil that is U235."

Cohen looked surprised, like a rabbit caught in the sweep of oncoming headlights, not sure whether to dart left or jump right.

"It's a significant step up, but I think you've proved you're up to the job, and you're certainly the most experienced commander I have. I hope you'll accept, but you can always serve under someone who's been stuck on the fringe for decades and hasn't fought the Deathless if you'd prefer to avoid the challenge?"

Cohen looked like he was about to be sick, but he nodded. "It would be an honour, sir. Thank you, I won't let you down."

"I bloody well hope not, since it'll be you and your crews on the line, Commodore. *Dreadnought* will be your flagship, Captain Warden your Marine contingent commander, and we'll discuss the details of the rest of your attack group later."

"Here's to a decisive strike against U235," said Denmead, raising her glass, "and to victory!"

"To victory!"

THANK YOU FOR READING

Thank you for reading Dreadnought, Book Five in the Royal Marine Space Commando series. We hope you enjoyed the book and that you're looking forward to the next entry in the series, Fleet.

It would help us immensely if you would leave a review on Amazon or Goodreads, or even tell a friend you think would enjoy the series, about the books.

In Fleet, Lieutenant Commander Cohen & Captain Warden will be launching an all out strike on the Deathless.

Immediately after Dreadnought, Ten will be going on a classified mission which begins in Incursion.

Incursion is the first book in the By Strength & Guile series with our new co-author, Paul Teague. Paul is the author of many books, including the popular Secret Bunker & The Grid series.

We think you'll love this trilogy that opens the door into the world of special forces operations in our Royal Marine Space Commandos universe.

All three books in the By Strength & Guild series should be out by the end of 2019 and we hope to have more collaborative efforts in the future.

SUBSCRIBE AND GET A FREE BOOK

Want to know when the next book is coming and what it's called?

Would you like to hear about how we write the books?

Maybe you'd like the free book, Ten Tales: Journey to the West?

You can get all this and more at imaginarybrother.com/journeytothewest where you can sign up to the newsletter for our publishing company, Imaginary Brother.

When you join, we'll send you a free copy of Journey to the West, direct to your inbox*.

There will be more short stories about Ten and his many and varied adventures, including more exclusive ones, just for our newsletter readers as a thank you for their support.

Happy reading,

Jon Evans & James Evans

We hope you'll stay on our mailing list but if you choose not to, you can follow us on Facebook or visit our website instead.

imaginarybrother.com

* We use Bookfunnel to send out our free books. It's painless but if you need help, they'll guide you through so you can get reading.

facebook.com/ImaginaryBrotherPublishing

ALSO BY JAMES EVANS AND JON EVANS

Also by James Evans

James is writing the Vensille Saga, an epic fantasy tale that began with A Gathering of Fools and continues with A Gathering of Princes. The third book is a work in progress.

A Gathering of Fools

Marrinek has fought his last war.

Once an officer in the Imperial Army, he has been betrayed, captured and named traitor. His future now holds only imprisonment and death - but that doesn't stop him dreaming of revenge.

Krant lives a clerk's life of paperwork and boredom until a chance meeting with an Imperial courier rips his world apart and sets him on a new course. Sent abroad with only the mysterious Gavelis for company, Krant faces an impossible task with no hope of success.

For two years, Adrava has hidden from her husband's enemies. But her refuge is no longer safe and she must venture forth to seek justice at the end of a blade.

In Vensille they gather, fools seeking shelter from a storm that threatens to drown the city in blood and fire.

A Gathering of Princes

War threatens the city of Vensille.

An unseen enemy strikes at the city and Duke Rhenveldt struggles to maintain control.

As the danger grows, Marrinek forms a desperate plan to save his household and the twins.

Adrava and Floost must embark on a dangerous journey, deep into the

Empire. Can they evade capture long enough to return to Vensille?

Far across the Empire, Tentalus marches west with his armies, bringing death and battle with him. Rumours of betrayal and conspiracy grow. Will the traitors spring their final trap before the Emperor can uncover their schemes?

And in the forests of Sclareme, an ancient horror awakens from its long slumber. Pursued and hunted, can Mirelle and her crew escape to bring a warning to Vensille?

Can anything save Vensille?

Also by Jon Evans

Jon is concentrating on the Royal Marine Commando series for the time being but is also writing a fantasy series. The Edrin Loft Mysteries follow the adventures of Edrin Loft, Watch Captain of the Thieftakers Watch House.

You can read the first book Thieftaker now.

Thieftaker

Why was the murder of a local merchant so vicious?

Mere days after he takes charge of the Old Gate Watch House, Captain Edrin Loft must solve a crime so shocking that even veteran Sergeant Aliria Gurnt finds it stomach turning. With no witnesses or apparent motive for the crime, finding the culprit seems an impossible task.

But Loft has new scientific methods to apply to crime fighting. His first successful investigation caused a political scandal that embarrassed the Watch. Promotion to his own command was the solution. Known as The Thieftakers, they are the dregs of the Kalider City Watch, destined to spend the rest of their careers hunting criminals in the worst neighbourhoods. After all, what fuss could he cause running down thieves and murderers in the slums?

Old Gate and this murder might be the perfect combination of place and crime to test his theories. The Thieftakers are the best Kalider has at tracking criminals, and Loft must teach them investigative skills to match.

Can he validate his theories and turn the Thieftakers into the first detectives in Kalider?

ABOUT THE AUTHORS JAMES EVANS

James has published the first two books of his Vensille Saga and is working on the third, A Gathering of Arms, as well as a number of other projects. At the same time, he is working on follow-up books in the RMSC series with his brother Jon.

You can join James's mailing list to keep track of the upcoming releases, visit his website or follow him on social media.

jamesevansbooks.co.uk

facebook.com/JamesEvansBooks

twitter.com/JamesEvansBooks

amazon.com/author/james-evans

goodreads.com/james-evans

bookbub.com/authors/james-evans-d81a33f8-688b-4567-a2c5-109cd13300fa

ABOUT THE AUTHORS JON EVANS

Jon is a new sci-fi author & fantasy author, whose first book, Thief-taker is awaiting its sequel. He lives and works in Cardiff. He has some other projects waiting in the wings, once the RMSC series takes shape.

You can follow Jon's Facebook page where you'll be able to find out more about the first quadrilogy of the RMSC series and the next book, Dreadnought.

If you join the mailing list on the website, you'll get updates about how the new books are coming as well as information about new releases and the odd insight into the life of an author.

jonevansbooks.com

facebook.com/jonevansauthor

amazon.com/author/jonevansbooks

goodreads.com/jonevans

bookbub.com/authors/jon-evans

instagram.com/jonevansauthor